BLOODFEVER

This Large Print Book carries the
Seal of Approval of N.A.V.H.

BLOODFEVER

KAREN MARIE MONING

THORNDIKE PRESS

A part of Gale, Cengage Learning

GALE
CENGAGE Learning·

Detroit • New York • San Francisco • New Haven, Conn • Waterville, Maine • London

GALE
CENGAGE Learning

Copyright © 2007 by Karen Marie Moning.
The Fever Series.
Thorndike Press, a part of Gale, Cengage Learning.

Thorndike Press® Large Print Basic.
The text of this Large Print edition is unabridged.
Other aspects of the book may vary from the original edition.
Set in 16 pt. Plantin.
Printed on permanent paper.

LIBRARY OF CONGRESS CATALOGING-IN-PUBLICATION DATA

Moning, Karen Marie.
  Bloodfever / by Karen Marie Moning.
    p. cm. — (Thorndike Press large print basic)
    ISBN-13: 978-1-4104-0526-5 (hardcover : alk. paper)
    ISBN-10: 1-4104-0526-5 (hardcover : alk. paper)
    1. Americans — Ireland — Fiction. 2. Magicians — Fiction. 3.
Magic — Fiction. 4 Ireland — Fiction. 5. Fairies — Fiction. 6.
Large type books. I. Title.
PS3613.O527B58 2008
813'.6—dc22   2007047229

Published in 2008 by arrangement with The Bantam Dell Publishing Group, a division of Random House, Inc.

Printed in the United States of America
1 2 3 4 5 6 7 12 11 10 09 08

This one's for Jessi for, among other things, tromping all over Ireland in the rain, taking such beautiful photographs. I'm so proud of you!

And for Leiha, who keeps the machine oiled and the wheels turning with a smile that makes the Cheshire cat look grumpy. Thanks for crossing the country for me.

And for Neil, who understands the soul of an artist because he has one. Thanks for the music and the months in Key West. It was heaven.

Dear Reader:

At the back of *Bloodfever* you will find a detailed glossary of names, items, and pronunciations.

Some entries contain small spoilers. Read at your own risk.

For additional information about the Fever series and the world of the Fae, visit www.sidhe-seersinc.com or www.karen moning.com.

I have seen the moment of my
greatness flicker,
And I have seen the eternal Footman
hold my coat, and snicker,
And in short, I was afraid.
— T. S. Eliot/*The Love Song of
J. Alfred Prufrock*

N

Antrim Coast
Bushmills ·
· Derry   Portrush ·

DONEGAL

NORTHERN
IRELAND Belfast   · Bangor

Belleek ·
· Drumcliff   Mourne
                    Mountains

· Strokestown

Knock ·   REPUBLIC
Westport ·   Bru Na
            OF   · Boinne
CONNEMARA
            IRELAND   · Trim
Galway ·

Dublin ·
Aran
Islands   Dun Laoghaire ·
    The Burren   WICKLOW
Cliffs of Moher CLARE
            · Ennis   Glendalough ·

                        · Kilkenny
            ■
        Rock
        of   · Waterford
· Tralee   Cashel
· Dingle   · Rosslare

    · Killarney   Ardmore ·
KERRY Blarney   · Cork
    · Kenmare
                · Cobh
    Kinsale ·   WALES
BANTRY
BAY

| 50 miles |
| 50 km |

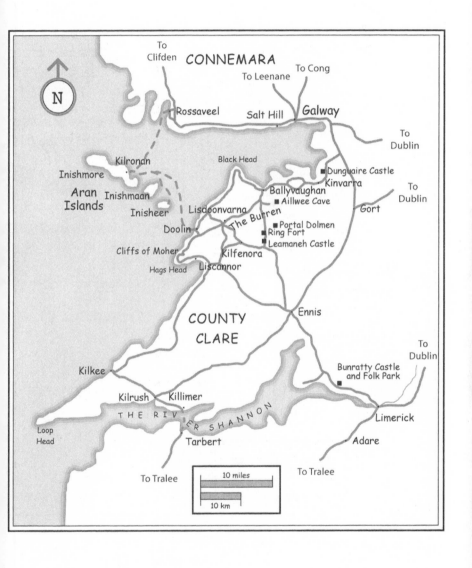

N

To Clifden
CONNEMARA
To Leenane
To Cong
Rossaveel
Salt Hill
Galway
To Dublin

Kilronan
Black Head
Dunguaire Castle
Inishmore
Kinvarra
To Dublin
Aran Islands
Inishmaan
Ballyvaughan
Aillwee Cave
Gort
Inisheer
Lisdoonvarna
The Burren
Doolin
Portal Dolmen
Ring Fort
Leamaneh Castle
Cliffs of Moher
Kilfenora
Hags Head
Liscannor
Ennis

COUNTY CLARE

To Dublin
Kilkee
Bunratty Castle and Folk Park
Kilrush
Killimer
THE RIVER SHANNON
Limerick
Loop Head
Tarbert
Adare
To Tralee
To Tralee

10 miles
10 km

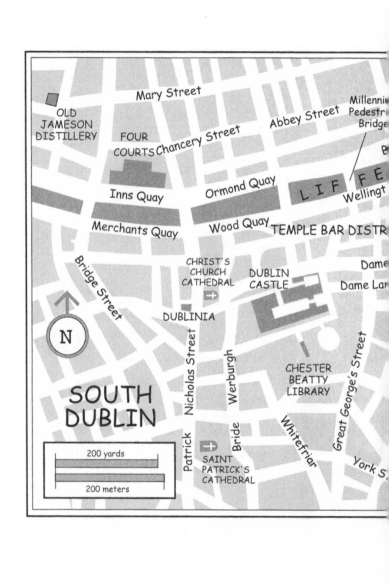

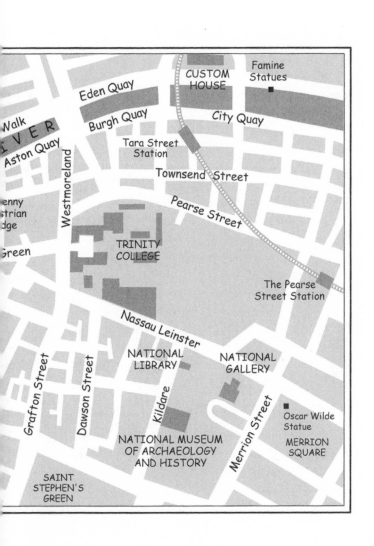

PROLOGUE

All of us have our little problems and insecurities. I'm no different. Back in high school when I used to feel insecure about something, I would console myself with two thoughts: I'm pretty, and my parents love me. Between those two, I could survive anything.

Since then I've come to understand how little the former matters, and how bitterly the latter can be tested. What's left then? Nothing about our appearance or who loves or hates us. Nothing about our brainpower — which, like beauty, is an unearned gift of genetics — nor even anything about what we say.

It's our actions that define us. What we choose. What we resist. What we're willing to die for.

My name is MacKayla Lane. I think. Some say my last name is really O'Connor. That's another of my insecurities right now:

who I am. Although, at the moment, I'm in no hurry to find out. *What* I am is disturbing enough.

I'm from Ashford, Georgia. I think. Lately I've realized I have some tricky memories I can't quite sort through.

I'm in Ireland. When my sister, Alina, was found dead in a trash-filled alley on Dublin's north side, the local police closed her case in record time, so I flew over to see what I could do about getting justice.

Okay, so maybe I'm not that pure.

What I really came over for was revenge. And now, after everything I've seen, I want it twice as bad.

I used to think my sister and I were just two nice southern girls who would get married in a few years, have babies, and settle down to a life of sipping sweet tea on a porch swing under the shade of waxyblossomed magnolias, raising our children together near Mom and Dad and each other.

Then I discovered Alina and I descend not from good, wholesome southern stock but from an ancient Celtic bloodline of powerful *sidhe*-seers, people who can see the Fae, a terrifying race of otherworldly beings that have lived secretly among us for thousands of years, cloaked in illusions and lies. Governed loosely by a queen, and even more loosely by a Compact few support and many ignore, they have preyed on humans for millennia.

Supposedly I'm one of the most powerful *sidhe*-seers ever born. Not only can I see the Fae, I can sense their sacred relics that hold the deadliest and most powerful of their magic.

I can find them.

I can *use* them.

I've already found the mythic Spear of Luin, one of only two weapons capable of killing an immortal Fae. I'm also a Null — a person who can temporarily freeze a Fae and cancel out its power with the mere touch of my hands. It helps me kick butt when I need to, and lately, every time I turn around, I need to.

My world began falling apart with the death of my sister, and hasn't stopped since. And it's not just my world that's in trouble; it's your world, too.

The walls between Man and Faery are coming down.

I don't know why or how. I only know they are. I know it in my *sidhe*-seer blood. On a dark Fae wind, I taste the metallic tang of a bloody and terrible war coming. In the distant air, I hear the thunderclap of sharp-bladed hooves as Fae stallions circle impatiently, ready to charge down on us in the ancient, forbidden Wild Hunt.

I know who killed my sister. I've stared into the murderous eyes of the one who seduced, used, and destroyed her. Not quite Fae, not quite human, he calls himself the Lord Master, and he's been opening portals between realms, bringing Unseelie through to our world.

The Fae consist of two adversarial courts with their own Royal Houses and unique castes: the Light or Seelie Court, and the Dark or Unseelie Court. Don't let the light and dark stuff deceive you: they're both deadly. Scary thing is the Seelie considered their darker brethren, the Unseelie, so abominable that they imprisoned them *themselves* a few hundred eons ago. When one Fae fears another Fae, you know you've got problems.

Now the Lord Master is freeing the darkest, most dangerous of our enemies, turning them loose on our world, and teaching them to infiltrate our society. When these monsters walk down our streets, you see only the "glamour" they throw: the illusion of a beautiful human woman, man, or child.

I see what they really are.

I have no doubt I would have ended up

every bit as dead as my sister shortly after I arrived in Dublin, if I'd not stumbled into a bookstore owned by the enigmatic Jericho Barrons. I have no idea who or what he is, or what he's after, but he knows more about what I am and what's going on out there than anyone else I've met, and I need that knowledge.

When I had no place to turn, Jericho Barrons took me in, taught me, opened my eyes, and helped me survive. Granted, he didn't do it nicely, but I'm no longer quite so picky about how I survive, as long as I do.

Because it was safer than my cheap room at the inn, I moved into his bookstore. It's well protected against most of my enemies with wards and assorted nasty tricks, and stands bastion at the edge of what I call a Dark Zone: a neighborhood that has been taken over by Shades, amorphous Unseelie that thrive in darkness and feed off humans.

Barrons and I have formed an uneasy alliance based on mutual need: We both want the *Sinsar Dubh* — a million-year-old book of the blackest magic imaginable, allegedly scribed by the Unseelie King himself, that holds the key to power over both the worlds of Fae and Man.

I want it because it was Alina's dying

request that I find it, and I suspect it holds the key to saving our world.

He wants it because he says he collects books. Right.

Everyone else I've encountered is after it, too. The hunt is dangerous, the stakes enormous.

Because the *Sinsar Dubh* is a Fae relic, I can sense it when it's near. Barrons can't. But he knows where to look for it, and I don't. So now we're partners in crime who don't trust each other one bit.

Nothing in my sheltered, pampered life prepared me for the past few weeks. Gone is my long blond hair, chopped short for the sake of anonymity and dyed dark. Gone are my pretty pastel outfits, replaced by drab colors that don't show blood. I've learned to cuss, steal, lie, and kill. I've been assaulted by a death-by-sex Fae and made to strip, not once but twice, in public. I discovered that I was adopted. I nearly died.

With Barrons at my side, I've robbed a mobster and his henchmen and led them to their deaths. I've fought and killed dozens of Unseelie. I battled the vampire Mallucé in a bloody showdown with the Lord Master himself.

In one short month I've managed to piss off virtually every being with magical power in this city. Half of those I've encountered want me dead; the other half want to use me to find the deadly, coveted *Sinsar Dubh*.

I could run home, I suppose. Try to forget. Try to hide.

Then I think of Alina, and how she died.

Her face swims up in my mind — a face I knew as well as my own; she was more than my sister, she was my best friend — and I can almost hear her saying: Right, Junior — and risk leading a monster like Mallucé, a death-by-sex Fae, or some other Unseelie back to Ashford? Take a chance that some of the Shades might cop a ride in your luggage and devour the charming, idyllic streets of our childhood, one burnt-out streetlamp at a time? When you see the Dark Zone that used to be our home, how will you feel, Mac?

Before her voice even begins to fade, I know that I'm here until this is over.

Until either they're dead or I am.

Alina's death *will* be avenged.

ONE

"You're a difficult woman to find, Ms. Lane," said Inspector O'Duffy as I opened the diamond-paned front door of Barrons Books and Baubles.

The stately old-world bookstore was my home away from home, whether I liked it or not, and despite the sumptuous furnishings, priceless rugs, and endless selection of top-rate reading material, I didn't. The comfiest cage is still a cage.

He glanced at me sharply when I stepped around the door, into full view, noting my splinted arm and fingers, the stitches in my lip, and the fading purple and yellow bruises that began around my right eye and extended to the base of my jaw. Though he raised a brow, he made no comment.

The weather outside was awful, and so long as the door was open, I was too close to it. It had been raining for days, a relentless, depressing torrent that needled me with sharp wind-driven droplets even where I stood, tucked beneath the shelter of the column-flanked archway of the bookstore's grand entry. At eleven o'clock on Sunday morning, it was so overcast and dark that the streetlamps were still on. Despite their sullen yellow glares, I could barely see the outlines of the shops across the street through the thick, soupy fog.

I backed up to let the inspector enter. Gusts of chilly air stepped in on his heels.

I closed the door and returned to the conversation area near the fire where I'd been wrapped in an afghan on the sofa, reading. My borrowed bedroom is on the top floor, but when the bookstore is closed on weekends I make the first floor, with its cozy reading nooks and enameled fireplaces, my personal parlor. My taste in reading material has become a bit eccentric of late. Acutely aware of O'Duffy on my heels, I surreptitiously toed a few of the more bizarre titles I'd been perusing beneath a handsome curio cabinet. *The Wee People: Fairy Tale or Fact?* was chased by *Vampires for Dummies* and *Divine Power: A History of Holy Relics.*

"Dreadful weather," he observed, stepping to the hearth and warming his hands before the softly hissing gas flames.

I agreed with perhaps more enthusiasm than the fact warranted, but the endless deluge outside was getting to me. A few more days of this and I was going to start building an ark. I'd heard it rained a lot in Ireland, but "constantly" was a smidge more than a lot, in my book. Transplanted against my will, a homesick, reluctant tourist, I'd made the mistake of checking the weather back home in Ashford this morning. It was a sultry, blue-skied ninety-six degrees in Georgia — just another perfect, blossom-drenched, sunny day in the Deep South. In a few hours my girlfriends would be heading up to one of our favorite lakes where they would soak up the sun, scope out datable guys, and flip through the latest fashion magazines.

Here in Dublin it was a whopping fifty degrees and so darned wet it felt like half that.

No sun. No datable guys. And my only fashion concern was making sure my clothes were baggy enough to accommodate weapons concealed beneath them. Even in the relative security of the bookstore, I was carrying two flashlights, a pair of scissors, and a lethal, foot-long spearhead, tip neatly cased in a ball of foil. I'd scattered dozens more flashlights and assorted items that

25

might second as arsenal throughout the four-story bookstore. I'd also secreted a few crosses and bottles of holy water in various nooks. Barrons would laugh at me if he knew.

You might wonder if I'm expecting an army from Hell.

I am.

"How *did* you find me?" I asked the inspector. When I'd last spoken to the Garda a week ago, he'd pressed for a way to reach me. I'd given him my old address at the Clarin House where I boarded for a short time when I first arrived. I don't know why. I guess I just don't trust anyone. Not even the police. Over here the good guys and the bad guys all look the same. Just ask my dead sister Alina, victim of one of the most beautiful men I've ever seen — the Lord Master — who also happens to be one of the most evil.

"I'm a detective, Ms. Lane," O'Duffy told me with a dry smile, and I realized he had no intention of telling me. The smile vanished and his eyes narrowed with a subtle warning: *Don't lie to me, I'll know.*

I wasn't worried. Barrons said the same thing to me once, and he has seriously preternatural senses. If Barrons didn't see through me, O'Duffy wasn't going to. I

26

waited, wondering what had brought him here. He'd made it clear he considered my sister's case unsolvable and closed. Permanently.

He moved away from the fire and dropped the satchel slung over his shoulder onto the table between us.

Maps spilled across the gleaming wood.

Though I betrayed nothing, I felt the cold blade of a chill at my spine. I could no longer see maps as I once had: innocuous travel guides for the disoriented traveler or bemused tourist. Now when I unfold one I half expect to find charred holes in it where the Dark Zones are — those chunks of our cities that have fallen off our maps, lost to the deadly Shades. It's no longer what maps show but what they *fail* to show that worries me.

A week ago I'd demanded O'Duffy tell me everything he knew about the clue my sister had left at the scene of her murder, words she'd scratched into the cobbled stone of the alley as she lay dying: 1247 LARUHE.

He'd told me they'd never been able to find any such address.

I had.

It had taken a bit of thinking outside the box, but that's something I'm getting better at every day, although I really can't take much credit for the improvement. It's easy to think outside the box when life has dropped a two-ton elephant on yours. What is that box anyway but the beliefs we choose to hold about the world that make us feel safe? My box was now as flat, and about as useful, as a tissue-paper umbrella in all this rain.

O'Duffy sat down on the sofa next to me, gently, for such an overweight man. "I know what you think of me," he said.

When I would have protested politely — good southern manners die hard, if at all — he gave me what my mother calls the "shush wave."

"I've been doing this job for twenty-two years, Ms. Lane. I know what the families of closed murder cases feel when they look at me. Pain. Anger." He gave a dry laugh. "The conviction that I must be a chuffing idiot who spends too much time in the pubs and not enough time on the job, or their loved one would be resting in vindicated peace while the perp rotted in jail."

Rotting in jail was far too kind a fate for my sister's murderer. Besides, I wasn't sure any jail cell could hold him. The crimson-robed leader of the Unseelie might draw symbols on the floor, stamp his staff, and disappear through a convenient portal. Though Barrons had cautioned against assumptions, I saw no reason to doubt the Lord Master was responsible for my sister's death.

O'Duffy paused, perhaps giving me a chance to rebut. I didn't. He was right. I'd felt all that and more, but weighing the jelly stains on his tie and the girth overhanging his belt as circumstantial evidence, I'd convicted him of loitering overlong in bakeries and cafés, not pubs.

He selected two maps of Dublin from the table and handed them to me.

I gave him a quizzical look.

"The one on top is from last year. The one beneath it was published seven years earlier."

I shrugged. "And?" A few weeks ago I would have been delighted for any help from the Garda I could get. Now that I knew what I knew about the Dark Zone neighboring Barrons Books and Baubles — that terrible wasteland where I'd found 1247 LaRuhe, had a violent confrontation with the Lord Master, and nearly been killed — I wanted the police to stay as far out of my life as I could keep them. I didn't want any more deaths on my conscience. There was nothing the Garda could do to help me anyway. Only a *sidhe*-seer could see the monsters that had taken over the abandoned neighborhood and turned it into a death trap. The average human wouldn't know they were in danger until they were knee-deep in dead.

"I found your 1247 LaRuhe, Ms. Lane. It's on the map published seven years ago. Oddly enough, it's *not* on the one published last year. Grand Walk, one block down from this bookstore, isn't on the new map, either. Neither is Connelly Street, a block beyond that. I know. I went down there before I came to see you."

Oh, God, he'd walked into the Dark Zone this morning? The day was barely bright enough to keep the Shades hunkered down wherever it was the nasty things hide! If the storm had blown in even one more dense, sky-obliterating cloud, the boldest of those life-suckers might have dared the day for a human Happy Meal. O'Duffy had just been waltzing cheek-to-cheek with Death, and didn't even know it!

The unsuspecting inspector waved a hand at the pile of maps. They looked well examined. One of them appeared to have been balled up in shock or perhaps angry disbelief, then re-smoothed. I was no stranger to those emotions. "In fact, Ms. Lane,"

O'Duffy continued, "none of the streets I just mentioned are on *any* recently published map."

I gave him my best blank look. "What are you saying, Inspector? Has the city renamed the streets in this part of Dublin? Is that why they're not on the new maps?"

His face tightened and his gaze cut away. "Nobody renamed the streets," he growled. "Unless they did it without notifying a single person in authority." He looked back at me, hard. "I thought there might be something else you wanted to tell me, Ms. Lane. Something that might sound . . . a bit . . . unusual?"

I saw it then, in his eyes. Something had happened to the inspector recently that had drastically changed his paradigm. I had no idea what had shaken the hard-boiled, overworked, fact-finding detective from his pragmatic view of the world but he, too, was now thinking outside his box.

I needed him back inside his box — ASAP. Outside the box in this city was a dangerous place to be.

I thought fast. I didn't have much to work with. "Inspector," I said, sweetening and softening my Georgia drawl, "putting on the southern," as we call it back home, a sort of verbal honey-butter that masks the unpalatable taste of whatever we're slathering it on, "I know you must think me a complete idiot, coming over here and questioning your investigative techniques when anyone can see you're the expert in the field and I don't have an ounce of training in detecting matters, and I appreciate how patient you've been with me, but I no longer have any concerns about your investigation into my sister's death. I know now that you did everything you could to solve her case. I meant to stop by and speak with you before I left, but . . . well, the truth is I was feeling a bit embarrassed about our previous encounters. I went back to the alley the other day and took a good look around, without crying and letting my emotions get away from me, and I realized that my sister didn't leave me any clues. It was grief and anger and a whole boatload of wishful thinking on my part. Whatever was scratched into that alley had been done years ago."

"Whatever was scratched into that alley?" O'Duffy repeated carefully, and I knew he was recalling how adamant I'd been only last week about *exactly* what was scratched into that alley.

"Really, I could barely make it out at all. It might have been anything."

"Is that so, Ms. Lane?"

"Yes. And I meant to tell you it wasn't her cosmetic bag, either. I got that mixed up, too. Mom said she gave Alina the silver one and it wasn't quilted. Mom wanted us to be able to tell them apart. We were forever arguing over whose was what and what was whose. The fact is I was grasping at straws and I'm sorry I wasted your time. You were right when you told me I should pack up, go home, and help my family get through these difficult times."

"I see," he said slowly, and I was afraid he really did — right through me.

Didn't overworked, underpaid civil servants only grease squeaky wheels? I wasn't squeaking anymore, so why wasn't he getting the message and holstering his oilcan? Alina's case had been closed before I'd come over, he'd refused to reopen it, and I'd be darned if he was reopening it now. He'd get himself killed!

I abandoned the oversweetened drawl. "Look, Inspector, what I'm saying is that I've given up. I'm not asking you or anyone else to continue the investigation. I know your department is overloaded. I know there are no leads. I know it's unsolved and I accept that my sister's case is closed."

"How . . . suddenly mature of you, Ms. Lane."

"A sister's death can make a girl grow up fast." That much was true.

"I guess that means you'll be flying home soon, then."

"Tomorrow," I lied.

"What airline?"

"Continental."

"What flight?"

"I can never remember. I've got it written down somewhere. Upstairs."

"What time?"

"Eleven thirty-five."

"Who beat you?"

I blinked, fumbling for an answer. I could hardly say I stabbed a vampire and he tried to kill me. "I fell. On the stairs."

"Got to be careful there. Stairs can be tricky." He looked around the room. "Which stairs?"

"They're in the back."

"How did you bang up your face? Hit the banister?"

"Uh-huh."

"Who's Barrons?"

"What?"

"This store is called Barrons Books and Baubles. I wasn't able to find anything in public records about an owner, dates of sale for the building, or even a business license. In fact, although this address shows on my maps, to all intents and purposes, the building doesn't exist. So, who's Barrons?"

"I'm the owner of this bookstore. Why?"

I jerked, stifling a gasp. Sneaky man. He was standing right behind us, the epitome of stillness, one hand on the back of the sofa, dark hair slicked back from his face, his expression arrogant and cold. No surprise there. Barrons *is* arrogant and cold. He's also wealthy, strong, brilliant, and a walking enigma. Most women seem to find him drop-dead sexy, too. Thankfully I'm not most women. I don't get off on danger. I get off on a man with strong moral fiber. The closest Barrons ever gets to fiber is walking down the cereal aisle at the grocery store.

I wondered how long he'd been there. With him you never know.

The inspector stood, looking mildly rattled. He took in Barron's size, his steel-toed boots, the hardwood floors. Jericho Barrons is a tall, powerfully built man. I knew O'Duffy was wondering how he could have failed to hear him approach. I no longer waste time wondering about that sort of thing. In fact, so long as he keeps watching my back, I'll continue to ignore the fact that Barrons doesn't seem to be governed by the natural laws of physics.

"I'd like to see some identification," growled the inspector.

I fully expected Barrons to toss O'Duffy from the shop on his ear. He had no legal compulsion to comply and Barrons doesn't suffer fools lightly. In fact, he doesn't suffer them at all, except me, and that's only because he needs me to help him find the *Sinsar Dubh.* Not that I'm a fool. If I've been guilty of anything, it's having the blithely sunny disposition of someone who enjoyed a happy childhood, loving parents, and long summers of lazy-paddling ceiling fans and small-town drama in the Deep South which — while it's great — doesn't do a thing to prepare you for life beyond that.

Barrons gave the inspector a wolfish smile. "Certainly." He removed a wallet from the inner pocket of his suit. He held it out but didn't let go. "And yours, Inspector."

O'Duffy's jaw tightened but he complied.

As the men swapped identifications, I sidled closer to O'Duffy so I could peer into Barrons' wallet.

Would wonders never cease? Just like a real person, he had a driver's license. Hair: black. Eyes: brown. Height: 6' 3". Weight: 245. His birthday — was he kidding? — Halloween. He was thirty-one years old and his middle initial was *Z.* I doubted he was an organ donor.

"You've a box in Galway as your address, Mr. Barrons. Is that where you were born?"

I'd once asked Barrons about his lineage, he'd told me Pict and Basque. Galway was in Ireland, a few hours west of Dublin.

"No."

"Where?"

"Scotland."

"You don't sound Scottish."

"You don't sound Irish. Yet here you are, policing Ireland. But then the English have been trying to cram their laws down their neighbors' throats for centuries, haven't they, Inspector?"

O'Duffy had an eye tic. I hadn't noticed it before. "How long have you been in Dublin?"

"A few years. You?"

"I'm the one asking the questions."

"Only because I'm standing here letting you."

"I can take you down to the station. Would you prefer that?"

"Try." The one word dared the Garda to try, by fair means or foul. The accompanying smile guaranteed failure. I wondered what he'd do if the inspector attempted it. My inscrutable host seems to possess a bottomless bag of tricks.

37

O'Duffy held Barrons' gaze longer than I expected him to. I wanted to tell him there was no shame in looking away. Barrons has something the rest of us don't have. I don't know what it is, but I feel it all the time, especially when we're standing close. Beneath the expensive clothes, unplaceable accent, and cultured veneer, there's something that never crawled all the way out of the swamp. It didn't want to. It likes it there.

The inspector apparently deemed an exchange of information the wisest, or maybe just the easiest course. "I've been in Dublin since I was twelve. When my father died, my mother remarried an Irishman. There's a man over at Chester's says he knows you, Mr. Barrons. Name's Ryodan. Ring a bell?"

"Ms. Lane, go upstairs," Barrons said, instantly, softly.

"I'm perfectly fine here." Who was Ryodan and what didn't Barrons want me to know?

"Up. Stairs. Now."

I scowled. I didn't have to look at O'Duffy to know he was regarding me with acute interest — and pity. He was thinking Barrons was the name of the flight of stairs I'd fallen down. I hate pity. Sympathy isn't quite as bad. Sympathy says, I know how it feels, doesn't it just suck? Pity means they think you're defeated.

"He doesn't beat me," I said irritably. "I'd kill him if he did."

"She would. She has a temper. Stubborn, too. But we're working on that, aren't we, Ms. Lane?" Barrons turned his wolf smile on me, and jerked his head up toward the ceiling.

Someday I'm going to push Jericho Barrons as far as I can and see what happens. But I'm going to wait a while, until I'm stronger. Until I'm pretty sure I've got a trump card.

I may have been forced into this war, but I'm learning to choose my battles.

I didn't see Barrons for the rest of the day.

A dutiful soldier, I retreated to the ditches as ordered and hunkered down there. In those ditches, I had an epiphany. People treat you as badly as you let them treat you.

Key word there: let.

Some people are exceptions, mostly parents, best friends, and spouses, though in my bartending job at The Brickyard, I've seen married people do worse things to each other in public than I'd do in private to someone I couldn't stand. Bottom line is most of the world will push you as far as you let them. Barrons might have sent me to my room, but *I'm* the idiot that went. What was I afraid of? That he'd hurt me, kill me? Hardly. He'd saved my life last week. He needed me. Why had I let him intimidate me?

I was disgusted with myself. I was still behaving like MacKayla Lane, part-time bartender, part-time sun-worshipper, and full-time glamour girl. My recent brush with death had made it clear that chick wasn't going to survive over here, a statement emphatically punctuated by ten unpolished, broken fingernails. Unfortunately, by the time I had my epiphany and stormed back downstairs, Barrons and the inspector were gone.

Worsening my already foul mood, the woman who runs the bookstore and carries a major torch for Barrons had arrived. Stunning, voluptuous, in her early fifties, Fiona doesn't like me at all. I suspect if she knew Barrons kissed me last week she'd like me even less. I was nearly unconscious when he did it, but I remember. It's been impossible to forget.

When she looked up from the numbers she was punching in on her cell phone, I decided maybe she *did* know. Her eyes were venomous, her mouth a moue fanned by delicate wrinkles. With each quick, shallow inhalation, her lacy blouse trembled over her full bosom, as if she'd just dashed somewhere in a great hurry, or was suffering great distress. "What was Jericho doing here today?" she asked in a pinched tone. "It's Sunday. He's not supposed to be here on Sunday. I can't imagine any reason for him to stop by." She scanned me from head to toe, looking, I think, for signs of a recent tryst: tousled hair, perhaps a missed button on my blouse, or panties overlooked in the haste of dressing, left bunched in the leg of my jeans. I did that once. Alina saved me before Mom caught me.

I almost laughed. A tryst with Barrons? Get real.

"What are *you* doing here?" I countered. No more good little soldier. The bookstore was closed and neither of them should have been here, raining on my already rainy parade.

"I was on my way to the butcher when I saw Jericho stepping out," she said tightly. "How long was he here? Where were you just now? What were the two of you doing before I came?" Jealousy so vibrantly colored her words I expected her breath to come out in little green puffs. As if conjured by the unspoken accusation that we'd been

41

doing the dirty, a vision of Jericho Barrons naked — dark, despotic, and probably flat-out ferocious in bed — flashed through my mind.

I found it staggeringly erotic. Disturbed, I performed a hasty mental calendar count. I was ovulating. That explained it. I get indiscriminatingly horny for three days when I am: the day before, the day of, and the day after; Mother Nature's sneaky little way of ensuring survival of the human race, I guess. I check out guys I wouldn't normally look at, especially ones in tight jeans. I catch myself trying to decide if they're left-ies or righties. Alina used to laugh and say if you can't tell, Junior, you don't want to know.

Alina. God, I missed her.

"Nothing, Fiona," I said. "I was upstairs."

She stabbed a finger at me, her eyes dangerously bright, and I was suddenly afraid she would cry. If she cried I'd lose all backbone. I can't stand older women crying. I see my mom in every one.

I was relieved when she snarled at me instead. "Do you think he healed your wounds because you matter to him? Do you think he cares? You mean nothing to him! You couldn't possibly understand that man and his moods. His needs. His desires.

42

You're a stupid, selfish, naïve child," she hissed. "Go home!"

"I'd *love* to go home," I shot back. "Unfortunately, I don't have that choice!"

She opened her mouth but I didn't catch what she was saying because I'd already turned and was banging through the connecting doors to the private residence part of the store, in no mood to get dragged any further into the argument she was spoiling to have. I left her shouting something about how she didn't have choices, either.

I went upstairs. Yesterday Barrons had told me to lose the splints. I'd told him bones didn't heal that fast, but my arm was itching like crazy again, so I went in the bathroom adjoining my bedroom and took it off.

I gingerly wiggled my wrist then flexed my hand. My arm had obviously never been broken, probably just sprained. It felt whole, stronger than ever. I peeled off the finger splints to find they were better than fine, too. There was a faint smudge of red and black on my forearm, like a smear of ink. While I rinsed it off, I turned my face from side to side in the mirror, wishing my bruises would heal as quickly. I'd spent most of my life as an attractive blonde. Now, a badly battered girl with short black hair stared back at me.

I turned away.

While I'd convalesced, Barrons had gotten me one of those little refrigerators college kids use in dorms, and stocked me up on snacks. I popped open a soda and sprawled across the bed. I read and surfed the Net the rest of the day, trying to educate myself on all the paranormal stuff I'd spent the first twenty-two years of my life belittling and ignoring.

For a week now, I'd been waiting for the army from Hell to come. I wasn't stupid enough to believe this little lull was anything but the calm before the storm.

Was Mallucé really dead? Though I'd stabbed the citron-eyed vampire during my aborted showdown with the Lord Master, and the last thing I'd seen before losing consciousness from the injuries he'd dished out in retaliation was Barrons slamming him into a wall, I wasn't convinced of his demise and wouldn't be, until I heard something from the empty-eyed worshippers that stuffed the vamp's Goth mansion to overflowing on the south side of Dublin. In the Lord Master's employ — while two-timing and withholding powerful relics from the Unseelie leader — Mallucé had tried to kill me in order to silence me before I could betray his dirty secret. If he was still alive, I had no doubt he'd be coming after me again, sooner rather than later.

Mallucé wasn't the only worry on my mind. Was the Lord Master really unable to get past the ancient wards laid in blood and stone around the bookstore, as Barrons assured me? Who'd been driving the car transporting the mind-bending evil of the *Sinsar Dubh* past the bookstore last week? Where had it been taken? Why? What were all the Unseelie recently freed by the Lord Master doing right now? And just how responsible was I for them? Does being one of the few people who can do something about a problem make you responsible for fixing it?

It was midnight before I slept, bedroom door locked, windows buttoned up tight, lights ablaze.

The instant I opened my eyes, I knew something was wrong.

Two

It wasn't just my *sidhe*-seer senses that tipped me off, screaming something Fae was very near.

My bedroom has hardwood floors and there's no threshold strip beneath the door. I usually wedge a towel into the gap — okay, several — packed in by books, fortified with a chair, topped by a lamp so if some bizarre new monster slithers in through the crack, the lamp breaking will startle me awake, and buy me just enough time to be almost conscious when it kills me.

Last night I forgot.

As soon as I roll over in the morning, I glance at the haphazard stack. It's my way of reassuring myself that nothing found me during the night and I live to see another day in Dublin, for whatever that's worth. This morning my observation that I'd forgotten to stuff the crack was accompanied by another that made my heart freeze:

The gap beneath the door was dark.

Black. As in pitch.

I leave all the lights on at night, not just inside my bedroom but inside the entire bookstore, and outside the building, too. The exterior of Barrons Books and Baubles is flanked front, sides, and back by brilliant floodlights, to keep the Shades in the adjacent Dark Zone at bay. The one time Barrons turned off those lights after dark, sixteen men were killed right outside the back door.

The interior is also meticulously lit, with recessed spotlights on the ceilings and dozens of table and floor lamps illuminating every nook and cranny. Since my run-in with the Lord Master, I've been leaving all of them on, twenty-four/seven. So far Barrons hasn't said a word to me about the pending astronomical utility bill and if he does I'm going to tell him to take it out of my account — the one he *should* be setting up for me for being his own personal OOP detector. Using my *sidhe*-seer talents to locate ancient Fae relics — Objects of Power, or OOPs for short — is hardly my idea of a dream job. The dress code leans toward black with stiletto heels, a style I've never gotten into; I prefer pastels and pearls. And the hours are lousy; I'm usually up all night, playing psychic lint brush in dark and scary places, stealing things from scary people. He can take my food and phone bills out of that account, and I could use a clothing allowance, too, for the things of my own that keep getting ruined. Blood and green goo are no friends of detergent.

I craned my neck to see out the window. It was still raining heavily; the glass panes were dark, and as far as I could tell from the warm cocoon of my bed the exterior floodlights weren't on, which hit me about as hard as getting dropped, bleeding, into a tank of hungry sharks.

I *hate* the dark.

I shot from bed like a rock from a slingshot — one moment lying there, next crouched battle-ready in the middle of the room, a flashlight in each hand.

Dark outside the store, dark inside, beyond my bedroom door: "What the fr— fuck?" I exclaimed, then muttered, "Sorry, Mom." Raised in the Bible Belt by a mother who'd firmly advocated the pervasive southern adage that "pretty girls don't have ugly mouths," Alina and I had created our own language for expletives at a young age. Ass was "petunia," crap was "fudge-buckets," the f-word was "frog." Unfortunately, when you grow up saying those words instead of

48

the actual cusswords, they prove every bit as hard a habit to break as cussing and tend to come out at inopportune moments, undermining your credibility in a big way. "Frog off, or I'll kick your petunia" just doesn't carry a lot of weight with the kind of people I've been encountering lately, nor have my genteel southern manners impressed anyone but me. I've been retraining myself, but it's slow going.

Had one of my deepest fears manifested while I'd slept, and the power had gone out? As soon as I had that thought, I realized that not only was the clock still blinking the time, 4:01 a.m., cheery and orange as ever, but, duh, my overhead was on, same as it was every night when I went to sleep.

Juggling two flashlights into one hand, I fumbled the phone from the receiver. I tried to think of someone to call but drew a complete blank. I didn't have any friends in Dublin, and although Barrons seems to keep a residence in the store, he's rarely around and I have no idea how to reach him. There was no way I was calling the police.

I was on my own. I replaced the receiver and listened hard. The silence in the store was deafening, fraught with terrible possibilities — monsters lurking with homicidal glee, right outside my bedroom door.

I wriggled into my jeans, swapped a flashlight for my spear, stuffed three more flashlights in the back of my waistband, and crept to the door.

I could feel that there was something Fae beyond it, but that was all I knew. Not what, how many, or even how close, just a deep malaise in my stomach accompanied by a foul itchiness in my brain that made me feel like a cat with its back up, claws out, fur spiked. Barrons assures me *sidhe*-seer senses improve with experience. Mine had better start improving fast or I won't live to see next week. I stared at the door. I must have stood there for five minutes trying to talk myself into opening it. The unknown is a vast paralyzing limbo. I'd like to tell you that the monster under the bed is rarely as bad as your fear of it, but in my experience it's almost always worse.

I slid the dead bolt, parted door from jamb in the narrowest of slivers, and knifed the sharp white beam of my flashlight through it.

A dozen Shades shrank back, retreating with oily swiftness to the edge of the light and not one inch further. Adrenaline kicked me in the teeth. I slammed the door shut and drove the dead bolt home.

There were Shades inside Barrons Books and Baubles!

How in the world had *that* happened? I'd checked the lights before I'd gone to bed — they'd all been on!

I pressed myself against the door, shaking, wondering if I'd really woken up or if I was still dreaming. I've had some bad dreams lately and this was certainly the stuff of nightmares. I might be a *sidhe*-seer and a mythic Null, I might have one of the Fae's deadliest weapons in my possession, but even I'm defenseless against the lowest caste of Unseelie. Ironic, I know.

"Barrons!" I shouted. For reasons my taciturn host refuses to divulge, the Shades leave him alone. That the deadly bottom-feeders of the dark Fae give Jericho Barrons a wide berth perturbs me immensely but I'd promise to never ask him another question about it again, if only he'd cut a swath through them right now and save me.

I shouted his name until my throat hurt, but no knight-errant rushed to my rescue.

Under normal circumstances, if the Shades had been outside the store in the streets, dawn would have driven the amorphous vampires back to wherever it is they hide during the day, but it was so stormy I doubted enough light could filter through the bookstore's alcoved windows to affect them in here. Even if the dense cloud cover passed and the sun came out, strong sunlight wouldn't enter the main floor of the bookstore before early afternoon.

I groaned. But Fiona would, long before that. This past week she'd begun working extended hours at the bookstore. Increased customer demand, she'd said. Lots of early morning clients. She'd been arriving at the shop at precisely eight-forty-five a.m. to open the bookstore at nine o'clock sharp.

I had to warn her off, before she walked into a waiting Shade ambush!

And now that I thought about it, I was pretty sure she knew how to reach Barrons, too. I snatched up the phone and rang the operator.

"County?" he inquired.

"All of Dublin," I said briskly. Surely Fiona lived nearby. If not, I'd try the outlying counties.

"Name?"

"Fiona . . . uh . . . Fiona . . ." With a sound of disgust, I dropped the phone back in the cradle. I was so panicked I hadn't realized I didn't know Fiona's last name until I'd needed it.

Back to square one.

I had two choices: I could stay up here,

safe with my flashlights while, in a few hours, the Shades devoured Fiona and any number of innocent, hapless patrons who might subsequently stroll through the door she unlocked, or get my panicked act together and stop that from happening.

But how?

Light was my only weapon against the Shades. Though I suspected Barrons might get positively hostile if I set his store on fire, I had matches, and it would certainly drive them out. However, I didn't want to be inside the building when it went up in flames, and since I could hardly jump from the fourth floor, and there was no fire escape or convenient stash of bed linens to knot into a rope, I filed that option away in the category "Last Resort." Unfortunately I could see only one other resort, and it wasn't a sunny spot in the Bahamas. I stared dismally at the door.

I was going to have to run the gauntlet.

How had the Shades gotten inside to begin with? Was the power out in part of the store and they'd slithered in through a crack? Could they do that? Or had the lights somehow gotten turned off? If so, I could creep from switch to switch, armed with flashlights, and turn them back on.

I don't know if you're familiar with the

child's game Don't Touch the Alligator, but Alina and I used to play it when Mom was too busy with something else to notice that we were hopping from the Sunday parlor sofa, to her favorite lace-covered pillows, to that awful chair Gram brocaded to match the curtains, and so on. The idea is that the floor is full of alligators and if you step on one of them, you're dead. You have to get from one room to the next, without ever touching the floor.

I needed to get from the top floor of the bookstore to the bottom without ever touching the dark, and I wasn't sure how completely I couldn't touch it. Barrons says they can only get you in full darkness, but did that mean a Shade could eat me, or part of me, if for one second, a single foot, or something so small as a toe protruded into shadow? The stakes in this game were significantly higher than a carpet-burned knee, or a scolding from Mom if I slipped up. I'd seen the piles of clothing and human rinds the Shades left behind after a meal.

Shivering, I pulled on my boots, zipped a jacket over my pajama top, and tucked two of my six flashlights into the waistband of my jeans, front and back, pointed up. I tucked two more into the snug elastic waistband of my jacket, pointed down to shine on my vulnerable toes. Those were iffy. If I moved too quickly they'd fall out, but I only had so many hands. I carried the other two. I slipped a pack of matches into my pocket and tucked the spear into my boot. I'd have no use for it against this particular enemy, but there might be others. It was possible the Shades were merely the vanguard, and there was worse to come.

I took a deep breath, squared my shoulders, and opened the door. When the overhead light arced into the hallway, the Shades repeated their oily retreat.

Shades come in all different shapes and sizes. Some are small and thin, others tall and wide. They have no real substance. They're hard to pick out from the darkness, but once you know what to look for you can spot them, if you're a *sidhe*-seer. They're areas that are darker and denser, and ooze malevolence. They move around a lot, as if they're hungry and restless. They make no noise. Barrons says they're barely sentient, but once I shook my fist at one of them and it bristled back at me. That's sentient enough to worry me. They eat anything that lives: people, animals, birds, right down to the worms in the soil. When they take over a neighborhood, they turn it into a wasteland. I'd christened those barren landscapes Dark Zones.

"I can do this. Piece of cake." Embracing the lie, I aimed my flashlights and stepped into the hall.

It *was* a piece of cake. Turned out the power wasn't off; the switches had been thrown. Initially, I worked my way cautiously from wall switch to lamp, but when I realized the Shades were consistently staying beyond the reach of direct light, I gained confidence. Even in a windowless hallway of utter blackness, the flashlights bathed my body in white radiance that protected me. With each switch I threw, more Shades bunched up, until I had fifty or more of them crammed into the darkness I was forcing to retreat, light by light.

By the time I reached the landing of the first-floor stairwell, I was feeling downright cocky about my ability to clear the store of the Unseelie infestation.

I stepped briskly into the back parlor, heading for the light switch on the opposite wall. Three steps into the room, a damp breeze ruffled my hair. I swung my flashlight in that direction. A window was open onto the alley behind Barrons Books and Baubles! The truth was inescapable —

interior and exterior lights off, a window propped open? Someone was trying to kill me!

I stomped toward the window and sprawled headlong over an ottoman that shouldn't have been there. My flashlights went flying in all directions, casting a dizzying strobe light effect as they spun out of control across the floor. Shades erupted like panicked pigeons, flocking through the open window to the sanctuary of night.

Ha. Good riddance. Now I just needed to slam the window on them.

I scrambled up onto my hands and knees and froze right where I was — face-to . . . er . . . blackness-where-a-face-wasn't — with a Shade that hadn't fled. It wasn't one of the smaller ones, either. It had contorted itself to occupy the darkness between the flashlights, coiling snakelike over, under, and around the beams. I didn't want to think about the frighteningly quick reflexes it must have to have managed the trick. It was as high as the ceiling in several places, at least twenty feet long, and pulsated like a dark cancer, pressing at the edges of the light.

I sucked in a breath. I'd seen one do this before — test the light. I'd not stuck around long enough to learn the outcome of its test.

I muttered a fervent prayer it had gotten an *F.* My flashlights were scattered across the floor. Two were shining on me, flanking me, left and right. I was far enough between them that the combined pool of light narrowly bathed my entire body, but if I were to crawl toward either one, the beam would dwindle the closer I got, leaving large parts of me in darkness. It was a risk I couldn't take with this abnormally aggressive, gigantic Shade crouching over me.

As I huddled there, it snaked inky tendrils of itself forward, one toward my hair haloed weakly in light, the other at my fingers splayed in a pale pool on the floor.

I yanked my hand back, fumbled the matches from my pocket, and struck one. The pungent smell of sulfur soaked the damp air.

The tendrils retreated.

Though it's tough to tell with something that has no face, I swear it studied me, seeking my weaknesses. The match was burning down between us. I dropped it to the floor and lit another. There was no way I could strip off my jacket to set it on fire without my arms and part of my torso protruding into the dangerous darkness. Likewise, the ottoman over which I'd fallen was too far behind me to be of use.

But . . . the priceless Persian rug beneath me was starting to smolder. I exhaled a gentle puff on the glowing embers of the dropped match. It went out.

If Shades snicker, this one did. It expanded and contracted, and I swear I felt its mockery. I really hope I'm wrong. I really hope they aren't capable of complex thought.

"It would seem you are in need of assistance, *sidhe*-seer." A musical baritone drifted through the window, otherworldly, sensuous, and punctuated by a forbidding growl of thunder.

THREE

Still no knight errant.

It was V'lane. And here I'd been thinking things couldn't get any worse.

Not a knight, but a Prince. Of the Seelie or Light Court, if anything he says can be believed. And hardly errant, V'lane is a death-by-sex-Fae. They don't wander in search of adventure and romance, they incite killing ardor.

I glanced down at myself to see if I still had my clothes on. I was relieved to find I did. Fae royalty exude such intense sexuality that they override every survival instinct we have, clouding a woman's mind, provoking her erotic senses beyond anything she was meant to experience, turning her into an inhumanly aroused animal, begging for sexual release. The first thing a woman does when one shows up is start stripping.

In a romance novelist's hands, that might come off as hot, campy, even sexy. In reality, it's icy, terrifying, and most often ends in death. *If* the woman is left alive, she's *Priya,* barely able to function, a Fae sex-addict.

I glanced back at the Shade and hastily lit another match. If anything, it was watching me even more intently now.

"So, assist me already," I snapped.

"Does that mean you accept my gift?"

During our first encounter several weeks ago, V'lane had offered me a mystical relic known as the Cuff of Cruce, a gesture of goodwill, he'd claimed, in exchange for my help finding the *Sinsar Dubh* for his ruler, Aoibheal, High Queen of the Seelie Court. According to *him,* the cuff protects the wearer from assorted nasties, including the Shades.

According to my intractable host and mentor, with a Fae, Light or Dark, there's always a catch, and they don't believe in full disclosure. In fact, they don't believe in disclosure at all. Would we disclose our intentions to a horse before we rode it, or a cow before we ate it?

Perhaps the cuff would save me. Perhaps it would enslave me.

Perhaps it would kill me.

During our last encounter, V'lane tried to rape me in the middle of a public place — not that being raped in a private place would have been any better, just that, adding insult to injury, I'd regained control of myself only to discover I was nearly naked in the middle of a crowd of voyeuristic jerks. It was a hurtful, hateful memory. I'd been racking up a lot of them lately.

Mom raised me better, I want that noted for posterity's sake: Rainey Lane is a fine, upstanding woman.

I told V'lane exuberantly and in vivid detail what I was going to do to him at the earliest opportunity, and exactly where I was going to shove my Fae-killing spear — razor-sharp tip first — when I was done. I sprinkled the expletives with colorful adjectives. I might not be much of a cusser, but a bartender gets an education whether she wants one or not.

I had fourteen matches left. I struck another.

Framed in the window beyond the Shade, V'lane rose, skin of shimmering gold, eyes of liquid amber, inhumanly beautiful against the backdrop of velvety night. I think he was floating in the air. He tossed his hair, a gilded waterfall glinting with metallic sparks, cascading over a male body of such sensual perfection, such hedonistic temptation that I had no doubt Satan had laughed on the day of his creation — and sounded pretty much like V'lane did now. When his laughter subsided he murmured, "And you were such a sweet thing when you got here."

"How do you know what I was like when I got here?" I demanded. "How long have you been watching me?"

The Fae prince raised a brow but said nothing.

I raised a brow back. He was Pan, Bacchus, and Lucifer, painted a thousand shades of to-die-for. Literally. "Why don't you come in?" I asked sweetly. I had a suspicion I wanted to test.

V'lane's mouth tightened and it was my turn to laugh. Barrons was amazing. "You can't get past the wards, can you? Is that why I'm not naked?" I dropped the match just as it began to burn my fingers and lit another one. "Do the wards somehow diminish your pow—"

I didn't even get to finish my sentence. A forest fire of debilitating sexual need blasted me — *i'mhungrystarvingdyingwithoutyou pleasewon'tyoupleasewon'tyougivemewhati need* — scorching the air in my lungs, flash-frying my brain, and charring my backbone.

I collapsed to the floor, human ashes.

As suddenly and unexpectedly as the sexual inferno had razed every cell in my body, it was gone, leaving me cold and, for brief moments, in agonizing pain, ravenous for delights that could only be sampled by eating from a banquet table at which humans were never meant to sit. Forbidden fruit. Poisonous fruit. Fruit a woman might sell her soul for. Perhaps even betray mankind.

"Careful, *sidhe*-seer. I have chosen to spare you. Do not press your luck."

I locked my jaw, pushed myself up, and lit another match, studying my enemies in the flickering light. Both would devour me. Just in different ways. If forced to choose, I'd take death-by-Shade.

"Why have you chosen to spare me?"

"I want us to be . . . what is your word? Friends."

"Psychotic rapists don't have friends."

"I was unaware you were a psychotic rapist or I would not have offered."

"Ha." I'd set myself up for that one.

He smiled, and I recognized the urge I suddenly felt to believe everything was wonderful with my world for the illusion it was. Royal Fae pack a psychic punch. Barrons says their entire being is designed to seduce on every level. Glamour piled upon illusion heaped upon deceit. You can't believe a word they say.

"I am unaccustomed to interacting with

humans, and have been known to under-estimate my impact upon them. I did not understand how deeply the *Sidhba-jai* would disturb you. I wish to start again," he said.

I dropped my match and lit another. "Start by getting rid of the Shade."

"With the cuff, you would be able to saunter among them freely, without fear. You would never be so vulnerable again. Why would you refuse such power?"

"Oh, gee, let's see . . . maybe because I trust you less than I trust the Shades?" At least the Shade was too stupid to be decep-tive. I think.

"What is trust, *sidhe*-seer, but expectation that another will behave in a certain fashion, consistent with prior actions?"

"Great definition. Examine your prior ac-tions."

"I did. It is you who do not see me clearly. I came to you offering a gift to protect your life. You are a beautiful woman who dresses to command male attention. I gave it to you. I did not know the *Sidhba-jai* would distress you as it did. I even offered to pleasure you without price. You refused me. Perhaps I was offended. You menace me with a weapon stolen from my race. You speak to me of reasons not to trust when you have given me a multitude. You are a suspicious larcenous being with homicidal tendencies. Despite your continued threats to do vile things to me, I remain here, withholding what offends you, offering aid."

I was getting low on matches. How cleverly he'd turned things around, as if he'd done nothing wrong, and *I* was the dangerous one. "Oh, drop the act, Tinkerbell, and get rid of my problem. Then we'll talk."

"Will we? Talk?"

I frowned and lit another match. There was a catch here somewhere but I wasn't sure what it was. "I said we would."

"As friends, we'll talk."

"Friends do *not* have sex, if that's what you're getting at." That wasn't true, but he didn't necessarily know that. I'm heir to the "sex is just sex" generation and I hate it. Not only friends have sex, people who don't like each other have sex. I'd once caught Natalie and Rick, two people I know for a fact can't stand each other, banging away in the bathroom at The Brickyard. When later I'd asked her what had changed, she'd said nothing, she still couldn't stand him, but he'd sure looked hot tonight. Doesn't anybody get that sex is what you make it, and if you treat it like nothing, it is? I don't clean the restrooms anymore. I leave that to Val. She's lower on the seniority totem pole.

For the past few years, I've been on a quest for a good old-fashioned date, the kind where the guy calls, makes the plans, picks you up in a car that's not his dad's or his other girlfriend's, and takes you somewhere that shows he put thought into what you might like, not what he might get off on like the latest how-many-naked-boobs-can-we-cram-into-this-movie-to-disguise-the-complete-lack-of-plot movie. I'm looking for the kind of date that starts with good conversation, has a sweet and satisfying middle, and ends with long, slow kisses and the dreamy feeling that you're walking on clouds.

"That is not what I was implying. We will sit, the two of us, and talk of more than threats and fears and the differences between us. We will spend one of your hours as friends."

I didn't like the careful way he'd phrased that. "One of *my* hours?"

"Our hours are much longer, *sidhe*-seer. See how freely I converse with you? Telling you of our ways. So trust begins."

Something about the Shade drew my attention. It took me a minute to figure out what it was. Its demeanor had changed. It was still predatory, but it was angry now. I could sense it the same way I'd felt its mockery earlier. I could also sense that its anger was not directed at me. I lit another match and contemplated it. I had four matches left, and an uneasy suspicion that V'lane might be doing something to rein in the amorphous life-sucker.

Was it possible this unnaturally strong Shade could take me, even in the light, if V'lane weren't here right now? Had he been holding it at bay since the beginning?

"One hour," I ground out. "But I'm not taking the cuff. And you won't do that sexing-me-up thing. And I need coffee before we begin."

"Not now. At a time of my choosing, Mac-Kayla."

He was calling me by name like we were friends. I didn't like it one bit. I lit my third-last match. "Fine. Fix my problem."

I was wondering just what I'd agreed to, and how many more demands V'lane would make before getting rid of the Shade — I had no doubt he'd draw it out until the last moment to scare and humiliate me as much as possible — when he mocked silkily, "Let there be light," and suddenly all the lights in the room popped on.

The Shade exploded, shattering into countless dark pieces. They scrabbled toward the night, frantic cockroaches fleeing a bombed room, and I could sense the Un-seelie was in unspeakable pain. If light didn't kill them, it was certainly their version of Hell.

After the last quivering fragment scuttled over the sill, I hurried to shut the window. The alley was once again brightly lit. And empty.

V'lane was gone.

I collected my flashlights, tucked them back into my waistband, and walked through the store, hunting for Shades lurking in corners or hiding in closets. I found none. All the lights were back on, inside and out.

It disturbed me deeply. As effortlessly as V'lane had helped me, he could dump me back into the dark if he felt like it, without ever even having to enter the store.

What else could he do? How powerful was a Royal Fae? Shouldn't the wards keep him from being able to influence physical matter beyond them? Speaking of wards, why hadn't they kept out the Shades? Had Barrons only warded the property against the Lord Master? If he could perform such tricks, why not ward the entire building against everything? Except, of course, store patrons, although it was obvious the bookstore was just a cover — Barrons needed more money like Ireland needed more rain.

I needed answers. I was sick of not getting any. I was surrounded by egotistical, unpredictable, moody, pushy jackasses, and my feeling was if you can't beat them, join them. I was confident I, too, could be a pushy jackass. I just needed a little practice.

I wanted to know more about Barrons. I wanted to know if he lived in this building or not. I wanted to know more about his mysterious garage. He'd slipped up not long ago, and mentioned something about a vault three floors beneath it. I wanted to know what a man like him stored in an underground vault.

I began with the store. The front half was just what it seemed, an eclectic and well-stocked bookstore. I dismissed it and moved to the rear half. The first floor was as impersonal as a museum, liberally and exorbitantly fitted with antiquities and artwork, but nothing that betrayed any real glimpse into the mind of the man who'd acquired the many artifacts. Even his study, the one room I expected to offer some personal portrayal of the man, presented only the cool, impersonal reflection of a large wood-framed mirror that occupied the wall between cherry bookcases, behind the ornate fifteenth-century desk. There was no bedroom, kitchen, or dining room on the first floor.

Every door on the second and third floors was locked. They were heavy, solid wood doors with complicated locks that I couldn't force or pick. I started out stealthily jiggling the doorknobs because I was afraid Barrons might be in one of the rooms, but by the time I got to the third floor, I was giving them good hard shakes and pissed-off kicks. I'd awakened tonight to find myself in the dark. I was tired of being in the dark. I was tired of everyone else having control of the lights.

I stomped back downstairs and outside to the garage. The rain had abated but the sky was still dark with thunderclouds, and dawn was a promise I wouldn't have believed, if I'd not lived through twenty-two years of them. Down the alley to my left, Shades restlessly shaped and reshaped the darkness at the edge of the abandoned neighborhood.

I flipped them off. With both hands.

I tested the garage door. Locked, of course.

I went to the nearest blacked-out window and smashed it in with the butt of my flashlight. The tinkle of breaking glass soothed my soul. No alarm went off. "Take that, Barrons. Guess your world isn't so perfectly controlled, after all." Perhaps it was warded like the bookstore, against other threats, not me. I broke out the jagged edges so I wouldn't get cut, hoisted myself over the sill, and dropped to the floor.

I flipped on the light switches by the door then just stood there a minute, grinning like an idiot. I've seen his collection before, even ridden in a few of the cars, but the sight of them all together, one gleaming fantasy after another, is a total rush to somebody like me.

I love cars.

From sleek and sporty to squat and muscley, from luxury sedan to high-performance coupe, from state-of-the-art to timeless classic, I am a car fanatic — and Barrons has them all. Well, maybe not *all*. I haven't seen him driving a Bugatti yet, and really, with 1003 horsepower and a million-dollar price tag, I'm hardly expecting to, but he's got pretty much every car of my dreams, right down to a sixty-four and a half Stingray, painted what else but British racing green?

There, a black Maserati crouched next to a Wolf Countach. Here, a red Ferrari stretched on the verge of a purr, next to a — my smile died instantly — Rocky O'Bannion's Maybach, reminding me of sixteen deaths that shouldn't have happened to men who hadn't deserved to die, and at least part of it was on my head: sixteen deaths I'd celebrated because they'd bought me a temporary stay of execution.

Where do you put such conflicting feelings? Is this where I'm supposed to grow up and start compartmentalizing? Is compartmentalizing just another way of divvying up our sins, apportioning a few here and a few over there, shoving our internal furniture around to hide some, so we can go on living with the weight of them individually, because collectively they'd drown us?

I shoved all thought of cars from my mind and began looking for doors.

The garage had once been some kind of commercial warehouse, and I wouldn't be at all surprised if it occupied nearly a city block. The floors were polished concrete, the walls poured concrete, the beams and girders steel. All the windows were painted black, from the glass-block apertures near the ceiling, to the two double-paned glass openings at ground level by the doors, one of which I'd busted. The garage had a single retractable dock door.

Other than that and a bunch of cars, there was nothing. No stairs, no closets, no trapdoors hidden beneath rubber mats on the floor. I know, I looked, there was nothing.

So where were the three subterranean levels and how was I supposed to get down to them?

I stood in the center of the enormous garage surrounded by one of the finest car collections in the world, tucked away in a nondescript alley in Dublin, and tried to think like its bizarre owner. It was an exercise in futility. I wasn't sure he had a brain. Perhaps there was only a coldly efficient microchip in there.

I *felt* more than heard the noise, a rumble in my feet.

I cocked my head, listening. After a moment, I got down on my hands and knees, brushed a thin veneer of dust from the floor, and pressed my ear to the cold concrete. Far beneath me, in the marrow of the ground, something bayed.

It sounded maddened, bestial, and it raised the fine hair all over my body. I closed my eyes and tried to picture the mouth capable of making such a sound. It bayed over and over, each soul-chilling howl lasting a full minute or more, echoing up from its concrete tomb.

What was *down* there? What kind of creature possessed such lung capacity? Why was it making such a sound? It was darker than a wail of despair, emptier than a funeral dirge; it was the bleak, tortured baying of a thing beyond salvation, abandoned, lost, condemned to the agony of hell without beginning or end.

Chicken flesh sprouted all over my arms.

There was a new cry then, this one more terrified than tortured. It rose in gruesome concert with that long, terrible howl.

They both stopped.

There was silence.

I rapped my knuckles on the floor in frustration, wondering just how far in over my head I was.

No longer feeling quite so jackassy or pushy, I left to go back to my room. As I stepped into the alley, the wind scooted trash along the pavement, and the dense cloud cover drifted apart to reveal a window of dark sky. Dawn was moments away, yet the moon was still bright and full. To my right, in the Dark Zone, Shades no longer crouched in the shadows. They'd fled something, and it wasn't the moon or the dawn. I'd watched them a lot from my window lately; they ceded the night in petulant degrees, the largest of them lingering until the last.

I glanced to my left and sucked in a breath.

"No," I whispered.

Just beyond reach of the building flood-lights a tall, black-shrouded figure stood, folds of midnight cloth rustling in the wind.

Several times over the past week, I'd thought I'd glimpsed something out a window, late at night. Something so trite and clichéd that I'd refused to believe it was real. And I wouldn't now.

Fae were bad enough.

"You're not there," I told it.

I dashed across the alley, vaulted up the stairs, kicked open the door, and burst through it. When I looked back, the specter was gone.

I laughed shakily. I knew better.

It had never been there to begin with.

I took a shower, dried my hair, got dressed, grabbed a chilled latte from the fridge, and made it downstairs just in time for Fiona to show up, and the police to arrive to arrest me.

FOUR

"I told you. He was working on my sister's case."

"And when did you see him last?"

"I told you that, too. Yesterday morning. He stopped by the bookstore."

"Why did he stop by the bookstore?"

"Oh, for heaven's sake, I told you that, too. To tell me he'd reviewed her case and there was still no new evidence and that he was sorry but it was going to have to stay closed."

"Do you expect me to believe Inspector O'Duffy, who incidentally has a lovely wife and three children he takes to church every Sunday, followed by brunch with his in-laws — a family outing he's missed only four times in the past fifteen years, and then for funerals — bypassed that in favor of making an early morning, personal visit to the sister of a deceased murder victim to tell her an already closed case was staying closed?"

Well, fudge-buckets. Even I was gripped by the illogic in that.

"Why didn't he use the phone?"

I shrugged.

My interrogator, Inspector Jayne, waved the two officers flanking the door from the room. He pushed up from the table and circled it, stopping behind me. I could feel him back there, staring down at me. I was acutely aware of the ancient stolen spear tucked into my boot, inside the leg of my jeans. If they charged and searched me, I was in big trouble.

"You're an attractive young woman, Ms. Lane."

"Point?"

"Was there something going on between you and Inspector O'Duffy?"

"Oh, please! Do you really think he's my type?"

"Was, Ms. Lane. Do I think he *was* your type. He's dead."

I glared up at the Garda looming over me, trying to use dominant body posture to intimidate me. He didn't know how bad my day had already been, or that there wasn't much in the human world that frightened me anymore. "Are you going to arrest me or not?"

"His wife said he'd been distracted lately.

Worried. Not eating. She had no idea why. You know?"

"No. I told you that, too. Half a dozen times now. How many more times do we have to go over this?" I sounded like a bad actor in a worse movie.

He did, too. "As many times as I say we have to. Let's take it from the beginning. Tell me again about the first time you saw him here at the station."

I took a deep breath and closed my eyes.

"Open your eyes and answer the question."

I opened my eyes and stared daggers up at him. I still couldn't believe O'Duffy was dead. Royally screwing up my world, he'd had his throat cut holding a scrap of paper with my name and the address of the bookstore written on it. It hadn't taken long for his brothers in — well, not exactly arms, the Dublin police don't carry guns — to come looking for me. I'd spent the morning battling Shades and a death-by-sex Fae, discovered something monstrous lived beneath Barrons' garage right behind my bedroom, and now I was in the police station being interrogated on suspicion of murder. Could my day get any worse? Oh, they'd not pressed formal charges, but they'd sure used scare tactics on me back at the bookstore, making them think they were. And they'd made it clear they'd jump on any reason they could find to back me up against a wall and start snapping mug shots. I was a stranger in this city, nearly all the answers I gave sounded evasive because they were evasive, and O'Duffy's Sunday morning visit to me really did look suspicious.

I repeated the story I'd told an hour ago, and an hour before that and an hour before that. He asked the same questions he and two men before him had asked, all morning and a good part of the afternoon — they'd let me stew for forty-five minutes while they went to lunch and came back smelling scrumptiously of vinegary fish and chips — phrased in minutely different ways, all designed to trip me up. The caffeine from my chilled latte had worn off hours ago and I was starving.

On one level, I could appreciate what Inspector Jayne was doing; it was his job, he was doing it very well, and it was obvious Patrick O'Duffy had been his friend. I hoped they'd done the same for Alina. On another level, it infuriated me. My problems were so much bigger than this. It was an epic waste of my time. Not only that, I felt exposed. With the exception of my trip across the back alley this morning, I hadn't set foot outside of the bookstore since I'd seen what I'd seen in the warehouse at 1247 LaRuhe a week ago. I felt like a walking target with a bull's-eye painted on my forehead. Did the Lord Master know where to find me? How high was I on his list of priorities? Was he still wherever he'd gone when he'd stepped through that portal? Was he watching the bookstore? Did he have his Rhino-boys, those watchdogs of the Fae — the lower caste of enormous, ugly, gray-skinned Unseelie with wide, squat, barrel-bodies, jutting underbites, and bumpy foreheads — waiting to grab me the moment I walked out of the police station by myself? Should I *try* to get myself formally arrested? I discarded that thought the instant I had it. Humans couldn't keep me alive. I blinked, startled to realize I no longer quite counted myself in that camp.

"He was my brother-in-law," he said abruptly.

I winced.

"Assuming you had nothing to do with his murder, I still have to find a way to tell my sister what the fuck he was doing with you the morning he died," he said bitterly. "So what the fuck was he doing, Ms. Lane? Because we both know your story's bullshit.

Patty didn't miss Mass. Patty didn't follow up on cases on his personal time. Patty stayed alive because Patty loved his family."

I stared dismally at my hands, folded neatly in my lap. I badly needed a manicure. I tried to imagine what the wife of an officer who'd died mere hours after visiting a pretty young woman, and was given the inane reason for the visit I was offering, would think and feel. She'd know she was being lied to, and the unknown always takes on greater, more terrible proportions than whatever truth is concealed behind the lie. Would she believe, as her brother did, that her beloved Patty had cheated on her and betrayed their marriage vows the morning he'd died?

I never used to lie. Mom raised us to believe that every lie puts something out there in the world that's inevitably going to come back and bite you in the petunia. "I can't explain Inspector O'Duffy's actions. I can only tell you what he did. He came by to tell me Alina's case was staying closed. That's all I know."

I drew comfort from the fact that if I came clean and told him everything, confessed every bit of it, down to my suspicion that O'Duffy had somehow learned that something big, nasty, and not human had moved into Dublin, and been killed because of it, he'd believe me even less.

The afternoon was endless: Who owns the bookstore? How did you say you met him? Why are you staying there? Is he your lover? If her case is closed, why haven't you gone home? How did you get those bruises on your face? Are you working somewhere? How are you supporting yourself? When do you plan to go home? Do you know anything about the three abandoned cars in the back alley behind Barrons Books and Baubles?

The whole time, I waited for Barrons to come and rescue me, the product, I suppose, of growing up in a world where nearly all the fairy tales I'd heard as a child had a prince rushing to the rescue of the princess. Men down south love to play up to that image.

It's a strange new world out there and the rules have changed: It's every princess for herself.

It was five-forty-five before they finally let me go.

O'Duffy's brother-in-law escorted me to the door. "I'm going to be watching you, Ms. Lane. Every time you turn around, it's my face you're going to see. I'm going to be tape to your ass."

"Fine," I said tiredly. "Can I get a ride

back to the bookstore?"

Okay, that was a no.

"How about the phone? Can I use it?" He gave me another hard look. "Are you *kidding* me? You guys wouldn't let me get my purse this morning. I don't have money for a cab. What if somebody out there mugs me?"

Inspector Jayne was already walking away. "You don't have a purse, Ms. Lane. What would somebody mug you for?" he tossed over his shoulder.

I glanced uneasily at my watch. When they'd picked me up at the bookstore, they'd made me remove the flashlights from the waistband of my jeans and leave them with Fiona.

Thunder rumbled, vibrating the glass panes in the windows.

It was going to be dark soon.

"Hey! You there, wait up!"

I didn't break stride.

"Beautiful girl, wait a minute! I was hoping I'd see you again!"

It was the "beautiful girl" part that flung a noose around my foot, the voice that snagged it tight. I raked a hand through my recently butchered hair and looked down at my dark, baggy clothes. The compliment

84

was balm to my soul, the voice young, male, and full of fun. I skidded to a halt. Shallow, I know.

It was the dreamy-eyed guy I'd seen in the museum the day I'd been searching it for OOPs.

I turned bright red. That was the day V'lane had amped up the death-by-sex thing and I'd stripped in the middle of Ireland's famous Ór exhibit, right there in front of God and everybody.

Flushing, I sprinted off again, splashing through puddles. It was raining — of frogging course — and the sidewalks of Dublin's *craic*-filled Temple Bar District were nearly empty. I had places to go, darkness to race, guys who'd watched me strip to avoid.

He dropped into a long-legged lope beside me and I couldn't help myself, I slanted a look at him. Tall, dark, dreamy-eyed, he was boy-on-the-cusp-of-man, in that perfect stage where guys are velvet skin over supple hard bodies, without an ounce of fat. I'd bet he had a six-pack. He was a serious leftie. Once upon a time in my life, I'd have given my eyeteeth for a date with him. I'd have dressed in pink and gold, swept my long blond hair up in a playful ponytail, and painted my nails and toes to match, Young-

85

Hearts-Beat-Free-Tonight Blush.

"Fine, I'll run with you then," he said easily. "Where you off to in such a hurry?"

"None of your business." Go away, pretty boy. You don't fit in my world anymore. How I wished he did.

"I was afraid I wouldn't see you again."

"You don't even know me. Besides, I'm sure you saw more than enough of me at the museum," I said bitterly.

"What do you mean?"

"You know."

He shot me a quizzical look. "All I know is I had to leave right after I saw you. I had to go to work."

He hadn't watched me strip? Some of the ugliness of my life melted away. "Where do you work?"

"Ancient Languages Department."

"Where?" Hunky and smart.

"Trinity."

"Cool. Student?"

"Yeah. You?"

I shook my head.

"American?"

I nodded. "You?" He didn't sound Irish.

"Little of this, little of that. Nothing special." He smiled and winked. Dreamy eyes, long dark lashes.

Wow. Right. This guy was special all the

way down to his toes. I wanted to know him. I wanted to kiss him. I wanted to feather my lips on those lashes. And he'd probably end up dead if he hung around with me. I killed monsters other people couldn't see and had just spent the entire day in the police station on suspicion of murder for the death of a man I hadn't killed instead of the sixteen I had. "Leave me alone. I can't be your friend," I said bluntly.

"That's way too intriguing to pass up. What's your story, beautiful girl?"

"I don't have a story. I have a life. And you don't fit in it."

"Boyfriend?"

"Dozens."

"Truth?"

"Is."

"Come on, don't dis me."

"Consider yourself dissed. Fuck off," I said coolly.

He held up both hands, "All right. I get it," and stopped.

I pounded down the sidewalk away from him and didn't look back. I wanted to cry.

"I'll be around," he called. "If you change your mind, you know where to find me."

Right. Ancient Languages Department at Trinity. I made a mental note never to go there.

"I think they know me," I said when I pushed through the front door of the bookstore. Barrons was behind the counter, not Fiona. That was weird. He was actually ringing up a purchase, like a real person doing a job. He cut me a look of warning — mute it, Ms. Lane — and jerked his head toward the customer.

"Flip the sign," he said when the patron left. He slapped a cardboard placard on the counter and began writing on it. "Who do you think knows you?"

"The Shades. They get . . . I don't know, agitated when they see me coming. Like they recognize me and I piss them off. I think they're more sentient than you know."

"I think you have an overactive imagination, Ms. Lane. Did you turn the sign over yet?"

I flipped over the sign. That was Barrons, autocratic down to his steel-booted toes. "Why? Wrapping up early?"

He finished writing, walked over, and handed me a placard to hang on the door next to the sign.

I read it. "For how long?" I was surprised. The bookstore was our cover and now he was closing it?

"At least a few weeks. Unless you want to start running the cash register, Ms. Lane."

"Where's Fiona?"

"Fiona turned off all the lights and left a window open last night."

I staggered — physically stumbled backward — and nearly fell from the impact of that mental blow. I caught myself on a display table, toppling a few baubles and stacks of the latest best-sellers. "Fiona tried to *kill* me?" I knew she didn't like me, but come on. Talk about excessive!

"She claimed she was only trying to frighten you off. She wanted you to go home. I was beginning to think she'd succeeded. Where were you all day?"

I was too busy reeling from Fiona's viciousness to answer him. It was bad enough that I had to watch my back with all the known nasties. I wasn't well versed enough in feminine wiles to see the subtler nasties coming. "God, what did she do?" I breathed. "Sneak back in late last night? How did she get out herself?"

"Same way you did, I imagine. Flashlights. I must admit, Ms. Lane, I'm impressed with how well you cleared the place. There must have been Shades everywhere."

"There were, and I didn't. I only cleared part of it. V'lane did the rest," I said absently. How ironic that I'd been so doggedly trying to save her from the very monsters she'd turned loose on me.

There was a moment of frozen silence, then Barrons exploded, "What? V'lane was here? In my store?" His fingers banded around my upper arm.

"Ow, Barrons, you're hurting me," I snapped.

He released me instantly.

Barrons is dangerously strong. I think he has to maintain constant awareness of what he's touching, or he'd end up breaking bones. I rubbed my arm. I would be bruised tomorrow. Again.

"My apologies, Ms. Lane. So?"

"No, of course he wasn't in the store; you have it warded, don't you? Speaking of which, why didn't your wards keep the Shades out?"

"It's only warded against certain things."

"Why don't you ward it against everything?"

"Wards demand . . . resources. Protection has a price. All power does. Lights serve well enough to keep the Shades out. Besides, they're stupid."

"I'm not so sure about that." I told him about the one that had faced off with me in the back room, how I'd lost my flashlights and been left with only a pack of matches that I'd nearly run through, how V'lane had appeared in the back alley and driven it off.

He listened intently, asked me many questions about our conversation, wrapping up with, "Did you fuck him?"

"Ah!" I yelled. "Of course not!" I rubbed my face with both hands and kept it buried there a minute. "Wouldn't I be an addict if I did?" I raised my face.

Barrons studied me, dark eyes cold. "Not if he protected you."

"They can do that? Really?"

"Try not to sound so intrigued, Ms. Lane."

"I'm not," I said defensively.

"Good. You don't trust him, do you?"

"I don't trust anybody. Not him. Not you. Nobody."

"Then you might just stay alive. Where were you today?"

"Didn't Fiona tell you?" I was learning from his tricks: answer a question with a question. Distract. Evade.

"She was hardly forthcoming when I . . . fired her." There was a hesitation before the word "fired," nearly imperceptible unless you knew the man.

"What if she comes back around and tries to hurt me again?"

"Not a worry. Where were you?"

I told him about the Garda, that I'd spent the day at the station, that O'Duffy was dead.

"And they think you slit the throat of a man nearly twice your size?" He snorted. "That's absurd."

A sudden, deep quietude blanketed my mind. I hadn't told Barrons how O'Duffy had died. "Yeah, well," I blustered around it, "you know how cops are. By the way, where have *you* been lately? I could have used help a few times in the past twenty-four hours."

"You seem to have done well enough on your own. You had your new friend, *V'lane,* to assist you." He said the name in a way that made the prince sound like a prancy little fairy, not the virile, lethally seductive Fae he was. "What happened to my window out back?"

I wasn't about to admit to a man who already knew how O'Duffy had died that I knew he was keeping some kind of monster under his garage. I shrugged. "I don't know. What?"

"It's broken. Did you hear anything last night?"

"Had my hands a little full, Barrons."

"Of Shades, not V'lane, one hopes."

"Ha."

"You weren't in my garage, were you?"

"No."

"You wouldn't lie to me, would you?"

"Of course not." No more than you would lie to me, I didn't add, honesty among thieves and all.

"Well, then, good night, Ms. Lane." He inclined his head and whisked silently through the connecting doors, into the rear of the building.

I sighed and began collecting the various books and baubles I'd knocked from the display table. I couldn't wrap my brain around the thought that Fiona had sneaked in last night and turned off all the lights. Chase me away, my petunia. That woman had wanted me dead. I couldn't imagine anyone knowing Barrons well enough to develop such strong feelings for him. Still, I knew there was something between the two of them, if only the intimacy and deep possession of long association.

From the rear of the building came a howl of outrage. A moment later Barrons exploded through the connecting doors, dragging a Persian rug behind him.

"What *is* this?" he demanded.

"A rug?" I batted my lashes, thinking what a stupid question.

"I know it's a rug. What are *these?*" He thrust it beneath my nose, stabbing a finger at the dozen or so burn marks.

I peered at them. "Burns?"

"Burns from dropped matches, Ms. Lane? Matches one might have dropped while flirting with a pernicious Fae, Ms. Lane? Have you any idea the *value* of this rug?"

I didn't think his nostrils could flare any wider. His eyes were black flame. "Pernicious? Good grief, is English your second language? Third?" Only someone who'd learned English from a dictionary would use such a word.

"Fifth," he snarled. "Answer me."

"Not more than my life, Barrons. Nothing is worth more than my life."

He glared at me. I notched my chin higher and glared back.

Barrons and I have a unique way of communicating. We have these little nonverbal conversations, where we say all those things we don't say with our mouths with our eyes instead, and we understand each other perfectly.

I didn't say, You are *such* a stuffy asshole.

And he didn't say, If you ever burn one of my quarter-of-a-million dollar rugs again I'll take it out of your hide, and I didn't say, Oh, honey, wouldn't you like to? And he didn't say Grow up, Ms. Lane, I don't take little girls to my bed, and I didn't say I wouldn't go there if it was the only safe place from the Lord Master in all of Dublin.

"You might reconsider that one day." His voice was low, fierce, on the verge of guttural.

I gasped. "What?" Intrinsic to our wordless free-for-alls was a tacit agreement never to elevate those conversations to a verbal level. It was the only reason either of us was willing to participate.

He gave me a cool smile. "That nothing is worth more than your life, Ms. Lane. Some things are. Don't put too high a premium on it. You may live to regret it."

He turned and walked away, dragging the rug behind him.

I went to bed.

The next morning I woke up, dismantled my haphazard monster alarm, opened the door, and found a small TV with a built-in VCR/DVD player sitting in the hallway.

Manna from heaven! I'd been thinking, since Fiona was gone, about swiping the one she kept behind the counter. Now I wouldn't have to.

There was a tape next to it.

I toted the TV into my room, plugged it into the wall, slipped in the tape, and turned it on. The program was already cued.

I winced and turned it back off. I kicked a chair.

Every time I think I'm getting smarter I realize that I've just done something stupid. Dad says there are three kinds of people in the world: those who don't know, and don't know they don't know; those who don't know and *do* know they don't know; and those who know and know how much they still don't know.

Heavy stuff, I know. I think I've finally graduated from the don't-knows that don't know to the don't-knows that do.

Barrons had security cameras in the garage. He'd just given me a tape of myself breaking into it.

FIVE

I flipped the sign, boldly lettered in hot pink Sharpie — Barrons Books and Baubles Summer Hours: 11 a.m. to 7 p.m., M.–F., it said — and locked the front door, feeling good about myself.

I'd just completed my first day on the new job.

Up until now, bartending had been my only marketable skill but today I'd broadened my employment horizons and could now add store clerk to my résumé. An opportunity had presented itself to make money, and I wasn't about to let it pass me by. Barrons had offered me the job last night — *unless you want to start running the cash register, Ms. Lane,* he'd said.

After only one day, I could see the job was far more complex than merely ringing up the occasional purchase. There was stocking to worry about, special ordering to be done, bookkeeping to stay on top of, and spending time with patrons, helping them find things they didn't know they wanted. The store carried some cool stuff but there were things that definitely needed changing. Some of the magazines had to go; I wasn't about to waste my precious time chasing teenage boys away from the Male Interest racks. The Female Interest racks were seriously lacking; I planned to add more high-end fashion magazines along with some eye candy, and the store definitely needed a more festive selection of writing implements. The hot pink Sharpie was mine. BB&B offered only your basic pens plus a few prissy-looking calligraphy sets, the kind that make it take forever to write a single letter. Barrons obviously didn't understand that shorthand — LMAO, IMHO, GFY — was the new longhand, and in a world where everything was high-speed and wireless, nobody wanted dial-up anymore.

My reasons for accepting the job were twofold: I was eventually going to run out of money, sooner rather than later; and if the Garda pushed their investigation, I could cite my job as the reason for my continued stay in Dublin. I was training to learn to run my own bookstore back in the States, I would tell them.

Fiona's recently extended hours were

absurd; there was no way I was working an eleven-hour day. Since I was in charge now, I'd made my first executive decision and chosen new hours of operation, opening late enough that I could either sleep in in the mornings or use them to take care of personal business. As far as State of the World business was concerned, I'd decided it wasn't my problem.

Vengeance for my sister — and only blood relative, as far as I knew, but those were murky waters I wouldn't swim in any more than I'd call home right now — was my first and only priority. Well, that and staying alive.

I'd had twenty-seven customers today, not counting the boys I'd run off, and I'd made good use of my time in between to begin putting the pictures I'd found at the Lord Master's, the ones of Alina in and around Dublin, into the new diary I'd purloined from the collection of hand-tooled leather journals sold at BB&B.

Alina.

God, why? I wanted to shout at the ceiling. Why *her?* There were millions of creeps in dozens of countries across the world — why hadn't he taken one of *them?* Now that I knew I was adopted, I resented God doubly. Other people had lots of relatives.

I'd only had one.

Would I ever stop hurting? Would I ever stop missing her? Would I ever live another day without this gouged-out place in my soul that I was desperate to fill with something, anything? Unfortunately, it was an Alina-shaped hole and nothing else would fit it.

But . . . maybe vengeance would soften the edges of it. Maybe killing the bastard who had killed her would make them less sharp, less jagged, and I could stop cutting myself on them.

Pasting the pictures of Alina into my journal had made the grief of losing her feel fresh all over again. With everything that had been happening to me lately, I'd actually woken up a time or two in the morning without the instant, crushing thought: *Alina's dead; how am I supposed to get through the day?* top on the list in my brain. I'd thought things like *I robbed a mobster yesterday and now he's going to kill me.* Or *vampires are real, whodathunk?* Or *I'm afraid Barrons was my sister's boyfriend.* Things like that. A week ago, I'd laid that last one to rest, much to my relief.

Now that weirdness in my life was the norm, grief and rage had resurfaced with a vengeance, on a level I couldn't deal with.

Inside me was a Mac I'd never met before. I couldn't dress her up. I couldn't make her take a bath. She wouldn't mix in pleasant society. I couldn't corral a single one of her thoughts. My only hope was she wouldn't suddenly sprout a mouth.

She was a bloodthirsty, primitive little savage.

And she hated pink.

I dug in my heels. "No way. I'm not going in there. I draw the line at grave-robbing, Barrons."

"It's not your pen."

"Huh? Whose is it?" What pen? I'd thought we were talking about crumbling gravestones, hallowed ground, and theft that was a crime against the tenets of church and man. We'd finished our discussion about pens on the way over, along with my plans for ordering new, cooler ones. He'd listened to me prattle in what I suspect was bemused silence. I get the feeling few women chat Barrons up.

And I'm paying you how much for running my bookstore? was all he'd finally asked. At the last minute, I'd tacked a little on to the sum I'd decided upon earlier. When he agreed, I almost whooped with joy except he'd stopped the Viper at that moment, and I'd taken my first good look around.

We were on the outskirts of the south side of Dublin, on a narrow lane, right next to a very dark, very old cemetery. The last time I'd been in a cemetery had been for Alina's funeral.

I closed my hands around the cold iron bars of the main entrance and swept a brooding glance over the headstones.

"The pen is a metaphor, Ms. Lane. Drawing lines isn't your prerogative. It's mine. You're the OOP detector. I'm the OOP director. You'll walk the cemetery. I'm particularly interested in the unmarked graves behind the church but make a thorough search of the building and the grounds, as well."

I sighed. "What exactly is it I'm looking for?"

"I don't know, perhaps nothing. This church was built on the site of an ancient meeting circle once presided over by the Grand Mistress of the *sidhe*-seers herself."

"In other words," I muttered, "it's probably a wild-goose chase."

"Remember the cuff V'lane offered you?"

"Is there anything you don't know?"

"Legend has it there are multiple cuffs, each with a different purpose. Legend also has it that, in ancient times, *sidhe*-seers collected every Fae relic they could get their hands on, and if it proved indestructible, secreted it away where they believed Mankind would never find it. Some say when Christianity came to Ireland, *sidhe*-seers encouraged the building of churches in specific places, even funded them, perhaps to keep their secrets safely buried on consecrated ground. Laws governing the digging up and relocating of remains are rigidly enforced."

It sounded plausible to me. "These *sidhe*-seers, were they like a club or something, back in the day?"

"As much as they could be. Times were very different then, Ms. Lane. Communication between enclaves took weeks, sometimes months, but in times of threat, they gathered in preappointed places and performed ritual magic. This was one of them."

"Where did all the *sidhe*-seers go? You said there are more of us out there?"

"When the Fae withdrew from our realms, the world no longer had any use for *sidhe*-seers. A once vaunted position became obsolete. Those accustomed to being highly valued lost their purpose overnight. In time, *sidhe*-lore was forgotten. Over the centuries, talents went fallow. As for where the ones who remain are, the next time you're out, look around. Watch. When you see something from Faery, look not at the Fae, but the crowd to see who else is watching it. Some know what they are. Some are on medication for psychological disorders. Some betray themselves to the first one they see and are killed by it. It's how I knew what you were. I saw you watching the Shades."

Psychological disorders? I tried to imagine seeing the monsters I'd recently encountered as a child, having no explanation for them, and realizing no one else could see them. I would have told my mother. She'd have been horrified, taken me for counseling. And if I'd told the counselor the truth? Drugs — a lot of them. I could see it happening all too easily. How many *sidhe*-seers were out there, too sedated to care what was going on in the world? "So this Grand Mistress, she ran things?"

He nodded.

"Is there still one today?"

"One would expect the bloodline that directed the *sidhe*-seers for millennia to have maintained the lore."

That was one evasive answer I wasn't willing to accept. "What does that mean? Do you or don't you know if there is one, and if so, who is she?"

He shrugged. "If there is one, her identity is tightly guarded."

"So, there's something you don't know. Amazing."

He smiled faintly. "Do your thing, Ms. Lane. You might be criminally young, but the night is not."

My "thing" entailed making like a brisk vacuum through the church, and when I'd finished with the spartan stone chapel, sweeping over the graves, up and down burial lanes, in and around mausoleums, searching with an inner antenna I'd not known I possessed, to collect things a few weeks ago I wouldn't have believed existed.

I saved the unmarked graves behind the church for last. I was armed to the teeth with flashlights, although I knew no Shades were here. Where Shades dwell, no night crickets chirp, not a blade of grass stirs, and tree limbs gleam bare and white as old bones.

I expected my stroll through the cemetery at night to be unnerving. I didn't expect to find the hushed world of the human dead soothing, peaceful, but there was an undeniable synergy here. Natural death was part of life. Only unnatural death — like Alina's — opposed the order of things and demanded retribution, a balancing of the scales on a cosmic level. I read the inscriptions as I passed. The epitaphs not worn to dust by time were heartfelt and warm. There were a surprising number of octogenarians and even centenarians interred here. Around these parts, life had once been simple, good, and unusually long, especially for the men.

Barrons waited in the car. I could see him in profile, talking on his cell phone.

Finding an object of power, or OOP, for short, is a talent not all *sidhe*-seers have. From what Barrons says it's rare. Alina had the gift, too, which is why the Lord Master used her.

Don't think I don't see the similarities between us: my sister and the Lord Master, Barrons and me. Difference is, I don't believe Barrons is out to destroy Mankind. I don't think he particularly *cares* much for Mankind, but I don't think he has any deep-seated desire to see us all wiped out. Another difference is he hasn't tried to seduce me, and I'm not in love with him. I have a clear head about what I'm doing and why. And, if one day, I learn Jericho Barrons did kill O'Duffy for snooping into his life, and *is* one of the bad guys, well . . . I'll cross that bridge if and when I come to it.

Revenge is a dish best served cold. I never

used to understand that saying, but I think I finally get it. I'm hotheaded and inexperienced right now. I need to know more about the Fae, and what I am. I need to be cooler, smarter, tougher, stronger, and packing better arsenal before I go after revenge. I need more OOPs, like the spear. I need Barrons. He's an endless source of information, and knows all the right places to look. Take this cemetery, for instance. I never would have known it existed, or what it had once been. I don't know the first thing about my heritage and even less about Irish history. Criminally young, he charged, and I can't argue. But I can change.

I stepped into the shadows beyond the church, swinging my flashlights left and right. This part of the graveyard was enclosed by a low, crumbling wall of stone, and had been fending for itself for years. No gardener toiled here. The grass grew tall and dense, and not one flower broke the stark pallor of many small cairns neglected beneath the heavy boughs of oak and slender limbs of yew. A broken wrought-iron gate swung from a single hinge that creaked a rusty protest when I pushed it open and stepped in.

So much for my talents — I was thigh-high in grass, and tripping over the darn thing before I sensed it.

In my defense, there wasn't much of it left.

"What is it?" I asked Barrons, horrified.

When I'd stumbled over the monstrosity, I'd screamed loud enough to wake the dead. Barrons had come at a run.

It was a misshapen lump at our feet, motionless but for the occasional, terrible shudder.

"I do believe it's what's left of a Rhino-boy," Barrons said slowly.

"What happened to it?"

"I believe, Ms. Lane that something has been . . . gnawing at it."

"What in the world eats Rhino-boys? And why?"

He glanced at me and I was stunned to see that he looked stunned himself, which was an exorbitant display of emotion for Barrons. "It had to be another Fae." He sounded appalled. "Nothing human could take down one of these things, and would certainly have no cause to eat it. As for the why, I have no idea. It goes against every-thing that is *Sidhe.* Fae do not savage one another. Even the lowest of the Unseelie would consider this an atrocity, an abomination. Packs of them would turn on the defiler."

"Will it die?" I asked. There was so little of it left. Yet it lived, and its agony was obvious.

"Not unless you stab it with your spear, Ms. Lane."

"Will it eventually regenerate or something?" It was missing major parts.

"No. Only the royal castes have that power. It will exist in this form forever, unless one of its own race stumbles across it and takes pity on it, which is unlikely. Or you do." His gaze was heavy on me. "Do you? Pity it?"

I stared into his dark eyes. Sometimes they seem bottomless, not entirely human, and this was one of those times.

"Tell me, Ms. Lane, will you walk away from it? Let it suffer for eternity? Or are you an angel of mercy?"

I bit my lip.

"Which will it be? Knowing one of these things murdered your sister. Perhaps not a Rhino-boy, but certainly one of its brethren."

"The Lord Master killed my sister." I was sure of it.

"So you say. He's not Fae and the marks on her body were."

There was that. Still, if he hadn't actually dealt the killing blow, he was the one who'd orchestrated it. I narrowed my eyes. Barrons was testing me. I had no idea what his twisted idea of a passing grade was. I only knew what I had to do. There is a synergy to life and death, and this did not fit.

I slid the spear from my boot and stabbed the Rhino-boy. Barrons smiled, but I don't know if he was mocking me for being weak or lauding me for being compassionate. Screw him. It was my conscience I had to live with.

As we were leaving the cemetery, I made the mistake of looking back.

The black-shrouded specter stood, dark folds rustling, one ghostly hand on the rusted gate, watching me. Its darkness was as enormous as the night. And like the night, it was all around me, pressing at me, caressing me, knowing me.

I cried out and stumbled over a low gravestone. Barrons caught my arm and saved me from a nasty spill. "What is it, Ms. Lane — pangs of regret? So soon?"

I shook my head. "Look back at the gate," I said numbly. It had never appeared to me before when someone else was around.

Barrons turned, scanned the old partitioned-off cemetery for several moments, then glanced back at me. "What? I see nothing."

I turned and looked. He was right. It was gone. Of course. I should have known. I sighed. "I guess I'm just a little spooked, Barrons. That's all. Let's go home. There's nothing here."

"Home, Ms. Lane?" His deep voice was gently amused.

"I have to call it something," I said morosely. "They say home is where the heart is. I think mine's satin-lined and six feet under."

He opened the car door for me — the driver's side. "Shall we dispel some of that youthful angst, Ms. Lane?" He offered me the keys. "Not far from here there's a road that goes on for miles, through positively desolate parts." His dark eyes gleamed. "Devilish curves. No traffic. Why don't you take us for a drive?"

My eyes widened. "Really?"

He brushed a curl from my forehead and I shivered. Barrons has strong hands with long, beautiful fingers, and I think he carries some kind of electrical charge because every time he touches me it shoots an unwelcome thrill through my body. I took the keys from his hand, being careful not to make contact with skin. If he noticed, he let it pass unremarked.

"Try not to kill us, Ms. Lane."

I slid behind the wheel. "Viper, SR10 coupe. 6-speed, V-10, 510 horses at 5,600 rpm, 0–60 in 3.9 seconds," I babbled happily. He laughed.

I kept us alive. Barely.

I think it's human nature to nest. Even the homeless stake out that special park bench or spot beneath the bridge, and feather it with items prized from someone's trash. Everybody wants their own safe, warm, dry place in the world and if they don't have one, they'll do their best to create one with what they've got.

I was nesting on the first floor of BB&B. I'd rearranged the furniture, stashed a boring brown throw in a closet, and replaced it with a silky yellow one, brought two peaches-and-cream candles down from my bedroom, plugged in my new sound dock behind the cash register and tuned it to a cheery playlist, and propped photos of my family on top of my predecessor's TV.

MacKayla Lane is here! it all said.

OOP-detector/monster-killer by night — bookseller by day was a much-needed respite. I liked the spicy fragrance of candles burning, the clean, new scent of freshly printed newspapers and glossily inked magazines. I liked ringing up sales and the sound the cash register made. I enjoyed the timeless ritual of taking money in exchange for goods. I liked the way the wood of the floors and shelves gleamed in the afternoon sun. I liked lying on my back on the counter when no one was around, trying to make out the mural on the ceiling, four floors above me. I enjoyed recommending great reads and discovering new ones from the customers. It all came together in a warm, nesty sort of way.

At four o'clock on Wednesday afternoon, I was surprised to find myself bustling around the store, humming beneath my breath, and feeling almost . . . it took me a few moments to identify the feeling . . . *good.*

Then Inspector Jayne walked in.

And if that wasn't bad enough — with him was my dad.

Six

"Is this your daughter, Mr. Lane?" said the inspector.

My dad stopped inside the door, and peered at me, hard.

I touched a hand to my butchered hair, abruptly, excruciatingly aware of the bruises on my face, and the spear tucked into my boot.

"Mac, baby, is that you?" Jack Lane looked shocked, appalled, and so relieved that I nearly burst into tears.

I cleared my throat. "Hey, Dad."

" 'Hey, Dad?' " he echoed. "Did you just say 'Hey, Dad'? After all I've been through to find you, you 'Hey, Dad' me?"

Uh-oh, I was in for it. When he gets that tone, heads roll. Six feet two inches of corporate tax attorney that manages the IRS on behalf of his clients and frequently bests it, Jack Lane is smart, charming, well spoken, and tough as a tiger when provoked.

And from the way he was raking back his silver-tipped dark hair and his brown eyes were flashing, he was currently *very* provoked.

He was lucky I was still calling him "Dad" at all, I thought bitterly. We both knew he wasn't.

He stalked toward me, eyes narrowed. "MacKayla Evelina Lane, what on earth did you do to your hair? And your face! Are those bruises? When was the last time you showered? Did you lose your luggage? You don't wear — Christ, Mac, you look awful! What happened —" He broke off, shaking his head, then aimed a finger at me. "I'll have you know, young lady, I left your mother with her parents four days ago! I dropped every case I was working on to fly over here and bring you home. Do you have any idea the heart attack it gave me to find out you hadn't been staying at the Clarin House for *over a week?* And nobody knew where you'd gone! Could you check your e-mail, Mac? Could you pick up a phone? I have been walking up and down these dreary, rainy, reeking-with-stumbling-drunks streets, staring into every face, searching trash-filled alleys for you, hoping and praying to God that I wasn't going to find you lying facedown in one of them like your sister and have to kill myself rather than take the news back home to your mother and kill *her* with it!"

The tears I'd been holding back came out in a waterfall. I might not have this man's DNA inside my body, but he couldn't be any more my father.

He swallowed up the room with long-legged strides and crushed me into that great, big, barrel-chested hug that always smelled like peppermint and aftershave, and it felt just like it always did — like the safest place on earth.

Unfortunately, I knew better. There was no safe place. Not for me. Not now. And certainly not for him. Not here.

He'd been walking around Dublin looking for me! I blessed the Fates that had spared him, steering him away from the Dark Zone, protecting him in those alleys from Unseelie. If anything had happened to him it would have been doubly on my head. What had I been thinking — avoiding my e-mail, refusing to call home? Of course he would come looking for me! Dad never took no for an answer.

I had to get him out of Dublin, fast, before something awful happened to him, and I lost another piece of my heart to that satin-lined box in the earth.

I had to make him fly home ASAP, and without what he'd come for — me.

"What happened to your face, Mac?" was the first question Dad asked me after Inspector Jayne left. Though there were still two hours to closing, I flipped the sign and stuck a Post-it next to it that said, SORRY, CLOSED EARLY, PLEASE COME BACK TOMORROW.

I led him to the rear conversation area where passersby couldn't see behind the shelves that someone was still inside, fingering my hair nervously. It was one thing to lie to the police, another to lie to the man who'd raised me, who knew I hated spiders and loved hot fudge sundaes topped with peanut butter and whipped cream.

"Inspector Jayne tells me you fell on the stairs."

"What else did the inspector tell you?" I fished. How much did I have to try to explain?

"That the police officer handling Alina's case was murdered. Had his throat cut. And that he'd been to see you the day it happened. Mac, what's going on? What are you doing here? What is this place?" He craned his head around. "Do you *work* here?"

I filled him in without filling him in at all.

117

I'd realized I liked it in Dublin, I told him. I'd been offered a job that came with lodgings, so I'd moved into the bookstore. Staying in Ireland and working gave me the perfect chance to keep the pressure on the new officer handling Alina's case. Yes, I fell on the stairs. I'd had a few beers and forgotten how much stronger their Guinness was than ours. No, I had no idea why Inspector Jayne didn't seem to think very highly of me. I gave Dad the same excuse I'd given Jayne for O'Duffy's visit. To make it more convincing, I embellished about how fatherly and kind O'Duffy had been and what a favor he'd been doing, stopping by. Crime was very high in Dublin, I told Dad, and I felt awful about O'Duffy's death but really, police officers died on the job all the time and Jayne was just being a jack-petunia about it to me.

"And your hair?"

"You don't like it?" It was hard to feign surprise when I hated it myself; I missed the weight of it, the different styles I'd been able to wear, the swish of it when I walked. I was just grateful he hadn't seen me when I'd still had all my splints on.

He gave me a look. "You are kidding, right? Mac, baby, you had beautiful hair, long and blond like your mother's . . ." He

118

trailed off.

And there it was. I looked him dead in the eye. "Which mother, Dad? Mom? Or the other one — you know, the one that gave me up for adoption?"

"You want to go get some dinner, Mac?"

Men. Do they all evade as first line of defense?

We ordered delivery. I hadn't had a good pizza in forever, it was starting to rain again, and I was in no mood to go out in it. I ordered, Dad paid, just like old times when life was simple, and Daddy was always there to be my Friday night date whenever my latest boyfriend had been a jerk. I gathered paper plates and napkins from Fiona's stash behind the register. Before sitting down with our pizza, I turned on all the exterior lights, and lit a cozy gas fire. For now, we were safe. I just had to keep him safe until morning, when I would somehow get him on a plane and send him home.

I keep a happy thought inside me at all times. I cling to it in my darkest moments: When all this is over, I'm going to go back to Ashford and pretend none of this happened. I'm going to find myself a man, get married, and have babies. I need both my parents at home, waiting for me because I'm going to make little Lane girls, and we're going to be a family again.

We kept the talk light through dinner. He told me that Mom was still lost in grief and not talking to anyone. He'd hated leaving her, but he'd taken her to Gram and Gramp's and they were giving her the best of care. Thinking about Mom was too painful, so I turned the conversation to books. Dad loves to read as much as I do, and I knew that in his opinion there were far worse places he could have found me working, like another bar. We talked about new releases. I told him some of my plans for the store.

When dinner was over we pushed our plates back and regarded each other warily.

He began a somber "You know your mother and I love you" spiel, and I hushed him. I knew. I didn't have any doubts on that score. I'd been forced to come to terms with so much in the past few weeks that making peace with my discovery that my parents were not my birth parents hadn't taken as long as I'd expected. It had rocked my world, brutally shifted my paradigm, but regardless of whose sperm and egg had resulted in my conception, Jack and Rainey Lane had raised me with more love and unwavering support than most people ever know in a lifetime. If my biological parents were alive out there somewhere, *they* were my second set.

"I know, Dad. Just tell me."

"How did you find out, Mac?"

I told him an old woman had insisted I was someone else, about brown eyes and blue not making green, about calling the hospital to check on my birth records.

"We knew this day might come." He pushed a hand through his hair and sighed. "What do you want to know, Mac?"

"Everything," I said in a low voice. "Every last detail."

"It's not much."

"Alina was my biological sister, wasn't she?"

He nodded. "She was almost three, and you were nearly a year when the two of you came to us."

"Where did we come from, Dad?"

"They didn't tell us. In fact, they told us virtually nothing while demanding everything."

"They" were people from a church in Atlanta. Mom and Dad couldn't conceive, and had been on an adoption waiting list for so long they'd nearly given up. But one day they got a call that two children had been left at a downtown church, and a friend of a friend of the church's pastor's sister knew their counselor, who'd suggested the Lanes. Not all couples were willing to accept, or had the financial means to take on two young children at once, and among the biological mother's lengthy list of requirements was that the children not be separated. She'd also insisted that if the adoptive couple did not already live in a rural area, they must move to a small town and agree to never live in or near a city again.

"Why?"

"We were told it was what it was, Mac, and we could take it or leave it."

"And you didn't think it was odd?"

"Of course we did. Extremely. But your mother and I wanted so badly to have children and couldn't. We were young and in love and would have done just about anything to have a family of our own. Since both of us came from small towns to begin with, we took it as a sign to return to our roots. We visited dozens of towns, finally settling on Ashford. I was a successful attorney and pulled every string I could to push the adoption through. We signed all the documents, including the list of requirements, and in no time, we were proud parents living in a great little town where everyone believed you were our biological daughters, leading the life we'd always dreamed of." He smiled, reminiscing. "We fell in love with you girls the moment we saw you. Alina was wearing this yellow skirt and sweater set, and you were dressed from head to toe in pink, Mac, with a little rainbow ribbon tied around a blond wisp of your hair."

I gaped. Does the infant mind remember? To this day, pink and rainbow hues are my favorite.

"What other strange requirements did the woman have?" I couldn't call her "our mother." She wasn't. She was the woman who'd left us.

He closed his eyes. "I no longer recall most of them. There's a legal document tucked away in a box somewhere that your mother and I signed. But there's one I never forgot."

I sat up a little straighter.

He opened his eyes. "The first promise we had to make to the adoption agency before they'd even consider putting us on the list of prospective parents was that under no circumstances would we ever let either of you set foot in Ireland."

I couldn't get him to go home.

I tried everything.

In his mind, he'd violated his most sacred trust the moment he'd caved in to Alina's radiant face when she'd announced that she'd won a full scholarship to study abroad — at Trinity, of all places! — by not locking her in her room and forbidding it. He should have threatened, he should have taken her car away, should have tempted her with the offer of a sporty new one if she stayed home. There were a thousand ways he could have stopped her from going, a thousand ways he'd failed.

She'd been so excited, he told me sadly. He hadn't been able to bring himself to stand in her way. Those conditions they'd agreed to so long ago had seemed as insubstantial as ghosts in the warm, sunny light of day. More than twenty perfect years had passed, and the odd demands accompanying us had lost their immediacy, become the phantom fears of a dying woman.

"She's dead, then?" I asked in a hushed voice.

"They never told us. We assumed. It was easier that way; we liked the finality of it. No worries that one day someone out there might come to their senses and try to take our girls away. Legal nightmares like that happen all the time."

"Did you and Mom ever go back and try

to find out more about us?"

Dad nodded. "I don't know if you recall, but Alina was very ill when she was eight and the doctors wanted more information about her medical history than we had. We found the church had burned to the ground, the adoption agency had closed, and the private investigator I hired to look into things couldn't locate a single ex-employee." He absorbed the look on my face and smiled faintly. "I know. Odd again. You must understand, Mac, the two of you were *ours*. We didn't care where you'd come from, only that you'd come. And that you're coming home with me now," he added pointedly. "How long will it take you to pack?"

I sighed. "I'm not packing, Dad."

"I'm not leaving without you, Mac," he said.

"You must be Jack Lane," said Barrons.

I nearly jumped out of my skin. "I wish you'd quit doing that." I craned my neck to shoot him an over-the-shoulder glare. How did such a large man move so silently? Once again, he was standing behind me while I was having a conversation, and neither of us had heard him approach. It aggravated me even more that he knew my father's first name. I'd never told him.

Dad rose in that way big, self-assured men

have, slowly, stretching to the last quarter inch of his height, and seeming to fill out even larger along the way. His expression was reserved but interested; he was curious to meet my new employer — despite the fact that he'd already decided I wouldn't be working for him anymore.

His expression changed the instant he saw Barrons. It frosted, shuttered, hardened.

"Jericho Barrons." Barrons extended his hand.

Dad stared at it, and for a few moments I wasn't sure he'd take it. Then he inclined his head and the men clasped hands, and held.

And held. Like it was some kind of pissing contest, and whichever man let go first might have to forfeit a ball.

I looked from one to the other, and realized that Barrons and my dad were having one of those wordless conversations he and I have from time to time. Though the language was, by nature, foreign to me, I grew up in the Deep South where a man's ego is roughly the size of his pickup truck, and women get an early and interesting education in the not-so-subtle roar of testosterone.

She's my daughter, you prick, and if you're thinking about your prick when you're looking at her, I'll rip it off and hang you by it.

Try.

You're too old for her. Leave her alone. (I wanted to tell my dad he was way off base with this one, but despite the dogged determination with which I tried to interrupt and force my ocular two cents' worth in, neither of them would look at me.)

You think? I bet she doesn't think I'm too old. Why don't you ask her? (Barrons said that just to irritate him. Of course, I think he's too old for me. Not that I think about him that way at all.)

I'm taking her home.

Try. (Barrons can be a man of annoyingly few words.)

She'll choose me over you, Dad told him proudly.

Barrons laughed.

"Mac, baby," my dad said without ever taking his eyes off Barrons, "get your things. We're going home."

I groaned. Of course, I'd choose my dad over Barrons, if given a fair choice. But it wasn't a fair choice. I hadn't been given many of them lately. I knew my refusal was going to hurt him. And I needed to hurt him, because I needed to make him leave.

"I'm sorry, Daddy, but I'm staying here," I said softly.

127

Jack Lane flinched. His gaze cut away from Barrons to stab at me with cool reproof, but not before I saw the hurt and betrayal beneath the lawyer-face he didn't paste on quick enough to mask.

Barrons' dark eyes gleamed. As far as he was concerned, the conversation was over.

I went with Dad to the airport the next morning to see him off.

Last night I wouldn't have believed I'd get him to go, and frankly I'm not sure *I'm* the one that did.

He'd stayed at the bookstore, in one of the extra fourth-floor bedrooms, and kept me up until three o'clock in the morning, arguing every angle he could think of — and believe me, attorneys can wear you out with them — trying to change my mind. We'd done something we never do: gone to bed mad at each other.

This morning, however, he'd been an entirely different man. I'd woken up to find him already downstairs, having coffee with Barrons in the study. He'd greeted me with one of those big all-encompassing hugs I love so much. He'd been relaxed, affectionate, his usual charismatic self, a man that, even at twice their age, had made most of my high school girlfriends giggle like morons. He'd been robust, cheerful, in all-around better spirits than I'd seen him since Alina's death.

He'd smiled and shaken Barrons' hand when we'd left, with what had looked like genuine friendliness, even respect.

I suppose Barrons must have confided something of himself in my father that revealed a hidden integrity of character I have yet to see, that set Jack Lane's legal-eagle mind at ease. Whatever he and Barrons had found to talk about, it'd worked wonders.

After a quick stop at Dad's hotel to grab his luggage, a bag of croissants, and coffee, we filled our time on the way to the airport discussing one of our favorite topics: cars and the new designs unveiled at the latest auto show.

At the terminal I soaked up another hug, sent my love to Mom, promised to call soon, and managed to make it back to the bookstore just in time to open up for business.

I had a good day, but I've begun to realize that's when life *likes* to kick you in the teeth — the moment you start to relax and let your guard down.

By six o'clock, I'd had fifty-six patrons,

rung up an impressive amount of sales, and discovered that I loved being a bookseller. I'd found my calling. Instead of serving drinks and watching people turn into drunken idiots, I was being paid to give people wonderful stories to escape into, full of mystery, mayhem, and romance. Instead of splashing anesthetizing alcohol into glasses, I was pouring fictional tonics to alleviate the stress, hardship, and drudgery of their lives.

I wasn't corroding anybody's liver. I didn't have to watch balding, middle-aged men hitting on pretty young coeds, trying to recapture their glory days. I wasn't deluged by the sordid sob stories of the recently and so often well deservedly jilted, while I stood behind my counter. I didn't have to watch a single person cheat on their spouse, urinate on the floor, or pick a fight all day.

At six o'clock, I should have counted my blessings and closed early.

But I didn't, and just when I was starting to feel almost happy and good about myself, my life went to hell again.

SEVEN

"Nice place you have here," said my latest customer, as the door banged shut behind him. "I wouldn't have thought the interior was so big from out on the sidewalk."

I'd had the same thought the first time I entered Barrons Books and Baubles. The building just didn't look large enough on the outside to contain all the room it held on the inside.

"Hi," I said. "Welcome to Barrons. Are you looking for something special?"

"As a matter of fact, I am."

"You've come to the right place, then," I told him. "If we don't have the book you want in stock, we can order it, and we've got some great collectibles up on the second and third floors." He was a good-looking man in his late twenties, maybe early thirties, dark-haired and nicely built. I seem to be surrounded by attractive men lately.

When I stepped around the counter, he

131

gave me an appreciative once-over, making me glad I'd dressed up. I hadn't wanted my dad to go home carrying a mental snapshot of his daughter, bedraggled, bruised, and gloomily attired, so I'd chosen my outfit with care this morning. I'd dug out a frothy peach skirt that kicked flirtatiously when I walked, a pretty camisole, and gold sandals that laced up my calves. I'd woven a brilliantly painted silk scarf through my short Arabian Night curls, and knotted it at my nape, letting the ends trail across my bare shoulders. I'd taken time with my makeup, concealing my bruises, and dusting a shimmery bronzer across my nose, cheeks, and breastbone. Dangly crystal earrings brushed my neck when I moved, and a single large teardrop rested in my cleavage.

Glam-girl Mac felt fantastic.

Savage Mac was pleased only by the spear strapped to the inside of my right thigh. And the short dirk I'd found on a display pedestal in Barrons' study and strapped to my left one. And the small flashlight tucked into my pocket. And the four pairs of scissors behind the counter. And the research I'd been doing in my spare time today on gun laws in Ireland and how to go about acquiring one. I thought the semiautomatics looked good.

"American?" he said.

I was beginning to get the hang of being a tourist in Dublin. In college the question was "What's your major?" Abroad everyone guesses your nationality. I nodded. "And you're definitely Irish." I smiled. He had a deep voice, a lilting accent, and looked like he'd been born to wear that thick, cream Irish fisherman's sweater, faded jeans, and rugged boots. He moved with easy grace, born of muscle and machismo. He was a rightie, I couldn't help but notice. Blushing, I busied myself neatening the evening newspapers on the counter.

For the next few minutes we indulged in the light banter of a male and female who find each other attractive and enjoy the timeless ritual of flirtation. Not everyone does, and frankly I think it's a lost art form. Flirtation doesn't have to go somewhere; it certainly doesn't need to end up in bed. I like to think of it as a little friendlier than a handshake, a little less intimate than a kiss. It's a way of saying hi, you look great, have a wonderful day. A tasteful flirtation, played out by people who understand the rules, leaves everyone feeling good and can perk up the bluest mood.

I was certainly feeling perky by the time I steered the conversation back around to business. "So what can I help you find, Mr . . . ?" I nudged delicately for a name.

"O'Bannion." He offered his hand. "Derek O'Bannion. And I'm hoping you can help me find my brother, Rocky."

Have you ever had one of those moments when time just freezes? You know, when the world suddenly goes deathly still, and you could hear a pin drop, and the squishing sound your heart makes is so loud in your ears you feel like you're drowning in blood, and you stand there in that suspended moment and die a thousand deaths, but not really, and the moment passes and dumps you out on the other side of it, with your mouth hanging open, and an erased blackboard where your mind used to be?

I think I've been watching too many old movies lately, in the middle of the night when I can't sleep, because the disembodied voice that offered counsel at that moment sounded a lot like John Wayne.

Buck up, little buckaroo, it said, in a dry, gravelly drawl. You wouldn't believe how many things that advice has gotten me through since. When everything else is gone, balls are all any of us really have left. The question is: Are yours made of flesh and blood, or steel?

When I shook Derek O'Bannion's hand, the spear I'd stolen from his brother before I'd led him to his unwitting death burned like a brand from hell against my inner thigh. I ignored it. "Goodness, is your brother missing?" I blinked up at him.

"Yes."

"How long?"

"He was last seen two weeks ago."

"How awful!" I exclaimed. "What brings you to our bookstore?"

He stared down at me, and I suddenly wondered how I could have missed the resemblance. The same cold eyes that had watched me two weeks ago from inside a mobster's den wallpapered with crosses and religious iconography gazed down at me now. Some would have pegged Rocky and his brother Derek as Black Irish, but I knew from Barrons, who knows everything about everyone, that the fierce, ruthless blood of a long-ago Saudi ancestor runs in O'Bannion veins.

"I've been stopping in at all the businesses along this street. There are three cars in the alley behind this shop. Do you know anything about them?"

I shook my head. "No. Why?"

"They belong to . . . associates of my brother. I was wondering if you knew when they'd been left there and why. If you heard or saw anything. Maybe a fourth black car? A very expensive one?"

I shook my head again. "I really don't go out back at all, and I don't much notice cars. My boss disposes of the trash. I just work here. I try to stay inside most of the time. Alleys scare me." I was babbling. I bit down lightly on the inside of my cheek to stop myself from talking. "Have you spoken to the police?" I encouraged. Go there, leave here, I willed silently.

Derek O'Bannion's smile was sharp as knives. "O'Bannions don't trouble the police with our problems. We take care of them ourselves." He studied me with clinical detachment, all flirtation gone. "How long have you been working here?"

"Three days," I said truthfully.

"You're new to town."

"Mm-hmm."

"What's your name?"

"Mac."

He laughed. "You don't look like a Mac."

Was this safer ground presenting itself? "What do I look like?" I asked lightly, leaning a hip against the counter and subtly arching my spine. Go back to flirting with me, my body posture invited.

He scanned me from head to toe. "Trouble," he said after a moment, with a faint, sexually charged smile.

I laughed. "I'm really not."

"Too bad," he parried. But I could tell his mind wasn't fully on flirting. It was on his brother. And something else I could completely understand; it was on a hunt for the truth, for retribution. What vagaries of fate had made kindred souls of us — me and this man? Oh, excuse me, it hadn't been vagaries. It was *me.*

He took a business card from his wallet, a pen from his pocket, and scribbled on the back. "If you should see or hear anything, you'll tell me, won't you, Mac?" He took my hand, turned it palm up, and dropped a kiss in it before the card. "Anytime. Day or night. Anything. No matter how inconsequential you think it seems."

I nodded.

"I think he's dead," Derek O'Bannion told me. "And I'm going to kill the fuck that did it."

I nodded again.

"He was my brother."

I nodded a third time. "My sister was murdered," I blurted.

His gaze sharpened with new interest. I was suddenly more in his eyes than another flirty, pretty girl. "Then you understand vengeance," he said softly.

"I understand vengeance," I agreed.

"Call me anytime, Mac," he said. "I think I like you."

I watched him leave in silence.

When the door closed behind him, I raced to the bathroom, locked myself in, and leaned back against the door, where I stood staring at myself in the mirror trying to reconcile dual images.

I was hunting the monster that had killed my sister.

I *was* the monster that had killed his brother.

When I came out of the bathroom, I glanced around, relieved to find no customers had entered the store. I'd forgotten to slap one of the BACK IN FIVE MINUTES signs that I'd made up yesterday to cover my bathroom breaks on the front door.

I hurried now to turn over the sign. Once again I was closing early. Barrons was just going to have to deal with it. It wasn't much early, and it wasn't like he needed the money.

As I flipped the placard, I made the mistake of glancing out the window.

It was nearly dark, that time of day folks around these parts call "gloaming," or twilight, when the day gently bruises into night.

And I was unable to decide which was worse: Inspector Jayne sitting on a bench a few doors down to the right not even pretending to be reading the newspaper he held; the black-shrouded specter standing directly across the street, watching me from beneath the ashy shadows of a dimly flickering streetlamp; or Derek O'Bannion exiting a shop two doors down, turning left, and heading straight into the Dark Zone.

"Where the *hell* have you been?" Barrons yanked open the cab door and pried me out with a hand around my upper arm. My feet left the ground for a moment.

"Don't start with me," I growled. Shaking off his grip, I pushed past him. Inspector Jayne's cab was just pulling up behind me. I wonder if he missed his family yet. I hoped he'd get tired of me soon and go home.

"I'm getting you a cell phone, Ms. Lane," he barked at my back. "You will carry it at all times, like the spear. You will do nothing without it. Need I remind you of all the things you won't be doing without it?"

I told him where he could put my as-yet-unpurchased cell phone — the sun didn't shine there and I didn't call it by a flower's name — and stomped into the store.

He stomped in after me. "Have you forgotten the dangers out there in the Dublin night, Ms. Lane? Shall we go for a little walk?" Once before when he'd thought I was being intractable he'd threatened to drag me into the Dark Zone at night. Tonight, I was too numb to care. Dead bolts rang out like bullets against steel as he slammed them home. "Have you forgotten your purpose here, Ms. Lane?"

"How could I?" I said bitterly. "Every time I try to, something worse happens."

I was halfway to the connecting doors when he caught me and spun me around. He gave me a furious once-over that seemed to get tangled up for a moment on the crystal dangling between my breasts. Or was it my breasts? "And there you are, dressed like a two-bit floozy, going out for a drink. What the fuck were you thinking? *Were* you thinking?"

"Two-bit floozy? Get with the times, Barrons. I don't look like a two-bit anything. In fact, I'm positively overdressed by lots of people's standards these days, and certainly

140

wearing more than that stupid little black dress you made me wear when we —" I broke off; where I'd worn that skimpy halter dress was hitting too close to home right now. "And for the record," I said stiffly, "I did *not* go out for a drink."

"Don't lie to me, Ms. Lane. I smell it on you. And other things. Who was the man?" His dark, exotic face was cold. His nostrils flared and constricted like an animal scenting prey.

Barrons has extraordinary senses. I'd not had even the tiniest sip of alcohol. "I said I didn't have a drink," I repeated. I'd had an awful night, one of the absolute worst of my life.

"You had something. What was it?" he demanded.

"An alcohol-laced kiss," I said tightly. "Two, to be precise." But only because I hadn't moved fast enough to avoid the second one. I turned away, hating myself, hating my choices.

His hand shot out and closed on my shoulder. He spun me back to him with such vehemence that I might have whirled in dizzying toplike circles if he hadn't caught me by the shoulders. He seemed to realize he was holding me too hard at the precise moment I was about to snap at him,

141

and his fingers relaxed on my skin, but his body seemed to doubly absorb the tension. His gaze dropped to my necklace again, to its soft cushion between my breasts. "From who?"

"From *whom*, I believe is the correct phrasing."

"All right, from-the-fuck-*whom*, Ms. Lane?"

"Derek O'Bannion. Any other questions?"

He regarded me a moment, then a slow half-smile curved his lips. Just as O'Bannion had earlier, he suddenly seemed to find me much more interesting. "Well, well." He brushed the pad of his thumb across my mouth, then cupped my chin and angled my face back up to the light, searching my eyes. For a moment, I thought he was going to kiss me himself, to taste the complexity and complicity of me. Or was that duplicity? "And you were kissing the brother of the man you killed — why?" he murmured silkily.

"*I* didn't kill him," I said bitterly. "You killed him without my permission."

"Ballocks, Ms. Lane," he said. "If I'd asked you that night if you wanted him dead so you could be safe, you'd have said yes."

I remembered that night. I would remember it forever. I'd been freaked out by the rapidity with which my life was unraveling, terrified of Rocky O'Bannion, and fully aware that if we didn't do something about him, he was going to do something very bad and no doubt unspeakably painful to me. I have no delusions about my ability to withstand torture. Barrons was right. I would have said "Do whatever you have to do to keep me safe." But I didn't have to like it. And I didn't have to admit it.

I turned and walked away.

"I want you to go to the Ancient Languages Department at Trinity College tomorrow morning, Ms. Lane."

I drew up like he'd yanked my leash, and scowled up at the ceiling. Was something Cosmic up there playing tricks on me? Was the whole universe in on a great big let's-mess-with-Mac joke? The Ancient Languages Department was the only place in all of Dublin I'd made a mental note never to go. "You're kidding, right?"

"No. Why?"

"Forget it," I muttered. "What do you want me to do there?"

"Ask for a woman named Elle Masters. She'll have an envelope for you."

"Why don't you go get it yourself?" What did he do all day?

"I'm busy tomorrow."

"So, go get it tonight."

"She won't have it until morning."

"Then have her send it by courier."

"Who's the employer here, Ms. Lane?"

"Who's the OOP detector?"

"Is there some reason you don't want to go to the university?"

"No." I was in no mood to talk about dreamy-eyed guys and dates I could never have.

"Then what, Ms. Lane, is your problem?"

"Shouldn't I be afraid the Lord Master might get me while I'm out and about?"

"Were you worrying about that tonight when you were letting Derek O'Bannion shove his tongue down your throat?"

I stiffened. "He was walking into the Dark Zone, Barrons."

"So? One less problem for us."

I shook my head. "I'm not you, Barrons. I'm not dead inside."

His smile was ten shades of ice. "So what did you do? Run after him and offer yourself on a silver platter to get him to turn around?"

Pretty much. And then I'd had to spend the next three and a half hours in a down-town club, dancing and flirting with him, and trying to keep his hands off me, while Inspector Jayne watched from a corner table. Trying to use up so much of his time that he would be disinclined to go back and search the Dark Zone tonight. Eventually trying to beg off nicely, and failing.

Like his brother, Derek O'Bannion was used to getting his way, and if he didn't, he pushed harder. In my blind determination to avert culpability in another death, I'd forgotten he was related to the man who'd brutally murdered twenty-seven people in a single night to get what he wanted.

By eleven-thirty, I'd had as much as I could take. With each drink he tossed back, he'd sprouted more hands and a worse attitude. I hadn't been able to extricate myself gracefully so, in a fit of desperation, I'd excused myself for the bathroom, and tried to sneak out a side door. I'd figured I would call him tomorrow, pretend I'd gotten sick, and if he asked me out again, evade, procrastinate, and lie. I really hadn't wanted another O'Bannion pissed off at me in this city. One had been bad enough.

He'd caught me outside the bathroom, shoved me into a wall, and kissed me so brutally that I hadn't been able to breathe. Flattened between his body and a brick wall, I'd grown light-headed from lack of oxygen. My mouth still felt swollen, bruised. I'd seen the excitement in his eyes and known he was a man turned on by a woman's helplessness. I'd remembered his brother's restaurant, the carefully coiffed and tightly controlled women, how the waiters were forbidden to serve a woman a meal or a drink unless a man ordered for them. O'Bannions were not nice men.

When I'd finally wrested myself free, I'd made a scene, loudly accusing him of forcing his attentions on me when I'd already told him a dozen times I wasn't interested. If he'd been anyone else, the bouncers would have tossed him out of the club, but in Dublin, nobody tosses an O'Bannion. They'd thrown me out instead. The tape-to-my-derriere inspector had watched it all through narrowed eyes, arms folded, without lifting a finger to help me.

I made another enemy in this city tonight, as if I didn't already have enough.

Still, I'd accomplished my goal and it hadn't been an easy one to tackle.

When I'd looked out the window and seen Derek O'Bannion heading straight for his deadly rendezvous with the Shades I'd wanted nothing more than to flip the sign, lock the door, curl up with a good book, and pretend nothing was out there, and nothing bad was about to happen. But it seems I've got this set of scales inside me that I never used to have, or at least I wasn't aware of, and I can't shake the feeling that if I don't try to keep them balanced, I'll lose something I won't be able to get back.

So I'd forced myself out of the bookstore and into the rapidly deepening dusk. I'd rolled my eyes at the inspector, and ground my teeth against the oppressive sense of dread that cloaked me every time I saw that terrifying black specter, watching, waiting. I'd notched my chin higher and made myself walk straight *past* it like it didn't even exist — and as far as I could tell, it didn't, because Jayne had ignored it and O'Bannion sure hadn't looked at it on the way back, but then again, I'd tugged my camisole down to reveal a shocking amount of cleavage to tempt him to turn around. I'd done for one O'Bannion what I'd failed to do for the other, and the scales inside me had leveled a little.

I hoped he'd continue his search tomorrow, in the daylight, and not stop in here on his way by. But if, despite my efforts, he went back into the abandoned neighborhood tonight, well, I'd done the best I could, and frankly I wasn't sure how important it was another O'Bannion remained among the living. Dad says Hell has a special place for men who abuse women.

There are Unseelie monsters and there are human ones.

"Was he a good kisser, Ms. Lane?" Barrons asked, watching me carefully.

I wiped my mouth with the back of my hand at the memory. "It was like being owned."

"Some women like that."

"Not me."

"Perhaps it depends on the man doing the owning."

"I doubt it. I couldn't breathe with him kissing me."

"One day you may kiss a man you can't breathe without, and find breath is of little consequence."

"Right, and one day my prince might come."

"I doubt he'll be a prince, Ms. Lane. Men rarely are."

"I'll get your envelope, Barrons. What then?" What crazy zig was my life going to zag down next?

"I took the liberty of placing garments in your room. Tomorrow evening we leave for Wales."

Turned out Elle Masters wasn't there the next day, nor, much to my relief, was the dreamy-eyed guy.

Instead, I met a fourth-year student who worked for Elle, and was holding the envelope for me. He was tall with dark hair, a great Scottish accent, a ton of curiosity about Barrons, who he'd heard about from his employer I guess, and pretty dreamy eyes himself, an unusual shade of amber, like tiger eyes, framed by thick, black lashes.

"Scotty" (we never got around to introducing ourselves, I was in too much of a hurry to get out of there and on with my day) told me Elle's six-year-old daughter was sick and she was keeping her out of school, so he'd swung by to pick up the envelope on his way into work.

I took it and hurried out the door. Scotty followed me halfway down the hall, making small talk with a charming Scots burr, and I got the distinct impression that he was working up to asking me out. Two gorgeous guys in the same department, two *normal* guys! I would only be torturing myself if I spared a second thought for either of them. The Ancient Languages Department at Trinity was off limits for me in the future. Barrons could run his own errands, or hire a courier service to do it for him.

On my way back to the bookstore, I pretended not to see nearly a dozen Unseelie Rhino-boys, escorting their new protégés down the streets, shaping them up for human society. They pointed and spoke, their charges nodded, and it was obvious they were being indoctrinated into their new world — *my* world. I wanted to stab every one of them with my spear as I walked by, but I refrained. I'm not in this for the little battles. I'm here for the war.

All of them were casting Fae glamours to make themselves appear human to varying degrees of attractiveness, but either they were rudimentary efforts, or I've gotten better at penetrating the Fae façade because aside from a momentary blurriness, a brief vacillation of color and contour, I saw them in their true forms. None were as revolting as the hideous Gray Man who'd preyed on women, stealing their beauty through the open sores in his flesh and hands, although all made me feel queasy, but that's just the effect of any Fae on my *sidhe*-seer senses; it's my early-warning system. I picked up a group of ten of them on my "radar" a full two blocks before encountering their little monster-posse. I counted three new types of Unseelie I would make notes on later in my journal, perhaps on the plane to Wales tonight.

When I got back to the bookstore, I steamed open the envelope. The adhesive edge curled quickly and the glue seemed sparse, making me wonder if I'd not been the first to do it.

It held an invitation, an exclusive one, extended by a host who denoted himself or herself with only a symbol, no address. On the back was jotted a partial list, intended to tantalize. It included an object long held to be mythical, two religious icons the Vatican was rumored to be looking for, and a painting by one of the Masters believed lost in a fire centuries ago.

Barrons and I were going to an auction tonight, a very private one, the kind of black market sale Interpol and FBI agents nurture sweet, career-making dreams of one day busting.

EIGHT

Wales is one of four constituent or home nations of the United Kingdom.

England, Scotland, and Northern Ireland are the other three.

Ireland — not to be confused with Northern Ireland — is a sovereign state, and a member of the European Union.

The entire United Kingdom, at about 94,000 square miles, is slightly smaller than the state of Oregon. The island of Ireland, both Northern and the Republic, is roughly the size of the state of Indiana.

At 8,000 square miles, Wales is tiny. To put Wales in perspective, Scotland has four times the land mass, and Texas is thirty-three times as big.

I know all of this because I looked it up. When my sister was killed and I was forced, wings untried, from my gently feathered nest in Ashford, Georgia, my eyes were opened in more ways than one. I took stock of myself and realized that among other things, I had no global awareness. I've been trying desperately to dispel my provinciality by teaching myself a bird's-eye view of things. If knowledge is power, I want all of it I can get.

The flight from Dublin to Cardiff took a little over an hour. We landed in Rhoose, about ten minutes from the capital city, at eleven-fifteen. A chauffeur fell into step beside us and ushered us into a waiting silver Maybach 62. I have no idea where we went from there because I'd never been inside such a car, and was too busy examining the luxurious interior to notice much more than city lights whizzing by, and finally darkness beyond the panoramic glass roof. I reclined my seat to nearly horizontal. I tested the massage option. I stroked the soft leather and the gleaming wood. I watched the velocity with which we hurtled into the night on the ceiling instruments.

"When we arrive, you will take your seat and not move," Barrons said for the fifth time. "Do not scratch your nose, fidget with your hair, rub your face, and no matter what I say to you, you must not nod. Speak to me, but softly. People will listen if they can. Be discreet."

"Still as a cat, quiet as a mouse," I replied,

flipping through the movie selections for my personal flat-screen TV. The car was capable of what critics called a "blistering performance," achieving 0–100 in five seconds. Barrons must be a serious collector for our hosts to have sent such a car after him.

I didn't become aware of my surroundings again until Barrons was helping me from the car, tucking my arm through his. I liked my attire tonight better than anything he'd chosen for me in the past. I had on a black Chanel suit that was all business, sexy heels that weren't, and fake diamonds at my ears, wrists, and throat. I'd sleeked my short dark curls with a leave-in conditioner and tucked it behind my ears. I looked like money and liked how it felt. Who wouldn't? Up until now the most expensive outfit I'd ever worn was my prom dress. I always figured the next expensive dress I'd get to wear would be the one my daddy bought me for my wedding, and if life was good, about half a dozen more between that and my funeral. I certainly never would have wagered on haute couture and fancy cars and illegal auctions and men who wore silk shirts and Italian suits, with platinum and diamond cuff links.

When I finally glanced around, I was

startled to find we were on a deserted country lane. Stiff men in stiffer suits herded us a short distance down a shadowy path through the woods, stopping us in front of an overgrown bank. I was perplexed until they parted the dense foliage, revealing a steel door in the side of an embankment. We were guided through it, down an endless, narrow flight of concrete stairs, through a long concrete tunnel lined with pipes and wires, and into a large rectangular room.

"We're in a bomb shelter," Barrons said against my ear, "nearly three stories beneath the ground."

I don't mind telling you it creeped me out more than a little, being so deep in the earth with only one way out, and that back the way we'd come, through a dozen heavily armed men. I'm not claustrophobic but I like the open sky around me, or at least the knowledge that it's right on the other side of whatever walls I'm enclosed by. This felt like being buried alive. I think I'd rather die in a nuclear holocaust than live in a concrete box for twenty years.

"Lovely," I murmured. "Is this kind of like your undergr— *Ow!*" Barrons' boot was on my foot and if he gave it any more pressure, it'd be flat as a pancake.

"There are times and places for curiosity, Ms. Lane. This is not one of them. Here, anything you say can and will be used against you."

"Sorry," I said and I really was. If he didn't want these people to know he had an underground vault, I could understand that, and if I'd not been so discombobulated by my surroundings, I would have thought of that before I'd brought it up. "Get off my foot."

He gave me a Barrons look that defies describing because he has several of them, and they speak volumes. "I'm alert, I swear," I said crossly. I hate being a fish out of water, and not only was I flopping around on the beach, I was a minnow among sharks. "And I won't say another word unless you speak to me, okay?"

He gave me a tight, satisfied smile and we headed for our seats.

The room was concrete from top to bottom, with no finishing touches. Exposed pipes and wires ran the length of the ceiling. Forty metal folding chairs had been set up in the room: five rows of four each on both sides of a narrow aisle. Most of the chairs were already filled with people in elegant evening attire. Those conversing did so in hushed murmurs.

At the front of the room was a center podium flanked by tables, covered with items draped in velvet. Additional draped items lined the wall behind it.

Barrons looked at me. I was careful not to nod. "Yes," I told him, as we took our seats in the third row on the right side of the room. I'd been feeling it ever since we'd entered the shelter but I'd had no way of knowing if it was a Fae relic, or an actual Fae, until I had the opportunity to examine all persons in the vicinity. There were no glamours being cast; the occupants of this room were human, which meant there was a very powerful OOP under all that velvet somewhere. On a nausea scale of one to ten — ten being the *Sinsar Dubh,* and most other things topping out at a three or four, with nothing so far between six and ten but the single ten that had made me lose consciousness — it was a five, and I thumbed from my pocket one of the Tums I'd begun taking to help with the discomfort of carrying the spear all the time, which, by the way, I'd left on Barrons' desk earlier at his direction, so he could strap it to his leg, not mine. I'd hated giving it up, but my sleek suit afforded no hiding places. Though there was little trust between us, I knew he would return it to me quickly if I needed it.

"The door closes at midnight." His lips brushed my ear and I shivered, which seemed to amuse him. "Anyone not inside by then doesn't get in. There are always a couple of last-minute stragglers."

I glanced at his watch. There were three and a half minutes to go and still half a dozen seats to fill. During the next minute, five were taken, leaving one empty up front. Though I craned my neck, studying every face, Barrons stared straight ahead. *You must be more than my OOP detector tonight, Ms. Lane,* he'd told me on the plane, *you must be my eyes and ears. I want you to analyze everyone, listen to everything. I want to know who betrays excitement over what item, who wins worriedly, who loses badly.*

Why? You always notice way more than me.

Where we're going tonight, noticing anyone other than yourself is considered a sign of uncertainty, weakness. You must notice for me.

Who noticed for you in the past? Fiona?

Barrons just ignores me when he doesn't feel like answering.

And so I was the green one, looking around. It wasn't as bad as I expected because no one would look back at me. Some of their gazes flickered a little, as if they resented being studied when the nature

158

of the game being played prevented them from returning the stare.

I found it silly that they all dressed up so much just to come sit in metal chairs in a dusty bomb shelter, but with people this wealthy, money wasn't something they had, it was who they were, and they would wear it to their graves.

There were twenty-six men and eleven women. They ranged in age from early thirties all the way up to a white-haired man who was ninety-five if a day, in a wheelchair, accompanied by an oxygen tank and bodyguards. His sallow skin was so thin and translucent I could see the network of veins behind his face. He was sick with something that was eating him alive. He was the only one that looked directly back at me. He had scary eyes. I wondered what a man so close to death wanted so badly. I hope when I'm ninety-five the only things I want are free: love, family, a good home-cooked meal.

Most of the conversation was about the inconvenience of their current location, the mud damage the short jaunt through the woods had done to their shoes, the dismal state of current political affairs, and the even more dismal weather. No one mentioned the items about to be auctioned, as if they couldn't have cared less about what was up for grabs. The entire time they pretended not to be interested in anyone or anything around them, they snatched greedy little glimpses by fabricating actions to justify movement. Two women withdrew jeweled compacts and checked their lipstick, but it wasn't their mouths they examined in those clever mirrors. Four people dropped various items from their laps for an excuse to move about and retrieve them. It was kind of funny in a sad way how many people dove for the goods, trying to use it as their own excuse.

Seven people got up and tried to go to the bathroom. The armed henchmen declined their requests, but at least they got a good look around.

I have never seen a more avaricious, paranoid assortment of people. Barrons didn't fit in any more than I did. If I was a minnow and they were sharks, he was one of those yet undiscovered fish that lurk in the deepest, darkest reaches of the ocean where sunlight and man never go.

A distinguished-looking gentleman with silver hair and a neatly trimmed beard entered the room and I thought for a moment he was the final attendee, but he headed straight for the podium. On the way there, he greeted many warmly and by name, with a clipped British accent and sparkling eyes.

When he arrived at the podium, he welcomed us, recounted a short list of conditions to which we'd all agreed to abide by by the mere virtue of our presence, and said that any could leave now that so chose (I wondered darkly if they would be permitted to live if they did). He then detailed accepted methods of payment, and just as the auction was about to begin, a very famous man you would recognize — you see him on TV all the time — slipped into the final seat.

The bidding opened with a Monet and grew more surreal to me from there. I learned that night that some of the finest art and artifacts in the world will never be seen by common man, but will continue to pass down through the ages via a hidden network of the uber-wealthy.

I saw paintings the world didn't know had been painted, artifacts I couldn't believe had survived the ages, the hand-penned copy of a play that has never been and will never be performed, much to our disastrous loss. I learned there are people that will pay a fortune to possess something that is one of a kind, for the sheer pleasure of possessing it and having a handful of their peers envy them the possession.

The bids were mind-boggling. A woman paid twenty-four million dollars for a painting the size of my hand. Another woman bought a brooch the size of a walnut for three point two million. The famous man bought the Klimt for eighty-nine million. There were jewels that had once belonged to queens, weapons owned by some of history's most notorious villains, even an Italian estate on the block, complete with a private jet and classic car collection.

Barrons acquired two ancient weapons and a journal written by a Grand Master of a secret society. I sat on my hands to keep myself from fidgeting and waited in breathless anticipation, as each treasure was unveiled, taking great pains not to move my head, which is considerably more difficult than it sounds. The urge to flip a curl of hair from my face that had escaped my sleek 'do became nearly debilitating. Until now I'd had no idea how frequently my body betrayed my thoughts until I repeatedly caught myself on the verge of shrugging, shaking, or nodding my head. It was no wonder Barrons read me so easily. It was not a comfortable night, but it was an unforgettable one. When the OOP was finally uncovered, I had no idea what it was, but Barrons knew — and he wanted it badly. I've learned to read him, too.

It was a jeweled amulet the approximate size of my fist — I have small hands — fashioned of gold, silver, sapphires, and onyx, and according to the information sheet, several unidentifiable alloys and equally mysterious gems. The amulet's lavish gilt casing housed an enormous translucent stone of unknown composition, and was suspended on a long, thick chain. It had a colorful history, dating farther back than it possibly could according to what we understood of *Homo sapiens'* development, and had been crafted for the coveted concubine of a mythical king known as Cruz.

Each auction participant was given a folder, detailing the item's provenance, a chain of custody that had my eyes popping out of my head when I read it over Barrons' shoulder. Every owner of the amulet down through time figured prominently in history or mythology — even I who'd slept through most of my history classes recognized them. Some had been heroically good, others epically bad. All had been immensely powerful.

The auctioneer's eyes twinkled as he spoke of the amulet and its "mystical" ability to grant its owners' deepest desires.

Is it good health you seek? he asked the wheezing, wheelchair bound man softly. *Longevity? One of its owners, incidentally a Welshman like yourself, sir, was reputed to have lived for hundreds of years.*

Perhaps you have political aspirations, he offered the famous man. *Would you like to guide your great nation? How about greater wealth?*

Could he get any wealthier? I wondered. If I were him, I'd go for better hair.

Perhaps you seek a return of sexual desire and desirability? he crooned to the faded beauty with bitter grooves bracketing her mouth and smoldering embers for eyes. *Your husband back? His new young wife . . . shall we say . . . receiving her comeuppance?*

Perhaps, he teased a man in the fourth row wearing the most haunted, hunted expression I'd ever seen, *you'd like to vanquish all your enemies.*

Bidding exploded.

The entire time Barrons sat motionless, staring straight ahead. I, on the other hand, rubbernecked shamelessly. My heart was pounding, and I didn't even have anything vested in the situation.

I kept waiting for Barrons to bid and grew increasingly alarmed when he didn't. Cruz was obviously Cruce, the legendary creator of the Cuff V'lane had offered me. It was a Fae relic, unbelievably powerful, and even if we weren't going to use it ourselves, it shouldn't be out there in the world. It was an OOP. Every *sidhe*-seer instinct in me wanted it withdrawn from the world of Man where it never should have been in the first place and in the wrong hands was capable of aiding great evil, as evidenced by a German dictator who'd once owned it.

I leaned into him and pressed my mouth to his ear. "Say something," I hissed. "Bid!"

He closed his hand around mine and squeezed. Bone ground gently upon bone. I shut up.

The bids reached astronomical proportions. There was no way Barrons had that kind of money.

I couldn't believe we were just going to let it go.

The bidding narrowed down to five fervent contenders. Then two: the famous man and the dying one. When the bidding reached eight figures, the famous man laughed and let it go. *I already have everything I want,* he said, and I was pleasantly surprised to see he actually meant it. In a room of malcontent, covetous people, he genuinely was happy with his Klimt, and his life overall. He rose considerably in my estimation. I decided I liked his hair and admired that he didn't care what anyone else thought of it. Good for him.

An hour later, the auction was over. A few hours after that, via a private plane — you can hardly transport illegal goods on a public one — we were standing outside the bookstore, shortly before dawn. Exhausted, I'd slept through the flight, waking only when we'd landed, to find my mouth slightly ajar on a soft snore and Barrons watching me with amusement.

I was pissed that he'd let the OOP go. I wanted to know the extent of the power it conferred. I wanted to know if it could have protected me even better than the Cuff V'lane was offering.

"Why didn't you at least bid on it?" I asked crossly, as he unlocked the front door.

He followed me inside. "I purchase what I must to maintain a façade, to continue receiving invitations. Any acquisition made at such an auction is observed and recorded. I don't like other people knowing what I have. I never buy the things I want."

"Well, that's just stupid. How do you get them, then?" I narrowed my eyes. "I am *not* helping you steal that thing, Barrons."

He laughed. "You don't want it? The auctioneer was incorrect, Ms. Lane. It's not the Amulet of Cruce. The Unseelie King himself fashioned that trinket; it's one of the four Unseelie Hallows."

A few months ago I'd never have believed in anything like the Hallows, but a few months ago I'd never have believed myself capable of killing, either.

The Hallows were the Fae's most sacred, powerful, and obsessively coveted relics. There were four Light or Seelie Hallows: the spear, the sword, the cauldron and the stone, and four Dark or Unseelie Hallows: the amulet, the box, the mirror, and the most terrible of them all, the *Sinsar Dubh.*

"You saw who owned it in the past," Barrons said. "Even if you don't want it, can you abide a Dark Hallow out there, loose in the world?"

"That's not fair, using my *sidhe*-seer-ness against me to get me to commit a crime."

"Life isn't fair, Ms. Lane. And you happen to be up to your ears in crimes. Get over it."

"What if we get caught? I could get arrested. I could end up in jail." I wouldn't survive prison. The drab uniforms, the lack of color, the rut of penitentiary existence would unravel me completely in a matter of weeks.

"I'd break you out," he said dryly.

"Great. Then I'd be on the run."

"You already are, Ms. Lane. You have been ever since your sister died." He turned and disappeared beyond the connecting doors.

I stared after him. What didn't Barrons know? *I* knew I'd been running since then, but how did he?

After Alina was murdered, I'd started to feel invisible. My parents had stopped seeing me. With increasing frequency, I'd caught them watching me with a heartbreaking mixture of longing and pain, and I'd known it was Alina they were seeing in my face, my hair, my mannerisms. They were *hunting* for her in me, summoning her ghost.

I'd stopped existing. I was no longer Mac. I was the one who'd lived.

He was right. Justice and revenge had been only part of my motivation for leaving Ashford. I'd run from my grief, from their pain, from being a shadow of another person, better loved for bitterly lost, and Ireland hadn't been nearly far enough.

The worst of it was that now I was caught up in a deadly marathon, running for my life, desperate to stay one step ahead of all the monsters behind me, and there was no finish line in sight.

NINE

Speaking of the better loved for bitterly lost, I had one day left to clean out her apartment. By midnight all of Alina's belongings had to be out, or the landlord had the right to set them to the curb. I'd packed the boxes up weeks ago. I just needed to drag them to the door, call a cab, and pay a little extra to have the cabbie help me load and transport them to the bookstore, where I could wrap them and ship them home.

I couldn't believe I'd so completely lost track of time, but I'd had monsters to fight, a police interrogation to deal with, a graveyard to search, my dad to send home, a mobster's brother's death to avert, a new job to learn, and an illegal auction to attend.

It was a wonder I got anything done, really.

And so Sunday afternoon, August 31, the last day of Alina's lease, the day she *should* have been packed and waiting for a cab to take her to the airport and, finally, home to me and Georgia, and endless summer beach parties on the cusp of fall, found me propping a dripping umbrella at the top of her stairs and wiping my shoes on the rug outside her door. I stood there a few minutes, shuffling aimlessly, taking deep breaths, digging for my compact to remove the speck from my eye that was making them water.

Alina's apartment was above a pub in the Temple Bar District, not far from Trinity, where she'd been studying, at least for the first few months that she'd been here, when she'd still been going to class, before she'd begun looking stressed and losing weight and behaving secretively.

I could understand how I'd forgotten about cleaning out her apartment, but now that I was standing outside it, I couldn't believe I'd forgotten about her journal. Alina was a diary addict. She couldn't live without one. She'd been keeping one ever since she was a little girl. She'd never missed a day. I know; I used to snoop and read them and torment her with secrets she'd chosen to confide to some stupid book over me.

During her tenure abroad, she'd confided the biggest secrets of her life to a stupid book over me, and I needed that book. Unless someone had beaten me to it and destroyed it, somewhere in Dublin was a record of everything that had happened to her since the day she'd set foot in this country. Alina was neurotically detailed. In those pages would be an account of all she'd seen and felt, where she'd gone and what she'd learned, how she'd discovered what she and I were, how the Lord Master had tricked her into falling for him, and — I hoped — a solid lead on the location of the *Sinsar Dubh:* who had it, who was transporting it, and for what mysterious reason. "I know what it is now," she'd said in her final, frantic phone message, "and I know where —" The call had ended abruptly.

I was certain Alina had been about to say she knew where it was. I hoped she'd written it down in her journal and hidden the journal somewhere she thought I, and only I, would figure out how to find it. I'd been finding them all our lives. Surely she'd left me a clue for how to find the most important one.

I slid the key into the door, jiggled the handle trying to turn it — the lock was sticky — pushed open the door, and gaped at the girl standing inside, glaring at me and wielding a baseball bat.

"Hand it over," she demanded, holding out a hand and nodding at the key. "I heard you out there and I already called the police. How'd you get a key to my place?"

I pocketed my key. "Who are you?"

"I live here. Who are you?"

"You don't live here. My sister lives here. At least she does until midnight today."

"No way. I signed a lease three days ago and paid up front. You have a problem with that, talk to the landlord."

"Did you really call the police?"

She assessed me coolly. "No. But I will if I have to."

That was a relief. I hadn't seen Inspector Jayne yet today and was savoring the respite. All I needed was for him to show up and arrest me for breaking and entering, or some other trumped-up charge. I glanced past her. "Where's my sister's stuff?" I demanded. All my carefully packed boxes were gone. There was no fingerprint dust on the floor, no broken glass scattered about, no sliced and diced furniture, no shredded drapes. All of it was gone. The apartment was spotless and had been tastefully redecorated.

"How should I know? The place was empty when I moved in."

"Who's the landlord?" I was stunned. I'd

been shut out. While I'd vacillated in indecision about whether or not to destroy the walls and floors in a thorough but damagingly expensive search for her journal, then been sidetracked by other things, I'd lost all my sister's personal possessions!

Someone was living in her apartment. It wasn't fair — I had one more day!

I would have continued to argue until the sun had gone down, the clock struck twelve, and the final bell finished chiming if the new tenant had said anything other than what she said next.

"The guy downstairs at the bar handles things for him, but it's probably the owner you'll need to talk to."

"And who's that?"

She shrugged. "I've never met him. Some guy named Barrons."

I felt like a rat in a maze and everyone else was human, wearing lab coats and standing outside my box, watching me run blindly up and down dead-end corridors, and laughing.

I left the new tenant without another word. I stepped outside, into the alley behind the pub, backed myself into an alcoved, bricked-up door to avoid the drizzle, and rang up Barrons on the cell phone he'd left outside my door last night with three numbers programmed in.

One was JB. That was the one I used now. The other two were mystifying: IYCGM and IYD.

He sounded angry when he answered. "What?" he snarled. I could hear the sound of things crashing, glass breaking.

"Tell me about my sister," I barked back.

"She's dead?" he said sarcastically. There was another crash.

"Where's her stuff?"

"Upstairs in the room next to yours. What's this about, Ms. Lane, and can't it wait? I'm a bit busy right now."

"Upstairs?" I exclaimed. "You admit you have it?"

"Why wouldn't I? I was her landlord and you didn't get the place cleaned out in time."

"I *was* on time. I had through today!"

"You were beat up and busy and I took care of it for you." A thunderous crash punctuated his words. "You're welcome."

"You were my sister's landlord and you never bothered to tell me? You said you didn't know her!" I shouted to make myself heard above the din coming out of the earpiece. Okay, maybe I shouted because I was furious. He'd lied to me. Baldly and blatantly. What else was he lying to me about? A clap of thunder above me made me even madder. One day I was going to escape Jericho Barrons and this rain. One day I was going to find myself a sunny beach, plant my petunia on it, and sprout roots. "Besides," I snapped, "your name wasn't on the letter we got about the damages to the apartment!"

"The man who handles my rentals sent the letter. And I didn't know your sister. I didn't know I was her landlord until my solicitor called a few days ago to tell me there was a problem with one of my properties." There was a soft thud and Barrons grunted. After a moment he said, "He'd been calling your house in Ashford and no one was answering. He didn't want to be responsible for setting a tenant's property to the curb. I heard the name, did the math, took care of it." There was a soft "oomph," and it sounded like Barrons' phone went clattering across the floor.

I was curiously deflated. I'd had one of those "aha" moments upstairs: I'd been immediately convinced he was hiding some personal connection between him and my sister, that I'd found evidence of it, it was proof of his villainy, and now things would fall miraculously into place and finally begin

175

making sense, but his reply was perfectly logical. Two of my patrons at The Brickyard owned multiple properties and never got personally involved in the running of them unless there was a problem. They didn't see any of the paperwork unless something had to go to court, and they never had any clue who was renting one of their apartments.

"You don't think it's terribly coincidental?" I demanded, when I heard him on the other end of the line again. He was breathing heavily, as if running, or fighting, or both. I tried to imagine who or what Barrons could be fighting that was giving him a run for the money and decided I didn't want to know.

"I've been choking on coincidences longer than I care to think about. You?"

"Yes," I agreed. "And I intend to get to the bottom of them."

"You do that, Ms. Lane."

He sounded positively hostile. I could tell he was about to hang up. "Wait a minute. Who's IYCGM?"

"If you can't get me," he gritted.

"And IYD?"

"If you're dying, Ms. Lane. But if I were you, I'd call that one only if I was sure I was dying, otherwise I'll kill you myself." I heard a man in the background laugh.

The line went dead.

"You see them, too," I said in a low voice, as I sank down onto the bench next to the lightly freckled redhead.

I'd found a *sidhe*-seer on the campus of Trinity — a girl, like myself.

On the way back to the bookstore the weather had cleared so I'd detoured to the college to people-watch. Although the sun was only weakly pushing through the clouds, the afternoon was warm and people had gathered on the commons, some studying, others laughing and talking.

When you see something from Faery, Barrons had advised me, *look not at the Fae, but the crowd to see who else is watching it.*

It had proved sound advice. It'd taken me a couple of hours, but I'd finally spotted her. It helped that there were so many Fae in the city. It seemed every half hour or so, a Rhino-boy walked by with one of his charges. Or I saw something totally new, like this one we'd both been watching.

The young girl glanced up from her book and gave me a blank look that was sheer perfection. A halo of curly auburn hair framed slight features, a small straight nose, a rosebud mouth, an impudent jaw. I pegged her for fourteen, fifteen at the most, and already her *sidhe*-seer façade was nearly flawless. It made me feel downright gauche. Had she taught herself or had someone else taught her?

"I'm sorry, what?" she said, blinking.

I glanced back at the Fae. It was stretched on its back on the edge of a multitiered fountain, as if soaking up the intermittent rays of sun. It was slender, diaphanous, lovely. Like those dreamy, translucent images of Fairy that are so popular in today's culture, it had a cloud of gossamer hair, a dainty face, and a petite, slim boy-body with small breasts. It was nude and not bothering with a glamour. Why should it? The normal human couldn't see it, and according to Barrons, many of the Fae believed *sidhe*-seers had died out long ago or dwindled to inconsequential numbers.

I handed the girl my journal, open to the page on which I'd been sketching it.

She flinched, clapped it shut, and glared at me. "How dare you? If you want to put yourself in danger, have a fine go at it, but don't be dragging me into it with you!" She grabbed her book, backpack, and umbrella, sprang up, and bounded off in a flash of feline grace.

I dashed after her. I had a million questions. I wanted to know how she'd learned what she was. I wanted to know who'd taught her, and I wanted to meet that person. I wanted to learn more about my heritage, and not from Barrons, who had agendas within agendas. Who was I kidding — even though she was years younger than me, it was lonely in this big city, and I could use a friend.

I was a good sprinter. It helped that I was wearing tennis shoes and she was in sandals. Though she dashed down one street after the next, pushing through tourists and vendors, I continued gaining, until finally she ducked into an alley, stopped, and whirled around. She tossed her fiery curls and shot me a glare. With a cat's luminous green-gold eyes, she performed a lightning quick scan of the alley, the pavement, the walls, the rooftops, finally the sky beyond.

"The sky?" I frowned, not liking that at all. "Why?"

"Blimey! How did you survive this fecking long?"

She was too young to be cursing. "Watch your mouth. My mother'd wash yours out."

She shot me a look of pure belligerence. "*My* mum would have turned you over to the council and had them lock you up for being a danger to yourself and others."

"Council? What council?" Could it be?

Were there that many of us? Were they organized, like Barrons said they'd been in olden days? "You mean a council of *sidhe*—"

"Stow it," she hissed. "You'll be the fecking death of us!"

"Is there one?" I demanded. "A council of . . . you know . . . people like us?" If so, I had to meet them. If they didn't already know about the Lord Master and his portal, they needed to. Perhaps I could turn this whole nasty affair over to someone else, a whole council of someone else's. Wash my hands of it, single-mindedly focus on my revenge, maybe get some help pursuing it. Had my sister known them, met with them?

"*Shoosh* it!" She scanned the sky again.

It was making me uneasy. "Why do you keep looking up?"

She closed her eyes, shook her head, and looked as if she were invoking Jesus, Mary, Joseph, and every last one of the saints in a bid for patience. When she opened them again, she hurried over and plucked the journal from beneath my arm. "Pen," she demanded. I dug one out of my purse and slapped it in her palm.

She wrote: *You and I are here, but the wind is everywhere. Cast no words upon it you don't wish followed back to you.*

"That's awfully melodramatic." I tried to make light of it, if only to dispel the chill inching up my spine.

"That's one of the first rules we ever learn," she said with a scathing glance. "I learned it when I was *three.* You're old. You should know better."

I bristled. "I'm not old. Who'd you learn it from?"

"My grandmum."

"Well, there you have it. I was adopted. Nobody told me anything. I had to learn it all myself and I think I'm doing a bang-up job. How well would you have done on your own?"

She shrugged and gave me a look that said she would have done way better than me because she was so smart and special. Oh, the cockiness of youth. How I missed mine.

"So what's with the sky?" I pressed. Was I the rat I'd been feeling like and there were owls above my head?

She turned the page to a blank one and wrote another word. Though the ink was pink, the word slashed, dark and ominous, across the page. *Hunters,* it said. The chill I'd nearly managed to dispel returned as an ice pick, pierced my back, and slid through my heart. Hunters were the terrifying caste of winged Unseelie whose primary purpose was to hunt and kill *sidhe*-seers.

She snapped the journal shut.

They've been spotted, she mouthed.

In Dublin? I mouthed back, horrified, glancing warily at the sky.

She nodded. "What's your name?"

"Mac," I said softly. Did I even want my name on the wind? "Yours?"

"Dani. With an *i*. Mac what?"

"Lane." That was good enough for now. How strange it was to feel like you didn't quite own your last name.

"Where can I find you, Mac?"

I started to give her my new cell phone number, but she shook her head briskly. "We stick to the old ways in times like these. Where are you staying?"

I gave her the address of Barrons Books and Baubles. "I work there. For Jericho Barrons." I searched her face for a sign of recognition. "He's one of us."

She gave me a strange look. "You think?"

I nodded and flipped the page in my journal. I wrote, *Are there many of us?*

It's not my place to answer your questions, she scribbled. *Someone will be in touch soon.*

"When?"

"I don't know. It's up to them."

"I need answers. Dani, I've seen things. Does your council know what's going on in this city?"

Her lucent eyes flared and she gave a single violent shake of her head.

I gave her an exasperated look. "Well, tell your 'someone' to hurry up. Things are getting worse, fast." I flipped my journal open again. *I'm a Null,* I wrote. *And I know about the Lord Master and the* Sinsar —

The journal was snatched from my hand and the page shredded before I could blink. She'd done it so smoothly and quickly that my pen was still poised in the air above a page that was no longer there, and I was still shaping the letter *D.*

Nothing normal could move that fast. She'd reacted with inhuman speed. I searched the pert, gamine face. "What are you?"

"Same as you. Latent talents awaken in times of need," she said, watching me. "You have your talents, I have mine. Every day we learn more about who we used to be and what we are again becoming."

"You let me catch you," I accused. She could have outrun me in a heartbeat. Who was I kidding? This kid could probably leap small buildings.

"So?"

"Why?"

She shrugged. "I wasn't supposed to, but

I was curious. Rowena sent a bunch of us out to find you, to learn where you were staying. Naturally, I'm the one that spotted you first. She made it sound like you were very powerful." She gave me a disdainful look. "I don't see it."

"Who's Rowena?" I had a hunch and didn't like it.

"Old woman. Silver hair. Looks fragile. Isn't."

Just as I'd suspected, the old woman I'd met my first night in Dublin, on the receiving end of her wrath when I'd stared overlong at the first Fae I'd ever seen. Later, she'd stood by and done nothing when V'lane had nearly raped me in the museum, then followed me, insisting I was adopted.

"Take me to her," I demanded. I'd hated her for tearing my world apart with her truth. I needed more of her truth. She'd called me O'Connor, mentioned someone named Patrona. Did she know where I came from? I almost couldn't let myself think the next thought; it frightened me as much as it fascinated me, felt like a betrayal of my parents, of all I'd been and done for the past twenty-two years: Did I have relatives somewhere in Ireland? A cousin, an uncle, dare I think it . . . a sister?

"Rowena will choose the time," Dani said.

When I scowled and opened my mouth to argue, she stepped back and raised her hands. "Hey, don't get mad at me. I'm just the messenger. And she'll box my ears for having given you any message at all." She flashed a sudden, brilliant grin. "But she'll get over it. She thinks I'm the cat's meow. I've got forty-seven kills."

Kills? Did she mean Fae? What was this cocky kid killing them *with*?

She turned to take off on feet that might as well have been winged, and I knew I had no chance of catching her. Why couldn't I have gotten superhuman speed? I could have used it dozens of times already.

"Mac," she shot over her shoulder, "one more thing, and if you tell Rowena I told you, I'll lie. But you need to know. There are no males among us. Never have been. Whatever your employer is, he's not one of us."

I made my way back through the Temple Bar District, with its snatches of music spilling from open windows and boisterous patrons stumbling from open pub doors.

The first time I'd ever walked into this part of the city, I'd gotten whistles and catcalls, and had enjoyed them all. I'd been the kind of girl who dressed for attention, in an eye-catching outfit with all the right accessories. Tonight, in baggy clothes and sensible running shoes, with no makeup and rain-slicked hair, my passage through the *craic*-filled party district went unnoticed, unremarked, and I was grateful for it. The only crowd I was interested in was the one in my head, thoughts crammed into every nook and cranny of my brain, elbowing each other out of the way to get my attention.

Up until now, Barrons had been my only source of information about what I was, and what was going on around me. But I'd just learned there was another source out there, and it was an organized one. There were other *sidhe*-seers battling and killing the Fae; spunky fourteen-year-olds, with super-hero speed, no less.

Up until now, without even knowing her name, I'd discounted Rowena as a cantankerous old woman who probably knew a few others like us and was old enough to recall a bit of *sidhe*-lore. I'd never dreamed she might be plugged into a community of *sidhe*-seers, an active network with a council and rules, and mothers who taught their children from birth how to cope with what they were. The ancient enclave Barrons had told me about in the graveyard still existed today!

I was angry that she hadn't invited me into that community the night we'd met, the night I'd seen my first Fae and nearly betrayed myself — would have, in fact, if she'd not intervened.

But no, far from taking me under her wing when I'd so desperately needed help, and teaching me how to survive, Rowena had chased me off and told me to go die somewhere else.

And that's exactly what I would have done — died — if I'd not crossed paths with Jericho Barrons.

Unguided, clueless about what I was, one or another of the Unseelie monsters I would have refused to believe was real would have killed me. Perhaps a Shade would have reduced me to a papery husk the next time I'd unwittingly wandered into the abandoned neighborhood. Perhaps the Gray Man would have made shorter work of my beauty than awful hair, bad clothes, and rapidly shifting priorities were managing to do quite nicely. Perhaps the Many-Mouthed Thing would have turned his many mouths on me, or perhaps I'd have been drawn to the attention of the Lord Master and ended up *his* personal OOP detector, not Barrons', and he'd have used and killed me just like Alina.

Whatever else Barrons may be — he was the one who'd saved me. He'd opened my eyes and turned me into a weapon. Not Rowena and her merry band of *sidhe*-seers. I'd take tough love any day over no love at all.

There are no male sidhe-*seers,* Dani had said. *Never have been.*

Well, I had news for her: Barrons could see them, he'd taught me about them, and we'd fought them side by side, and that was more than Rowena or anyone else had ever done for me.

I had no doubt she'd send for me soon. She'd had *sidhe*-seers out hunting for me. She knew I had one of the Seelie Hallows. That day in the museum when V'lane had forced his deadly sexuality on me, she'd seen me threaten him with the spear. When I'd finally escaped, she'd caught up with me and tried to get me to go somewhere with her. But it had been too little, too late. She'd abandoned me for the second time that day in the museum, letting me strip in public and back up like a mindless mare in heat to a death-by-sex Fae and not lifting a finger to help me. When I'd demanded to know why she hadn't tried to do something — anything — she'd said coldly, *One betrayed is one dead. Two betrayed is two dead . . . we cannot take risks that might betray more of us, especially not me.*

She was important, this old woman. And she had information about me, about who I was. And when she sent someone for me, I would go.

But only with guarded thoughts and cautious tread.

At our third encounter, things were going to be very different: *She* was going to have to prove herself to *me.*

It was dark by the time I got back to the bookstore. I made my way down the side alley and around to the back entrance, a flashlight clutched in each hand. I noticed Barrons had boarded up the broken window in the garage.

I was not developing a full-blown obsession with the Shades. I was merely checking to make sure the status quo was still . . . well, quo. One of my enemies had set up a base camp right outside my back door. The least any good soldier would do was scout it on a regular basis to make sure there were no new developments.

There were no new developments. The floodlights were on, the windows were closed. I dragged the back of my hand across my brow with a sigh of relief. Ever since the Shades had gotten into the store,

I'd not been able to get them off my mind, especially the big, aggressive one that had menaced me in Barrons' parlor, and was currently moving restlessly back and forth at the edge of the darkness.

I blinked.

It was shaping a tendril of itself into something that looked suspiciously like a fist with a single upright human finger — you know which one. Surely it wasn't learning from me, was it? I refused to entertain the thought. There was no room for it in my head; my brain was full. It had been a trick of the shadows, nothing more.

I turned for the stairs and was on the top step, my hand on the doorknob, when I felt its presence behind me.

Dark.

Empty.

Vast as the night.

I turned, as inexorably drawn as if a black hole had opened at my back and I was being sucked into its event horizon.

The specter stood motionless, watching me in silence, still as death. The inky folds of its voluminous, cowled robe rustled in the breeze.

I narrowed my eyes. There was no breeze. Not the merest hint of wind stirred the back alley. Not a hair on my head moved. I licked my finger and held it up. The air was flat, stagnant.

Yet the specter's robe rippled, buffeted by a draft that wasn't there.

Great. If I'd been looking for proof that the ghoulish vision haunting me was a delusion, I'd just gotten it. I'd obviously Photoshopped this thing in from stills stored in my memory compiled from movies, childhood ghost stories, and books. In my mind's media banks its robes always rustled, I never saw its face, and it always carried a sharply curved, lethal blade mounted on a tall pole of ebony wood like the one it was toting now. It was perfect. *Too* perfect.

Why was I doing this to myself?

"I don't get it," I said. Of course, the specter said nothing. It never did and never would. Because Death wasn't standing in this alley with me, waiting, with patience born of perpetuity, for the right moment to punch my ticket, call in my chip. The Eternal Footman wasn't holding out my coat, a subtle yet irrefutable signal that the dance, for me, was over, the ball done, the night through.

And if I wanted further evidence that this clichéd spirit was just that — an apparition, a figment of an overwrought imagination — I had only to remind myself that Barrons,

Jayne, and Derek O'Bannion hadn't seen it, when they'd been in its vicinity. Jayne and O'Bannion weren't necessarily conclusive evidence, but Barrons was. Good grief, the man could smell a kiss on me. He didn't miss anything.

"Is it because I killed Rocky O'Bannion and his men? Is that why I keep seeing you? Because I collected their clothes and threw them in the trash instead of sending them to the police, or back to their wives?" I'd had my share of psych courses in college. I knew a perfectly healthy human mind could play tricks on itself, and mine wasn't healthy. It was burdened by vengeful thoughts, regrets, and rapidly multiplying sins. "I know it's not because I killed all those Unseelie in the warehouse or stabbed Mallucé. I feel good about those things." I studied it a moment. How honest did I have to be with myself to get rid of it? "Is it because I left Mom back home in Ashford, grieving, and I'm afraid she'll never get better without me?"

Or had this thing's dark conception taken place long before that? Had the seeds of it been planted on a warm sunny day by the side of a swimming pool, while I was stretched out, tanning my pampered hide and listening to happy, mindless music while four thousand miles away my sister was stretched out, bleeding to death in a dirty Dublin alley?

Was it because I'd talked to Alina every week for hours, over the course of months, and never once clued in to anything in her voice, never pulled my head out of my happy little world far enough to sense that something was wrong in hers? Because I'd dropped my stupid cell phone in the pool, been too lazy to get a new one, and missed her dying call, and my last chance for the rest of my life to hear her voice? "Is it because I failed her? Is that it? Am I seeing you because I'm ashamed that I'm the one that lived?"

Darkness yawed beneath the specter's cowl, a nameless, blameless, silken darkness that promised oblivion. Was I subconsciously seeking it? Had my life become so foreign and awful that I wanted out and — contrary to torturing myself with fear of death, a death I thought I deserved — was I actually comforting myself with the promise of it?

Nah, that was way too complicated for me. There wasn't a suicidal bone in my body. I believed in silver linings and rainbows, and all the monsters and guilt in the world weren't going to change that.

What, then? I couldn't think of anything else I felt bad about, and frankly, I wasn't in the mood to keep hunting; psychoanalyzing myself ranked right up there with getting an unnecessary root canal.

I hadn't eaten since breakfast, my feet hurt from walking all day, and I was tired. I wanted comfort food, a warm fire, and a good book to read.

Wasn't I supposed to be able to banish my own demons? I felt like the biggest idiot, but gave it a try. "Begone, dastardly fiend!" I flung one of my flashlights at it.

It sailed straight through it and bounced off the brick wall behind it. By the time it clattered to the cobbled street, my Grim Reaper was gone.

I just wished I believed it would stay gone.

TEN

"Why hasn't the Lord Master come after me yet? It's been two weeks." When Barrons stepped into the bookstore Monday evening, an hour earlier than was his usual custom, I voiced the worry that had been on my mind all day.

It was raining again. Unlike the streets, the customers had dried up. Despite the lack of patrons, I felt guilty about having closed early more often than not since I'd started my new job, and was determined not to lock the doors this evening until seven o'clock on the dot. I'd been staying busy restocking shelves and dusting displays.

"I suspect, Ms. Lane," he said, closing the door behind him, "our reprieve is a matter of convenience. Note the 'our' in that sentence, in case you were foolhardily considering striking out on your own again."

He was never going to let me forget that I would have died that day I'd gone off into the Dark Zone by myself, if he hadn't come after me. I didn't care. He could dig at me all he wanted to. His heavy-handedness was beginning to roll off me. "Convenience?" It was certainly convenient for me, but I didn't think that was what Barrons meant.

"His. He's probably occupied with something else at the moment. If, when he disappeared through his portal, he went to Faery, time moves differently there."

"That's what V'lane said." I emptied the cash drawer, counted the bills into stacks, then began punching in numbers on an adding machine. The store wasn't computerized, which made bookkeeping a real pain in the neck.

He gave me a look. "The two of you are getting downright chatty, aren't you, Ms. Lane? When did you last see him? What else did he tell you?"

"I'm asking the questions tonight." One day I was going to write a book: *How to Dictate to a Dictator and Evade an Evader,* subtitled *How to Handle Jericho Barrons.*

He snorted. "If an illusion of control comforts you, Ms. Lane, by all means, cling to it."

"Jackass." I gave him a look modeled on his own.

He laughed, and I stared, then blinked

and looked away. I finished rubber-banding the cash, put it in a leather pouch, and punched the final numbers in, running the day's total. For a moment there he hadn't looked dark, forbidding, and cold, but dark, forbidding, and . . . warm. In fact, when he'd laughed he'd looked . . . well . . . kind of hot.

I grimaced. Obviously I'd eaten something bad for lunch. I inked the day's earnings into the ledger, tucked the pouch into a safe behind me, then skirted the counter, and flipped the sign on the door. I waved to Inspector Jayne as I locked the door. I saw no point in pretending he wasn't there. I hoped he was wet, cold, and bored to tears. I certainly hadn't needed the reminder of O'Duffy's death staring me in the face all day.

"What about Mallucé?" I asked. "Is he definitely dead?" I'd been so busy worrying about the enemies I was seeing on a regular basis that I hadn't gotten around to worrying about the ones I hadn't seen in a while.

Mallucé — born John Johnstone, Jr., to a wealthy British financier — had conveniently lost both his parents in a hit-and-run car accident that had never been resolved to the insurance company's satisfaction, and gained a nearly billion-dollar fortune at the same time, all at the tender age of twenty-four. He'd promptly divested himself of his redundant name, assumed the singular Mallucé, and reentered society as one of the recently undead. That had been eight or nine years ago. Since then, he'd acquired a worldwide cult following of true believers who traveled in droves to the south-side Goth mansion where the citron-eyed, steampunk vamp held court.

Whether or not he was really a vampire — Barrons didn't seem to believe it — was anyone's guess. All I knew for sure was that he was *something* more than human. Icy pale, tall with the slim, muscled body of a dancer, I'd watched him fling a nearly seven-foot, massively bulked bodyguard across the room, to his death, with a single backhanded blow. I still wasn't sure how I'd survived the blow I'd taken that day in the Dark Zone, after I'd stabbed him with my spear.

"There was a memorial service at his compound last week," Barrons replied.

Yes! This was what I'd been waiting for, his worshippers to mourn him! "So, he's dead." I encouraged him to say the words. Despite how certain his news made me, I wanted Barrons' verbal confirmation that there was one less bad guy out there after me now.

He said nothing.

"Oh, why won't you just say it? If you hold a memorial service for someone who's undead then he must be no longer 'un,' which means he's dead. Right? Otherwise they would have held a creepy welcome-back-to-life service, not a weepy we'll-always-remember-you service."

"I told you, Ms. Lane, never believe anything's dead —"

"— I know, I know, until you've 'burned it, poked around in its ashes, and then waited a day or two to see if anything rises from them,' I shot back at him dryly, with a roll of my eyes. According to Barrons, some things couldn't be killed. He'd strongly hinted that vampires fell into that category. Obviously Barrons hadn't read *Vampires for Dummies.* According to the VFD's authors, who'd allegedly interviewed hundreds of undead in their quest for the truth even dummies could follow (Mallucé was so famous they'd devoted an entire chapter to him), vampires were easily staked and tidily dispatched and subject to all kinds of worldly limitations and afflictions.

"His solicitor was at the auction, Ms. Lane, bidding heavily on several items, including the amulet."

My hopes went flat as a tire on nails. "He's alive?"

"It would be unwise to speculate. It could be that someone else is pursuing his interests, using his name and representatives as a front. Perhaps the Lord Master has assumed control of Mallucé's finances and following. There would be little to stop him."

That was a frightening thought. Whatever fanatic worshippers Mallucé had managed to acquire, I had no doubt the Lord Master could increase tenfold. Though I'd seen him only once, his face was permanently etched in my memory, in fine detail. I'd studied the photos that had been taken of him and my sister in and around Dublin, for hours. He was inhumanly beautiful, like a Fae, but not Fae. My *sidhe*-seer take on him had been as confused as my take on Mallucé. Human . . . but . . . not quite human.

Of one thing I was certain: On a charisma scale of one to ten, my sister's ex-boyfriend was an eleven. Mallucé's followers wouldn't stand a chance. They'd fall on their knees, supplicant in a heartbeat. The night I'd stolen the OOP that Mallucé had been hiding from the Lord Master, I'd seen enough of his groupies to know they were so desperate for something to live for that they'd die to get it. That was more oxymoronic than jumbo shrimp in my book. Not to mention just plain moronic.

"Go put these on." Barrons tossed a parcel at me.

I regarded it warily. Barrons' clothing choices were never simpatico with mine. He and I could walk into the same store and shop all day, and by the end of it, I still wouldn't have gotten around to selecting the one outfit that would have been his first choice. He goes for stark versus accessorized, dark over bright, jewel tone instead of pastel, carnal over flirty. I rarely recognize myself when he dresses me. Deep inside I'm still my daddy's rainbow and pink girl.

"Let me guess," I said dryly, "it's black?"

He shrugged.

"Tight?"

He laughed. That was twice in one night. Barrons rarely laughed. I narrowed my eyes. "What's with you?" I asked suspiciously.

"What do you mean, Ms. Lane?" He stepped closer. Too close. Was he looking at my breasts again? I could feel the heat of his big body, along with the energy that always seemed to roll off him, that strange electrical current that bristled, omnipresent beneath his golden skin. There was something different about him tonight. Control was Barrons' middle name. Why then was I getting this feeling of . . . wildness . . . of an emotion I couldn't identify but was surely kin to violence. And there was something more . . .

If he'd been any other man and I'd been any other girl, I'd have called the narrowing of his heavy-lidded dark eyes lust. But he was Barrons and I was Mac, and a blossoming of lust was about as likely as orchids blooming in Antarctica.

"I'll just go change." I turned away.

He caught my arm, and I glanced back. Backlit by wall sconces, he didn't look like Barrons at all. Light glanced off the sharp planes and shadowed the angles of his face, merging his bones together into a fierce, brutal mask. Though he was looking directly at me, it was with a thousand-yard stare and if he was seeing me at all, it was not a me I knew. To dispel the profound tension of the moment, I said, "Where are we going tonight, Jericho?"

He shook himself, as if stirring from a dream. "Jericho? Are you kidding me, Ms. Lane?"

I cleared my throat. "I meant Barrons and you know it," I said crossly. I had no idea why I'd just called him by his first name.

The one time I'd tried to elevate our bizarre relationship, for lack of a better word, to a first-name basis — in my defense he'd just saved my life and I was narcotized by gratitude and nearly unconscious at the time — he'd mocked and flatly refused me.

"Forget it," I said stiffly. "Let go of my arm, Barrons. I'll be ready in twenty minutes."

His gaze dropped, skimmed my breasts.

I pulled away.

If he'd been any other man and I'd been any other girl, I'd have said Barrons was looking for some action tonight. Maybe, despite the age difference, he and Fiona had been lovers and now that she was gone, he was getting horny. That was a scary thought. One that proved more recalcitrant than I'd have liked when I tried to shove it from my mind.

Forty-five minutes later, we were on a private plane destined for Wales, and the commission of yet another felony. Inspector Jayne followed us to the airport, and looked furious when he realized we were taking not a plane he might have boarded himself, but a private charter.

I'd been right about black and tight. Beneath a raincoat I had no intention of removing until I absolutely had to I was wearing a clingy catsuit that fitted me so snugly I might as well have been naked for all it revealed. Barrons had secured a work belt around my waist with myriad pockets and pouches into which he'd stuffed my spear, flashlights, and half a dozen other gadgets and gizmos I couldn't identify. It weighed a ton.

"What is this amulet, anyway?" I asked as I settled back into my seat. I wanted to know what I was risking life, limb, and modesty to steal.

He took the seat opposite me. "You never really know what a Fae relic is until you get your hands on it. Even then, it may take time to figure out how to use it. That includes the Hallows."

I raised a brow and glanced down at my spear. I hadn't had any problems figuring it out.

"That's what most would call a no-brainer, Ms. Lane. And I can't guarantee that it doesn't have another purpose entirely to a Fae. Their history is sketchy, full of inaccuracies, and planted liberally with lies."

"Why?"

"Multiple reasons. For one, illusion amuses them. Two, they frequently re-create themselves, and each time they do so, they divest all memory."

"Huh?" Divest memory? Could I get in on this? I had a few I'd like to lose and they didn't all begin with my sister's death.

"A Fae will never die of natural causes. Some of them have lived longer than you could possibly fathom. Extreme longevity has an unfortunate and inescapable by-product: madness. When they feel it approaching, most choose to drink from the Seelie Hallow, the cauldron, and wipe their memories clean so they can start over. They retain nothing of their former existence and believe they are born the day they drink. There is a record-keeper; one who scribes the names of each incarnation each Fae has borne, and maintains a true history of their race."

"Doesn't the record-keeper eventually go mad, too?"

"He or she drinks before that happens and the duty changes hands."

I frowned. "How do you know all this, Barrons?"

"I've been researching the Fae for years, Ms. Lane."

"Why?"

"The amulet," he said, ignoring my question, "is one of the gifts the Unseelie King fashioned for his favored concubine. She was not of his race and possessed no magic.

He wished her to be able to weave illusions for her amusement, like the rest of his kind."

"But the auctioneer made it sound as if the amulet did more than weave illusions, Barrons," I protested. I wanted it to work. I wanted it. "He made it sound like it impacted reality. Just look at the list of prior owners. Whether they were good or bad, they were all incredibly powerful."

"Another problem with Fae relics is they often transmute over time, especially if they are used near or corrupted by other magic. They can take on a life of their own, and turn into something other than what they were meant to be. For example, when the Sifting Silvers were first made they rippled like the silver of a sun-kissed sea. In those hallowed halls was beauty beyond compare. They were pure, magnificent. Yet now they're —"

"Black around the edges," I exclaimed, thrilled to have some nugget of knowledge to contribute to the conversation, "like they're going bad from the outside in."

He looked at me sharply. "How do you know that?"

"I've seen them. I just didn't know what they were."

"Where?" he demanded.

"In the Lord Master's house."

He stared.

"You didn't go inside the house?"

"I was in a bit of a hurry that day, Ms. Lane. I went straight to the warehouse. So that's how he's been getting in and out of Faery. I wondered."

"Not following," I said.

"With the Silvers a human can enter the Fae realms, undetected. How many did he have?"

"I don't know. I saw at least half a dozen." I paused before adding, "There were things in those mirrors, Barrons." Things I saw in my nightmares sometimes.

To my surprise, Barrons didn't ask what. "Were they open?"

"What do you mean?"

"Did you have to uncover the glasses to look into them, Ms. Lane?"

I shook my head.

"Did you see any runes or symbols in the mirrors, on the surface?"

"No, but I didn't really look." After I'd glanced into the first few, I'd refused to regard the others with anything more than peripheral vision. "So you're saying these mirrors are doorways into Faery? I could have walked into one?"

"It's not quite that simple, but under certain circumstances, yes. The Silvers are one of the Unseelie Hallows. Most believe the first Dark Hallow the King created was a single mirror. A few of us know it was actually a vast *network* of mirrors, linking dimensions and connecting realms. The Silvers were the Tuatha Dé's first method of locomotion between dimensions, before they evolved to the point where they could travel by thought alone, although some say they were created for a more personal purpose of the dark king's that history failed to record. At some point in the Fae time-line, this Cruce we keep hearing about cursed the Silvers."

When I regarded him expectantly, he shook his head. "I don't know what curse, nor do I know who Cruce was or why he cursed them. I only know that not even the Fae dared to enter the Silvers, under the direst of circumstances, after he'd done it. Once they started to turn dark, the Seelie Queen banished the glasses from Faery, not trusting them in their realms, for fear of what they were becoming."

I felt that way about myself lately; turning dark and afraid of what I was becoming. At that moment, I had no idea how light I still was. But then we so rarely understand the value of what we possess until it's gone.

I shook off the spell of Barrons' story. I

needed some sunshine in my life, and soon. In the interim, a lighter topic would do. "Let's get back to the amulet."

"In a nutshell, Ms. Lane, it's rumored to amplify human will."

"If you visualize it, it will come to pass," I said.

"Something like that."

"Well, it certainly seems to work. You saw the list."

"I also saw the long gaps between ownership. I suspect only a handful of people possess a will strong enough to make it work."

"You mean you have to be epic already, for it to make you more epic?" I was supposed to be epic, wasn't I?

"Perhaps. We'll know soon enough."

"He's dying, you know." I meant the old man. He wanted the amulet to live. When we took it from him, it would be one more inadvertent death on my conscience.

"Good for him."

I don't always get Barrons' sense of humor, and sometimes I don't bother trying. Since he was being so voluntarily informative, I broached another line of inquiry. "Who were you fighting when I called you?"

"Ryodan."

"Why?"

"For talking about me to people he

shouldn't be talking to."

"Who's Ryodan?"

"The man I was fighting."

I took a detour around the dead end. "Did you kill the inspector?"

"If I were the type of person to kill O'Duffy, I would also be the type of person to lie about it."

"So, did you, or didn't you?"

"The answer would be 'no' in either case. You ask absurd questions. Listen to your gut, Ms. Lane. It may save your life one day."

"I heard there are no male *sidhe*-seers."

"Where did you hear that?"

"Around."

"And which one of those are you in doubt about, Ms. Lane?"

"Which one of what?"

"Whether I see the Fae, or whether I'm a man. I believe I've laid your mind to rest on the former; shall I relieve it on the latter?" He reached for his belt.

"Oh, please." I rolled my eyes. "You're a leftie, Barrons."

"Touché, Ms. Lane," he murmured.

Tonight I didn't know the name of our unwitting victim, and I didn't want to. If I didn't know his name, I couldn't scribe it on my list of sins, and perhaps one day the old Welshman I'd robbed of his last hope for life would disappear from my memory and cease to trouble my conscience.

We rented a car at the airport, drove through gently rolling hills, and parked down a forested lane. I parted reluctantly with my raincoat and we hiked from there. When we crested a ridge and I got my first glimpse of the place we were planning to rob, I gaped. I'd known he was rich, but knowing was one thing, seeing another.

The old man's house was palatial, surrounded by elegant outbuildings and illuminated gardens. It soared, a gilded ivory city, above the dark Welsh countryside, lit from all directions. Its focal point was a tall, domed entry; the rest of the house unfolded from there, wing to turret, terrace to terrace. It was topped by a brilliantly mosaicked rooftop pool surrounded by sculptures displayed on pedestals of marble. Four-story windows framed glittering chandeliers in elaborate panes. Amid the lush foliage of manicured gardens, fountains splashed from one exquisitely inlaid basin to the next and pools shimmered the color of tropical surf, steaming the cool night air. For a moment I indulged in the fantasy of being the pampered princess that got to sunbathe in this fairy-tale world. I quickly exchanged that fantasy for another: being the princess that got to shop with the old man's credit card.

"Sale price of one hundred and thirty-two million dollars, Ms. Lane," Barrons said. "The estate was originally built for an Arab oil prince who died before it was completed. At forty-eight thousand square feet, it's larger than the private residence at Buckingham Palace. It has thirteen en-suite bedrooms, an athletic center, four guesthouses, five pools, a floor of inlaid gold, an underground garage, and a helipad."

"How many people live here?"

"One."

How sad. All this and no one to share it with. What was the point?

"It has state-of-the-art security, two dozen guards, and a panic room in case of terrorist attacks." He sounded perversely pleased by those facts, as if he relished the challenge.

"And just how do you plan on getting us in there?" I asked dryly.

"I called in a favor. The guards won't be a problem. But make no mistake, Ms. Lane. It still won't be easy. The security system must be disarmed, and there are half a dozen wards to be broken between us and him. I suspect the old man will be wearing the amulet. We may be here for some time."

We made our way down the hill, and were nearly to the house when I spotted the first body, partially concealed by a bank of thick shrubbery. For a moment, I couldn't make out what it was. Then I couldn't believe what I was seeing. Gagging, I turned away.

It was one of the guards, not simply dead, but badly mutilated.

"Fuck," Barrons cursed. Then his arm was behind my knees, and I was over his shoulder, and he was running with me, away from the house. He didn't stop until we'd reached one of the outlying guesthouses.

He dropped me to my feet and pushed me back into the shadows beneath the eaves. "Don't move until I return for you, Ms. Lane."

"Tell me that was not the favor you called in, Barrons," I said in a low, careful voice. If it was, he and I were through. I knew Barrons wasn't entirely on the up-and-up, but I had to believe such butchery was beyond him.

"They were supposed to be unconscious, that's all." His face was grim in the moonlight. When I would have spoken again, he pressed a finger to my lips then moved off into the night.

I huddled in the shadows of the guesthouse for a small eternity until he returned, though by my watch a mere ten minutes had passed.

His voice preceded him. "Whoever did it is gone, Ms. Lane." He stepped into view and I smothered a sigh of relief. The only thing I hate worse than the dark is being alone in it. I didn't used to be that way, but I am now and it seems to be getting worse. "The guards have been dead for hours," he told me. "The security system is disarmed and the house is wide open. Come."

We moved directly for the front entrance, not bothering with stealth. We passed four more bodies on the way. The front doors were open, and beyond them I could see an opulent round grand foyer with a dual staircase that unfurled gracefully up each side and met in a landing suspended beneath a domed skylight hung with a glittering chandelier. I stared straight ahead. The marble floor had once been polished pearl. It was now splashed with crimson, strewn with bodies, some of them women. The housekeeping staff had not been spared.

"Do you sense the amulet, Ms. Lane? Are you picking up anything?"

I closed my eyes to shut out the carnage, and stretched my *sidhe*-seer senses, but carefully, very carefully. I no longer thought of my ability to sense OOPs as a benign talent. Last night, after finishing yet another book on the paranormal — *ESP: Fact or Fiction?* — I'd been unable to sleep so I'd lain there thinking about what I was, what it meant, wondering where the ability came from, why some people had it and others didn't. Wondering what was different about me, what had been different about Alina. The authors contended that those with extrasensory abilities utilized parts of their brains that were dormant in other people.

Wondering if that was true, and bored out of my gourd — late-night TV is lousy in any country — I'd fingered my spear and gone poking around in my own skull.

It hadn't been hard to find the part of me that was different, and now that I knew it was there, I couldn't believe I'd been unaware of it for twenty-two years. There was a place in my head that felt as old as the earth, as ancient as time, always wakeful, ever watching. When I focused on it, it pulsed hotly, like embers in my brain. Curious, I'd played with it a little. I could fan it into a fire, make it expand outward, consume my skull, and pass beyond it. Like the element it resembled, it knew no morality, didn't understand the word. Earth, fire, wind, and water are what they are. Power.

At best, impartial. At worst, destructive. I shaped it. I controlled it. Or didn't.

Fire isn't good or bad. It just burns.

Now I skimmed it, a stone skipping the surface of a placid sea; a deep, dark sea I intended to keep placid. There would be no stirring of still waters on my watch.

I opened my eyes. "If it's here, I can't feel it."

"Could it be somewhere in the house and you just aren't close enough?"

I shrugged. "I don't know, Barrons," I said unhappily. "It's a big estate. How many rooms are there? How thick are the walls?"

"One hundred and nine, and very." A muscle worked in his jaw. "I need to know if it's still here, Ms. Lane."

"What are the odds of that?"

"Stranger things have happened. Perhaps the massacre was the result of a foiled robbery attempt."

It certainly looked like an expression of rage. Incensed, inhuman fury.

I told him the truth, although I knew it would seal my fate and the last thing in the world I wanted to do was pass through those doors. "I couldn't sense Mallucé's stone until I was in the same room with it. I didn't pick up on the spear until I was above it, and I only sensed the amulet once I was inside the bomb shelter door." I closed my eyes.

"I'm sorry, Ms. Lane, but —"

"— I know, you need me to walk the house," I finished for him. I opened my eyes and notched my chin higher. If there was the slightest chance the amulet could still be in there, we had to look.

And I'd thought the graveyard was bad. At least those bodies had been bloodless, embalmed, and tidily interred.

Barrons made the rooms more bearable for me as we went, by going ahead, entering them first, draping the bodies with sheets or blankets, and when none were available, stowing them behind furniture. Only after he'd "secured" a room, did he exit it and send me in alone, the better to focus on my search, he said.

While I appreciated his efforts, I'd already seen too much and frankly, it was hard not to glance behind a sofa or a chair, at the bodies he hadn't covered. They exerted the same gruesome hold over me as the husks left by the Shades, as if some wholly ir-rational part of me thought by staring long and hard enough, immersing myself in the horror of it, I might learn something that would help me avoid the same fate.

"They have no defensive wounds, Barrons," I said, exiting another room.

He was leaning up against the wall a few doors down, arms crossed over his chest. He was getting bloody from moving the bodies. I focused on his face, not the stains on his hands, or the dark, wet splotches on his clothes. His eyes were intensely bright. He seemed harder, larger, more electric than ever. I could smell the blood on him, the metallic tinge of old pennies. When our gazes locked, I jerked. If there was a man behind those eyes, I was a Fae. Jet, bottomless pools regarded me; on those glossy obsidian surfaces tiny Macs stared back at me. His gaze dropped, raked over my clingy catsuit, then worked back up very slowly.

"They were unconscious when they were slaughtered," he said finally.

"Then why kill them?"

"It would appear for the pleasure of it, Ms. Lane."

"What kind of monster does that?"

"All kinds, Ms. Lane. All kinds."

We continued our search. Whatever fascination the house might once have held for me was gone. I hurried through an art gallery that would have made any major metropolitan museum curator swoon with envy, and felt no more than the bitterness of the man who'd been driven to acquire the spectacular collection only to hang it in a windowless, vaultlike room where none but him could ever see it. I passed over a solid gold floor, and saw only the blood.

Barrons found the old man — who'd paid over a billion dollars for the amulet, blissfully ignorant that he'd not only *not* postponed his death, but had just spent an obscene amount of money to hasten it — dead in his bed, his head half ripped off from the force with which the amulet had been torn from his neck, chain marks scored into the shredded skin of his throat. So much for longevity; by trying to cheat death, he'd succeeded only in expediting it.

Our search was fruitless. Whatever had once been housed there — the amulet, perhaps other OOPs — was gone. Someone had beaten us to it. The Unseelie Hallow was out there in the world, amplifying the will of a new owner, and we were back at square one. I'd really wanted that amulet. If it was capable of impacting reality, and I could figure out how to use it . . . well, the possibilities were endless. At the least, it could protect me; at best it could help me get my revenge.

"Are we done here, Barrons?" I asked, as we descended the rear stairs. I suddenly felt as if I couldn't get out of the marble mausoleum fast enough.

"There's a basement, Ms. Lane."

We turned at the bottom of the final flight, and began walking toward a set of doors in the wall past the base of the stairwell.

At that very moment, they began to swing open.

Abruptly, I was no longer in the house at all, but standing on a white powder beach with a warm, salty breeze tangling my hair.

The sun was shining. Alabaster birds swooped low, gliding along lapis lazuli waves.

And I was naked.

ELEVEN

"V'lane!" I snarled.

I was naked — he was near.

"It is time for our hour, MacKayla," said a disembodied voice.

"Put me back right now! Barrons needs me!" How had he so cleanly swapped one reality for the next? Had he moved me, or worlds? Had I just been "sifted"? But I hadn't even seen him, or felt him touch me, or anything!

"At the time of my choosing was our deal. Will you dishonor it? Should I undo my part of it as well?"

Could he do that? Rewind time and dump me back into the Shade-infested bookstore, crouching before my enemy with too few matches left? Or did he mean to let the Shades back in right now, and when I got home from Wales, I'd have to clear it again, this time, without his help? I had no desire to face either. "I'm not dishonoring it. *You* are. Give me my clothes back!"

"We discussed nothing of attire in our bargain. We are on equal footing, you and I," he purred, behind me.

I whirled, fury in my eyes, murder in my heart.

He was naked, too.

All thought of Barrons and basement doors opening and potential dangers behind them vanished. Nor did it matter how I'd gotten here. I was here.

My knees turned to ash. I collapsed to the sand.

I looked away but my eyes didn't. My central nervous system was currently serving another master and had no interest in will. Will? What was will? Papers you signed in case you died, that was it. Nothing to do with my current situation. All I needed to do now was entrust my body to the Maestro before me who would play it like no other, stroking it to unimaginable crescendos, plucking chords no man had ever sounded before, or would ever match again.

A Fae prince naked is a vision that renders all other men eternally inadequate.

He stepped toward me.

I trembled. He was going to touch me. Oh, God, he was going to touch me.

Over the course of my many encounters

with V'lane, I would attempt repeatedly to describe him in my journal. I would use words like: terrifyingly beautiful, godlike, possessing inhuman sexuality, deadly eroticism. I would call him lethal, I would call him irresistible, I would curse him. I would lust for him. I would call his eyes windows to a shining heaven, I would call them gates to Hell. I would fill entries with scribblings that would later make no sense to me, comprised of columns of antonyms: angelic, devilish; creator, destroyer; fire, ice; sex, death — I'm not sure why those two struck me as opposites, except perhaps sex is both the celebration of life and the process whereby we create it.

I would make a list of colors, of every shimmering shade of bronze, gold and copper, and amber known to man. I would write of oils and spices, scents from childhood, scents from dreams. I would indulge in lengthy thesaurus-like entries trying to capture the sensory overload that was Prince V'lane of the Fae.

I would fail at every turn.

He is so beautiful that he makes a part of my soul weep. I don't understand those tears. They aren't like the ones I cry for Alina. They aren't made of water and salt. I think they're made of blood.

"Turn. It. Off." I gritted.

"I am doing nothing." He stopped in the sand next to me, towered above me. The parts of him I needed, those perfect, incredible parts I burned to have inside me, slaking my terrible, inhuman lust, were within arm's reach. I fisted my hands. I would never reach. Not for a Fae. Never. "Liar."

He laughed and I closed my eyes, lay shuddering on the soft white sand. The fine grains against my skin were the hands of a lover, the breeze at my nipples a hot tongue. I prayed the ocean wouldn't begin to lap at any part of me. Would I come apart? Would my cells lose the cohesion necessary to maintain the shape of my humanity? Would I scatter to the far reaches of the universe, flakes of dust borne off on a fickle Fae wind?

I rolled so my nipples pressed against the beach. As I turned, my thigh grazed the tender, aching flesh of my mons. I came, violently. "You bastard . . . I . . . *hate* . . . you," I hissed.

I was standing again. Fully clothed in my clingy catsuit, spear in hand. My body was cool, remote; not one ounce of passion stirred in what had an instant ago been enflamed loins. I was master of my will.

I lunged for him without hesitation.

He vanished.

"I sought only to remind you of what you and I might share, MacKayla," he said behind me. "It is extraordinary, is it not? As befits an extraordinary woman."

I spun and lunged again. I knew he would only vanish once more, but I couldn't help myself.

"What part of 'no' don't you understand? The *n* or the *o?* No is not maybe. It is not I like to play rough. And it is never, never, *never* yes."

"Permit me to tender my apologies." He was in front of me again, clothed in a robe that was a color I'd never seen before and couldn't describe. It made me think of butterfly wings against an iridescent sky, backlit by a thousand suns. His eyes, once molten amber, burned the same strange hue. He could not have looked more alien.

"I'll permit you nothing," I said. "Our hour is up. *You* dishonored our deal. You promised you wouldn't sex me up. You broke that promise."

He regarded me a long moment and then his eyes were molten amber, and he was the tawny Fae prince again. "Please," he said, and from the way he said it, I knew there was no such word in the Fae tongue.

To the Tuatha Dé there is no difference between creating and destroying, Barrons had said. *There is only stasis and change.* Nor to these inhuman beings was there any such thing as apologizing. Would the ocean apologize for covering the head and filling the lungs of the man who fell in it?

He'd used the word for me. Perhaps learned it for me. He'd used it in supplication. It gave me pause, as he'd meant it to do.

"Please," he said again. "Hear me out, MacKayla. Once more I have erred. I am trying to understand your ways, your wants." If he'd been human I would have said he looked embarrassed. "I have never before been refused. I do not suffer it well."

"You don't give them the chance to refuse. You rape them all!"

"That is untrue. I have not used the *Sidhba-jai* on an unwilling woman in eighty-two thousand years."

I stared. V'lane was eighty-two thousand years old?

"I see I have made you curious. That is good. I am curious about you as well. Come. Join me. Let us talk of ourselves." He stepped back and waved a hand.

Two chaise longues appeared between us. A wicker table between them offered a plate with a pitcher of sweet tea and two ice-filled glasses. There was a bottle of my favorite suntan oil stuck in the sand next to the chair closest me, near a pile of thick pastel towels. Sheets of brilliantly striped silk wafted from nowhere, billowed once in the breeze and draped themselves over the chairs.

Salt air kissed my skin. I glanced down.

My catsuit was gone and I was again spearless. I was wearing a hot pink string bikini, with a gold belly chain from which dangled two diamonds and a ruby.

I blinked.

A pair of designer sunglasses appeared on the bridge of my nose.

"Stop it," I hissed.

"I am merely trying to anticipate your needs."

"Don't. It's offensive."

"Join me for an hour in the sun, Mac-Kayla. I will not touch you. I will not . . . as you say . . . sex you up. We will talk, and at our next encounter, I will not make the same mistakes again."

"You said that last time."

"I made new mistakes this time. I will not make those, either."

I shook my head. "Where is my spear?"

"It will be returned to you when you leave."

"Really?" Why would he return a Fae-killing Hallow fashioned by his race to me,

227

knowing I would use it to kill more Fae?

"Consider it a gesture of our goodwill, MacKayla."

"Our?"

"The queen and I."

"Barrons needs me," I said again.

"If you insist I prematurely terminate our hour because you feel I have dishonored it, I will not return you to Wales, and you will still be of no use to him. Stay or go, you won't be with him. And MacKayla, I believe your Barrons would tell you he needs no one."

That much was true. I wondered how he knew Barrons. I asked him. They must have trained with the same master of evasion because he said only, "It rains in Dublin incessantly. Look."

A small square in the tropical vista opened before me, as if he'd peeled back the sky and palms, and torn a window open onto my world. I saw the bookstore through it. The streets were dark, wet. I would be alone there.

"It is raining now. Shall I return you, Mac-Kayla?"

I looked at the tiny bookstore, the shadowy alleys to either side of it, Inspector Jayne sitting across the street beneath a street-lamp watching it, and shivered. Was that the dim outline of my private Grim Reaper down the block? I was so tired of the rain and the dark and enemies at every turn. The sun felt heavenly on my skin. I'd almost forgotten the feel of it. It seemed my world had been wet and gloomy for months.

I glanced away from the depressing view, and up at the sky. Sun has always made me feel strong, whole, as if I get more than vitamins from it; its rays carry something that nourishes my soul. "Is it real?" I nodded up at the sun.

"As real as yours." The window closed.

"*Is* it mine?"

He shook his head.

"Are we in Faery?"

He nodded.

For the first time since I'd so unceremoniously arrived, I examined my surroundings. The sand was radiantly white and soft as silk beneath my bare feet, the ocean azure, and the water so clear I could see entire cities of rainbow-colored coral beneath it with tiny gold and pink fish swimming the reefs. A mermaid danced on a crest of a wave before disappearing beneath the sea. The tide tossed sand to the beach in a surf of glittering silver foam. Palm trees rustled in the breeze, dropping lush scarlet blossoms on the shore. The air smelled of rare spices, exotic flowers, and salt sea spray. I bit my lip on the verge of saying *It's so beautiful here.* I would not compliment his world. His world was screwing up mine. His world didn't belong on our planet. Mine did.

Still . . . the sun has always been my drug of choice. And if he would play fair — meaning not try to rape me again — who knew what I might learn? "If you touch me, or in any way try to affect my will, our time together stops. Got it?"

"Your will, my command." His lips curved with victory.

I took off my shades and glanced briefly at the sun, hoping to sear the devastating beauty of that smile from my retinas, scorch it from my memory.

I had no idea who or what V'lane really was, but I knew this: He was a Fae, and an immensely powerful one. In this battle where knowledge was so evidently power, where information could keep me alive, where Barrons pretty much ruled his far-reaching world because of how much he knew, I couldn't afford to pass up a chance to interrogate a Fae, and it looked like V'lane, for whatever reason, might just let me.

Perhaps he would lie. Perhaps he wouldn't about some things. I was getting better at sorting through what people told me. Learning to hear the truth in their lies and the lies in their truth.

"Have you really been alive for eighty-two thousand years?"

"Longer. That was merely the last time I used glamour to seduce a woman. Sit and we will talk."

After a moment's hesitation, I perched stiffly on the edge of the chaise.

"Relax, MacKayla. Enjoy the sun. It may be your last chance to see it for some time."

I wondered what he meant by that. Did he consider himself a weather prognosticator? Or could he actually control it, make it rain? Against my better judgment, I stretched out my legs and lay back. I stared at the sapphire sea, watched graceful alabaster birds pluck fish from the waves. "So, how old are you?"

"That," he said, "is anyone's guess. In this incarnation, I have lived one hundred and forty-two thousand years. Are you aware of our incarnations?"

"You drink from the cauldron."

He nodded.

How long, I wondered, did it take to go mad? My short twenty-two years were sorely testing me. It seemed forgetting might be a comfort. I considered the ramifications of divesting memory, and realized why a Fae might put it off. If he'd spent fifty or a hundred thousand years watching, learning, building alliances, making enemies, the moment he divested memory he would no longer even know who those enemies were.

But they would know who he was.

I wondered if any Fae had ever been forced to drink by others of their race, to rescue them from the vast, desolate steppes of insanity. Or perhaps for more nefarious reasons.

I wondered, considering V'lane had known exactly where I was and what I'd been doing, if he'd been responsible for the massacre at the Welshman's estate.

"Did you steal the amulet?"

He laughed. "Ah, so that was what you were after. I wondered. It amplifies the will, MacKayla."

"Your point?"

"I have no use for it. My will needs no amplifying. My will shapes worlds. The amulet was fashioned for one like you with no will of which to speak."

"Just because we can't manipulate reality with our thoughts doesn't mean we don't have will. Maybe we *do* shape reality, just on a different scale, and you don't see it."

"Perhaps. The queen suspects such might

be the case."

"She does?"

"That is why she sent me to help you, so that you may help us, and together we may ensure the survival of both our races. Have you learned anything about the *Sinsar Dubh?*"

I thought about that a moment. Should I tell him? What should I tell him? Perhaps I could use it as leverage. "Yes."

The palm trees stopped swaying, the waves froze, the birds halted mid-dive. Despite the sun, I shivered. "Would you please start the world again?" It was creepy frozen. Things moved once more.

"What have you learned?"

"Did you know my sister?"

"No."

"How could that be? You knew about me."

"We learned of you because we were watching Barrons. Your sister, who we've since become aware of, did not know Barrons. Their paths never crossed, ergo nor did ours. Now, tell me of the *Sinsar Dubh.*"

"Why were you watching Barrons?"

"Barrons needs watching. The book, Mac-Kayla."

I wasn't done yet. The book was big information, surely worth more of an exchange. "Do you know the Lord Master?"

"Who?"

"You're kidding, right?"

"No. Who is this Lord Master?"

"He's the one bringing the Unseelie through. He's their leader."

V'lane looked astonished. No more so than I felt. He and Barrons both knew so much yet were missing chunks of essential information. They were so smart in some ways, and so blind in others.

"Is he Fae?" he demanded.

"No."

He looked incredulous. "How can that be? A Fae would not follow a *hu*man."

I hadn't said he was human. He was something more than that. But the way V'lane had just sneered the word human — as if a life-form just couldn't get any lower — pissed me off so I didn't bother correcting him. "You're the one who's supposed to be all-knowing."

"Omnipotent not omniscient. We are frequently blinded by how much we see."

"That's absurd. How can you be blinded by vision?"

"Consider being able to see the atomic structure of everything around you, Mac-Kayla, past, present, and part of the future, and exist within that skein. Consider possessing awareness of infinite dimensions.

Imagine being able to comprehend infinity — only a handful of your race has yet achieved such awareness. Consider seeing the possible ramifications of each minute action you might make, from your slightest exhalation upon the breeze, in all realities, but you cannot piece them together into a guaranteed finale because every living thing is in constant flux. Only in death is there stasis and even then, not absolute."

I had a hard enough time functioning on my tiny little nearsighted human level. "So, what you're saying in a nutshell," I distilled, "is that for all your superiority and power, you're no smarter or better off than we are. Perhaps worse."

A heartbeat stretched into half a dozen. Then he smiled coolly. "Mock me if you will, MacKayla. I'll sit at your deathbed and ask you then if you would rather be me. Where is this human fool that fancies himself master of anything?"

"1247 LaRuhe. Warehouse behind it. Huge dolmen. He brings them through there. Would you mind squashing it for me?"

"Your wish, my command." He was gone.

I stared at the empty chaise. Had he really gone to destroy the dolmen through which the Unseelie were being brought? Would he kill the Lord Master, too? Would my vengeance be achieved so anticlimactically? And without me there as witness? I didn't want that. "V'lane!" I shouted. But there was no reply. He was gone. And I was going to *kill* him if he killed my sister's killer without me. The dark fever I'd caught that first night I'd set foot in Dublin had turned into a fever of a different kind: a bloodfever — as in I wanted blood, spilled for my sister. Spilled by my hand. That savage Mac inside me still hadn't found an audible voice, still wasn't speaking with my tongue, but we spoke the same language, she and I, and agreed on critical things.

We would kill my sister's killer together.

"Junior?" said a soft, lilting voice. A voice I'd never expected to hear again.

I shuddered. It had come from my right. I stared out at the waves. I would not look. I was in Faery. Nothing could be trusted.

"Junior, come on, I'm over here," my sister coaxed, and laughed.

I nearly doubled over from the pain of it. It was exactly Alina's laugh: sweet, pure, full of endless summer and sunshine and the sure knowledge that her life was charmed.

I heard the slap of a palm on a volleyball. "Baby Mac, let's play. It's a perfect day. I brought the beer. Did you get the limes from the bar?"

My name is MacKayla Evelina Lane. Hers is Alina MacKenna Lane. I was Junior on two levels. Sometimes she'd called me Baby Mac. I used to pilfer limes from the condiment tray at The Brickyard on Saturdays. Cheap, I know. I never wanted to grow up.

Tears burned my eyes. I gulped deep breaths and forced air in and out of my lungs. I fisted my hands. I shook my head. I stared out at the sea. She was not there. I did not hear the thud of a ball hitting sand. I did not smell Beautiful perfume on the breeze.

"The sand's perfect, Junior. It's powder. Come *on!* Tommy's coming today," she teased. I'd had a crush on Tommy for years. He was dating one of my best friends so I pretended I couldn't stand him, but Alina knew.

Don't look, don't look. There are ghosts and there are worse things than ghosts.

I looked.

Behind the volleyball net, buffeted by a gentle tropical breeze, my sister stood, smiling, waiting to play. She was wearing her favorite neon lime bikini, and her blond hair was pulled back in a bouncy ponytail through the flap of the faded Ron Juan ball cap she'd gotten in Key West on spring break two years ago.

I began to cry.

Alina looked stricken. "Mac, honey, what's wrong?" She dropped the volleyball, ducked under the net, and hurried across the sand to me. "What is it? Did somebody hurt you? I'll kick their frogging petunias. Tell me who. What did they do?"

My tears turned into sobs. I stared up at my sister, trembling from the violence of my grief.

She dropped to her knees next to me. "Mac, you're *killing* me. Talk to me. What's wrong?" Her arms went around me, and I was crying against her neck, lost in a cloud of peach shampoo, Beautiful perfume, Hawaiian Tropic suntan oil, and the bubble gum she'd always chewed on the beach to hide the smell of beer on her breath from Mom.

I could feel her warmth, the silkiness of her skin.

I was touching her.

I buried my fingers in her ponytail and sobbed.

I missed her hair. I missed mine. I missed her. I missed me.

"Tell me who did this to you," she said, and she was crying, too. We'd never been able to stand each other's tears. We'd always ended up crying with each other. Then made pacts that we would stand up for each other forever, take care of each other forever. Pacts that I now knew we'd started making when she was three and I was one, and we'd been left in a world that wasn't ours — to hide us, I'd begun to suspect.

"Is it really you, Alina?"

"Look at me, Junior." She pulled away, and used one of the towels to dry my tears, then dried her own. "It's me. It's really me. Look, I'm here. God, I've missed you!" She laughed again and this time I laughed with her.

When you lose someone you love abruptly, without warning, you dream of getting the chance to see them, just one more time, please God, one more time again. Every night after her funeral I'd lay awake in my bedroom, down the hall from hers, and call good night, even though I knew it would never be answered again.

I'd lay there clutching photographs, re-creating her face in my mind in exacting detail, as if — if I got it exactly perfectly right — I could take it into my dreams, and use it as a road map to lead me to her.

Some nights, I couldn't see her face and I cried, begged her to come back. I offered all kinds of deals to God — He doesn't make them, by the way. In my despair, I offered deals to anyone or anything that would listen.

Something had heard me. Here was my chance to see her again. I didn't care how. I didn't care why. I absorbed every detail.

There was the mole high on her left cheek. I touched it. There were the freckles on her nose that drove her crazy, the tiny scar on her lower lip from where I'd accidentally bashed her in the mouth with a guitar when we were kids. There were those sunny green eyes, like mine but with more gold flecks. There was the long blond hair, so much like mine used to be.

She was wearing the tiny sterling silver heart earrings I'd saved for six months to buy her from Tiffany's for her twenty-first birthday.

This was Alina, right down to her toenails painted her favorite summer shade, Cajun Shrimp. It clashed horribly with her lime bikini and I told her so.

She laughed and took off across the sand. "Come on, Junior, let's play."

I sat, frozen for a long moment.

I can't tell you all the thoughts that went through my head then: *This isn't real, it can't be. Maybe it is. Maybe it's dangerous. Could this be my sister in another dimension, another version of her, but Alina all the same? Hurry up and ask her questions about her journal and the Lord Master and what happened in Dublin. Don't ask her questions; she might disappear.* All those thoughts passed swiftly and left a single directive in their wake: Play with your sister right here, right now. Take it for what it is.

I stood and ran across the sand, kicking up white powder with my heels. My legs were long, my body strong, my heart complete.

I played volleyball with my sister. We drank Coronas in the sun. I hadn't brought the limes, of course, but we found a margarine bowl of them in the cooler, and squeezed them into the bottles, pulp slipping down the frosty sides. A beer would never taste so good again as it did that day with Alina in Faery.

Eventually, we sprawled on the sand and soaked up the sun, toes teasing the edge of the surf. We talked about Mom and Dad, we talked about school, we talked about the hot guys that walked by and tried to coax us into another game of volleyball.

We talked about her idea of moving to Atlanta, and how I would quit my job and go with her. We talked about me getting serious about life finally.

It was that thought that sobered me. I'd always been planning to get serious about life and here I was, being exactly who I'd been back then, taking the path of least resistance, the easy way out, doing what made me feel good right now, consequences be damned.

I rolled over and looked at her. "Is this a dream, Alina?"

She turned toward me and smiled. "No."

"Is it real?"

She smiled again, sadly. "No."

"Then what is this?"

She bit her lip. "Don't ask me, just enjoy the day."

"I need to know."

"It's a gift from V'lane. A day on the beach with me."

"An illusion," I said. Water to a man stranded for two and a half days in the desert without a drink. Beyond refusing, even if it was poisoned. I knew better but it didn't stop me from trying: "So if I were to ask how you met the Lord Master, or where to find the *Sinsar Dubh?*"

She shrugged. "I don't know those things."

I wasn't surprised. V'lane must have lifted her from my memories, which meant she would know only what I knew, and made questions about anything other than experiences I recalled, or my current situation, pointless. "How long have I been here?" As V'lane's creation, she should know that.

She shrugged again.

"Longer than a human hour?"

"Yes."

"Can I leave?"

"Yes."

"Could I choose to stay?"

"And have anything you wanted, Mac-Kayla. Forever."

Alina *never* called me MacKayla. In fact, neither did my parents or any of my friends. Only V'lane did. Was he behind those sunny eyes? And still, I wanted to stay here, lose myself on this beach, in this sun, live this day over and over again for the rest of my life. Forget the rain and the fear, the pain and my uncertain future. I could die happily on a hammock in the sun, seventy years from now, surrounded by lost dreams.

"I love you, Alina," I whispered.

"I love you, too, Mac," she whispered back.

"I'm sorry I failed you. I'm sorry I missed your call. I'm sorry I didn't figure out something was wrong."

"You never failed me, Mac. You never will."

Tears filled my eyes. Where had those

words of absolution come from? Did the icy Fae prince understand more about human emotion than he let on?

I hugged Alina, inhaled deeply, and memorized every sensory detail I could greedily gather.

Then I squeezed my eyes shut and went to that place in my head that was so alien, and I fed the foreign fire. When I'd stoked it hot enough and high enough, I murmured, "Show me what is true," and opened my eyes.

My arms were empty. Alina was gone.

V'lane knelt in the sand before me.

"Never do that to me again," I said in a low voice.

"You did not enjoy your time with her?"

"It wasn't her."

"Tell me you did not enjoy it."

I couldn't.

"Then thank me for it."

I couldn't do that either. "How much time has passed?"

"I would have retrieved you but I was loath to disrupt your pleasure. You have had so little of it lately."

"You said you would take no more than one hour of my time."

"And I meant it. You *chose* to stay in Faery when you followed her across the sand. I understand freedom is a commodity humans prize highly. I permitted you yours."

When I would have argued his under-handed methods he pressed a finger to my lips. It was warm, strong, but there was absolutely nothing Fae in his touch. He was muting himself for me. He felt like a man, a strong, solid, sexy man, nothing more. "Some wounds need salve to heal. Illusion is the great salve. Tell me, has your grief for your sister lessened?"

I considered his words and was startled to realize it was true. Although I knew the Alina I'd just played with, and cried with, and hugged and begged forgiveness of had not been real, my day in the sun with her had given me a degree of closure I'd not had before. Although I knew the Alina who'd absolved hadn't been *my* Alina, her words had comforted me all the same.

"Never again," I repeated. Illusion might be a salve, but it was also dangerous. There was enough danger in my life.

He flashed a smile. "Your wish."

I closed my eyes a moment, trying to clear Alina from my thoughts; the sight, scent, and sound of her lingered all around me. From hugging her, I still smelled Beautiful on my skin. Later I would re-live every mo-ment, and it would comfort me again. I opened my eyes. "What of the Lord Master?"

"The warehouse was deserted. I destroyed the dolmen. It did not appear anyone had been there in weeks. I suspect he never returned to that location once it had been discovered. Tell me everything you know of him."

"I'm tired," I said. "Our hour is up." Plus some. "Return me now."

"Tell me of the *Sinsar Dubh.* You owe me that."

I told him what I knew, that I'd felt it pass me in the streets of Dublin, moving rapidly in a car of some kind, past the bookstore, a little over two weeks ago. He asked me many questions that I couldn't answer because the mere nearness of the Dark Book had knocked me out, a fact he seemed to find amusing.

"We will see each other again, MacKayla," he said.

Then he was gone and I was somewhere else. I blinked. Although I'd not terminated our time together prematurely, V'lane still hadn't returned me to Wales; he'd deposited me in Barrons Books and Baubles. Probably just to irritate Barrons.

It took me a few moments to adjust and focus. Having realities swapped so quickly and completely seems to exceed what the human mind can process — we were not fashioned for such a method of travel — and it goes blank, like the static on late-night television, for a few seconds. It's a vulnerable time. A person could be ambushed in such a moment.

My hand went instantly to my spear. I was relieved to find it was once again there, in the belt draped around my — "Ha-ha, V'lane," I muttered, pissed — hot pink bikini. "Jackass." It was no wonder I was cold.

Then my brain processed what I was seeing and I gasped.

Barrons Books and Baubles had been ransacked!

Tables were overturned, books torn from shelves and strewn everywhere, baubles broken. Even my little TV behind the counter had been destroyed.

"Barrons?" I called warily. It was night and the lights were on. My illusory Alina had told me more than an hour had passed. Was it the same night, nearly dawn? Or was it the night following our theft attempt? Had Barrons come back from Wales yet? Or was he still there, searching for me? When I'd been so rudely ripped from reality, who or what had come through those basement doors?

I heard footsteps, boots on hardwood, and turned expectantly toward the connecting doors.

Barrons was framed in the doorway. His eyes were black ice. He stared at me a moment, raking me from head to toe. "Nice tan, Ms. Lane. So, where the fuck have you been for the past month?"

Twelve

"One afternoon," I insisted. "I spent maybe six hours there, Barrons!"

I'd lost a month of my life, on a beach in the sun with Alina. It was incomprehensible. Had I aged a month or stayed the same? What if I'd chosen to hang out with Alina for a week? Would I have lost a year? Ten? What had changed since I'd been gone? I glanced out the window. One thing hadn't — it was still raining.

"In Faery, you fool," he snarled. "You know time doesn't move the same there! We talked about that!"

"V'lane promised it would be only an hour of my time. He tricked me," I said hotly.

" 'V'lane promised. He tricked me,' " he mocked in falsetto. "What did you expect? He's a bloody Fae, Ms. Lane, and one of the — what do you call them — death-by-sex ones. He seduced you and you fell for it. What else did you fall for? Why did you agree to give him an hour in Faery in the first place?"

"I didn't agree to give him an hour in Faery! I agreed to spend an hour with him at a time of his choosing. He didn't say anything about where it would be spent."

"Why did you agree to spend an hour with him at all?"

"Because he helped me clear the Shades from the bookstore!"

"*I* would have helped you clear the Shades!"

"*You* weren't there!" We were shouting at each other.

"Deals with the devil, Ms. Lane, never go well. That's a given. You will not make one again. Do you understand me? If I have to chain you to a fucking wall to protect you from your own stupidity, I will!" He glared at me.

I rattled my chains. "Wrists. Beam. Chained already, Barrons. Come up with a new threat." I glared back.

He tried to stare me down, make me quail and look away. I didn't. Not even with my arms chained behind me, wearing only a string bikini. I was losing the ability to quail and I would never again be the kind of girl that looked away.

"Who trashed the bookstore, Barrons?" I

250

demanded. I had a lot of questions and so far I'd not gotten the chance to ask a single one. The moment he'd seen me, he'd charged me, roughly bundled me over his shoulder, hauled me to the garage, stripped off my tool belt, and chained me to a support beam. I hadn't even tried to fight him off; there was more steel inside Barrons than the post behind me.

A muscle in his jaw worked. He turned away, walked to a small metal worktable on wheels, and rolled it over next to me. Then he retrieved a long, flat wooden box from one of the many tool shelves.

"What are you doing?" I said warily. He removed items from the box and began placing them on the table next to me. First came two tiny bottles that contained liquids: one crimson, one black. Were they poisons? Drugs? Next came a knife, very sharp, with a long, deadly point. "Are you going to torture me?" I said incredulously. He withdrew a sooty candle with a long black wick. "Or cast a spell on me?" Could he do that?

"What I am going to do, Ms. Lane, is tattoo you." He opened the bottles, unwrapped a set of needles bound in embossed leather, and lit the candle. He began heating a needle in the flame.

I gasped. "No, you're not. Mom'll kill

me." The liquids were inks, not drugs. I wasn't sure if that was better or worse. Drugs wore off. Inks were permanent.

He gave me a hard look. "Grow up."

I *was* growing up and doing a fine job of it, whether he thought so or not. It wasn't immature that I considered my mother's feelings. In my book, it was just the opposite. Besides, I felt the same way she did. Heir to a generation that tattooed, pierced, and performed cosmetic surgery on themselves as casually as they shaved their heads, I'd vowed years ago to go to the grave the same way I'd been born, just a lot more wrinkly. "You are *not* tattooing me," I repeated.

"Stop me." His smile was so cattish that I felt twitchy mouse ears sprout from the top of my head. He was serious. He'd chained me up, and now he was going to tattoo me. He was going to stand close to me, work slowly and methodically on my naked skin for what might be hours depending on the complexity of the tattoo. The thought made me feel lightheaded, queasy.

I told myself to be calm. I would get to the bottom of this. I would talk him out of it. "Why are you going to tattoo me, Barrons?" I asked in the most reasonable, soothing voice I could muster.

"The design contains a spell, so I can find you the next time you decide to indulge yourself in a childish whim."

"A whim?" I rattled my chains angrily. "It was no whim. You weren't there to help me with the Shades so I made the best bargain I could with who was available."

"I wasn't talking about V'lane. I was talking about choosing to stay in Faery."

My temper flared white hot. "You have no idea what it was like! My sister died without warning and suddenly there she was again, standing right in front of me. I got to see her, touch her, hear her voice again! Do you know what it's like to lose someone? Actually, probably the right question for you is have you ever loved anyone other than yourself? Loved them so much that you couldn't stand to go on living without them? Do you even know what love is? I did *not* indulge myself. I had a weakness." And I'd gotten over it. I'd made the illusion disappear with my will. I'd seen through it. I was proud of myself for that. "People who feel things sometimes have weaknesses, but you wouldn't know the first thing about that, would you?" I said bitterly. "The only things you feel are greed, mockery, and occasionally you probably get a hard-on, but I bet it's not over a woman, it's over money or an artifact or a book. You're no different than any other player in this game. You're no different than V'lane. You're just a cold, mercenary —"

His hand was on my throat, and he was crushing me back with his body into the cold steel beam behind me. "Yes, I have loved, Ms. Lane, and although it's none of your business, I have lost. Many things. And no, I am not like any other player in this game and I will never be like V'lane, and I get a hard-on a great deal more often than occasionally." He leaned fully against me and I gasped. "Sometimes it's over a spoiled little girl, not a woman at all. And yes, I trashed the bookstore when I couldn't find you. You'll have to choose a new bedroom, too. And I'm sorry your pretty little world got all screwed up, but everybody's does, and you go on. It's *how* you go on that defines you." His hand relaxed on my throat. "And I *am* going to tattoo you, Ms. Lane, however and wherever I please." His gaze dropped down over my sun-kissed, lightly oiled, very bare skin. The delicately strung together hot pink triangles covered very little, and while I'd not minded so much on the beach, being nearly naked around Barrons felt a lot like going to a shark convention lightly basted in blood.

This was a line I couldn't let him cross. I had to own myself. I had to win this one. "If you do this, Barrons, I'm going to walk out of this place as soon as you're done and never find another OOP for you. If you force this on me, you and I are through. I'm not kidding. I'll find someone else to help me." I stared into those jet eyes. I didn't throw V'lane's name at him because I had no desire to wave the red cape at the bull. The calm of unshakable resolution settled over me, and I injected it into my voice. "Don't do it. I let you push me pretty far sometimes, but not this time. I will not have you put your" — it took me a moment to find the right words — "sorcerer's brand on me, so you can hunt me down whenever and wherever you please. And that, Jericho Barrons, is non-negotiable."

There are some lines you just can't let another person cross. They don't always make sense, they might not always seem like the most important things, but only you can know what they are, and when you butt up against one, you have to defend it. Besides, who knew what else the tattoo might do?

We stared at each other in silence.

This time, if we had one of those wordless conversations of ours I couldn't hear a thing he said because I was too busy broadcasting a single, deafening word: *No.* As an after-thought, I felt for that strange place inside my skull, stoked it up into a furnace of flames, and tried to channel everything it would give me into the implacable refusal I was throwing his way. Tried to magic-up my "no," in a manner of speaking, to amplify it.

I was astonished when Barrons suddenly smiled.

Even more so when he began to laugh, softly at first, but the rumble grew. I felt it deep in his chest, expanding. His hands moved from my throat to my shoulders, his teeth flashed in his dark face. He was electric, a live current up against my body, humming with vitality, burning with energy.

"Well done, Ms. Lane. Just when I think you're all useless fluff and nails, you show me some teeth."

I didn't know if he was talking about my vocal refusal, or if my freshman effort to use that *sidhe*-seer place in my head to shove at him had worked, but he reached around me and worked at the chains binding me to the post. After a few moments, they dropped to the concrete with a clatter of steel.

"You win. This time. I won't tattoo you. Not today. But in lieu of that, you will do something for me. Refuse and I tattoo you.

And, Ms. Lane, if I chain you up one more time tonight, there'll be no more talking. I'll gag you."

He unbuttoned his shirtsleeve, rolled it back, removed a wide silver cuff from his wrist, and handed it to me. I had a déjà vu moment, flashback to V'lane and the Cuff of Cruce, although this cuff was very different. I'd seen it on him many times. I accepted it and turned it in my hand. It was hot from his skin. Forged of thick silver, ornately embossed with Celtic knotwork, runes, and symbols, and lightly blackened, it looked ancient, like something out of a museum. "Put it on. Never take it off."

I glanced up. He was too close. I needed distance. I stepped out from between him and the beam, skirting the pile of chains. "What does it do?" I asked.

"It will allow me to locate you if you disappear again."

"Could you really have found me in Faery if I'd been tattooed?"

He looked away and said nothing. Then, "I would have at least known you were alive. I didn't even know that."

"Why didn't you offer me the cuff first, instead of trying to tattoo me?"

"Because, Ms. Lane, a cuff can be removed or forgotten. A tattoo can't. I still

257

prefer the tattoo. The cuff is a concession, and one I'm making only because you've finally pulled your head out and begun exploring your . . . talents." He smiled faintly.

Aha, so what I'd tried to do with that strange place in my skull *had* had some effect on him! That was something. It wasn't exactly bending spoons with a thought, but it was a start. "Couldn't somebody cut a tattoo off me?" Didn't the ink go only so many layers of skin deep?

"It would be risky and immensely painful. I intended to hide it."

I looked down at myself. "Just where were you planning to hide a" — I veered sharply away from that cliff — "I don't want to know." I examined the cuff. "Does it do anything else?"

"Nothing you need to worry about. Put it on. Now."

I saw all kinds of nonnegotiable in his eyes and I knew he would tattoo me, and I would have to leave, and despite my bravado, I wasn't ready to be on my own in this dark world.

I slipped it on my wrist. It was huge. I pushed it up my arm but it just slid back down, and fell off over my hand. He caught it before it hit the floor, and forced the ends apart. He placed it above my biceps and squeezed it until the ends met. I had just enough muscle to keep it where it was.

"What did you and V'lane do in Faery?" he asked casually.

I shrugged, in no mood to talk about Alina, and I suspected telling him I'd had the most intense orgasm of my life on a beach beneath a Fae sun probably wouldn't go over real well. I glanced at the floor. It occurred to me the garage had been silent tonight. I wondered if his monster slept. Barrons had watched me break into the place on his video cameras. He knew I knew. "What do you keep under your garage, Barrons?" I countered. I was so certain of his answer that I mouthed it along with him.

"Nothing you need to worry about." He gave me a cold look. "If you already know the answer, Ms. Lane, don't waste my time. You just wasted a month of it."

"Fine, Barrons, keep your secrets but know this: I'll only confide in you to the extent that you confide in me. You keep me in the dark, I'll keep you in the dark, and you know what that does? Leaves us both bumbling around in the dark. Seems pretty stupid to me."

"My night vision's just fine. Burn the

bikini, Ms. Lane. Trust nothing he gives you."

I snorted and shrugged my cuff-bound arm at him. "But I can trust what *you* give me? Give me a break."

"If you think to stand between V'lane and me, and play both ends against the middle, you'll get ripped to pieces. If I were you, Ms. Lane, I'd choose a side, and fast."

I began restoring order to the store the next morning: sweeping, dusting, tossing broken baubles in the trash, and re-stocking books. Barrons had suggested I leave the shop closed, but I needed the store. Illusion was one salve, purpose and routine were another.

He hadn't broken my iPod and sound dock; thankfully I'd had them safely tucked away in a cabinet beneath the register, so I listened to old Beach Boys music while I cleaned. I sang along to "Sloop John B." at the top of my lungs: *I want to go home. This is the worst trip I've ever been on.*

Every now and then, I'd glance out the window at the blustery fall sky, and try to deal with the fact that while I'd sunned with my pseudosister, summer had turned to fall overnight — literally; it was now October. I consoled myself with the thought that six hours of good sun was probably all I'd have gotten in a month in Dublin anyway.

The store was nearly presentable by lunchtime, after which I turned my attention to the month of newspapers that had piled up in my absence, delivered but not sold. I gathered a couple of packing boxes and began tossing the dailies in to drag out to the trash later. After a few moments, I stopped pitching them, riveted by the headlines.

While I'd been gone, Dublin had suffered an unprecedented hike in crime, and the media was crucifying the Garda over it. (On a personal note, I hoped that meant Inspector Jayne would be too busy with other cases to continue harassing me.) The incidence of unsolved muggings and rapes was up by sixty-four percent, and homicides by nearly one hundred and forty-two percent year-to-date — but that was only half the story the papers were telling: The brutality of the crimes had intensified as well.

I read paper after paper, digested one alarming news story after the next. These were no straightforward murders. They were vicious, sadistic killings, as if the darkest, most disturbed part of people was boiling to the surface and spilling over. Every few days, the headlines announced some new, shockingly more violent multiple-homicide-cum-suicide.

Was it possible that Unseelie walking among humans — even unseen — was changing people? Unlocking their ids? Unleashing the most depraved in us all?

What else had happened while I'd been gone? I glanced uneasily to my right, as if I could somehow see through the wall to know if the cancerous Dark Zone had metastasized in my absence. If I went searching through maps, would I find more parts of the city missing?

"This is awful," I told Barrons, later that night, as we got into the only nondescript vehicle he owned, the dark sedan we'd used the night we'd robbed Rocky O'Bannion. "Have you seen the news lately?"

He nodded.

"And?"

"A great deal happened while you were gone, Ms. Lane. Perhaps it will make you think twice about spending time with V'lane."

I ignored the jibe. "I called my dad today. He acted like we'd just talked a few days ago."

"I sent him a few e-mails from your laptop. He called once. I covered for you."

"You hacked into my laptop? That's personal!" I was outraged. I was also glad he'd kept my dad from worrying in my absence, and curious how he'd gotten past my security measures. "How?"

He gave me a dry look. "Your general password, Ms. Lane, was 'Alina.' Your e-mail password was 'rainbow.' "

I huffed into the passenger seat. It was stiff and cold. There were no seat heaters. I preferred the Viper, or the Porsche or the Lamborghini or pretty much anything else, but it seemed anonymity was the name of the game tonight. "Where are we going, Barrons?" I asked irritably. For a change, he hadn't specified my clothing, and left to my own devices I'd chosen jeans, a sweater, and boots, with a jacket.

"An old abbey, Ms. Lane. A simple drive-by. No need to walk it. It won't take long, but it's a few hours' drive from the city."

"What do you think might be there? Are we looking for something specific?"

"Just looking."

"Was the abbey built on an ancient *sidhe*-seer site like the graveyard?" Barrons did nothing without good reason. Something about the abbey made him think there might be an OOP there. I wanted to know what it was.

He shrugged.

"Well, why aren't we going to walk it?"

"It's occupied, Ms. Lane. I doubt they would welcome us."

"Monks?" I knew monasteries often had strict rules about permitting women on the grounds. "Or nuns?" They'd take one look at Barrons and decide the devil himself had come knocking. He not only looked dangerous, he emanated something that made even *me* feel like crossing myself sometimes, and I'm not religious. I see God in a sunrise, not in repetitious ritual. I went to a Catholic church once — sit, stand, kneel, kneel, stand, sit — and got so stressed out trying to anticipate how next to position myself that I'd missed most of what was being said.

He grunted noncommittally in that way that meant he was done answering my questions, so I might as well save my breath. I wondered what he thought we were going to accomplish with a mere drive-by at this mysterious abbey, considering how close I had to be to sense an OOP. That thought raised another *very* belated one — and I smacked myself in the forehead. I couldn't believe I'd forgotten until now. "Who came through the basement door that night in Wales, Barrons?" He hadn't mentioned a thing about it.

From the immediate tension in his body I

knew the memory was not a pleasant one. "More bloody thieves."

"Are you kidding me? You mean besides us and whoever got the amulet? There were *three* of us after it that night?"

"Bloody damned convention."

"Well, who were they? Someone else from the auction?"

"I have no bloody idea, Ms. Lane. Never seen them before. Never heard of them. As far as I knew, there weren't any bloody Scots in the game. It's as if they dropped from the bloody damned sky." He paused then added darkly, "And they knew too bloody much for my liking."

All those "bloodys" was a veritable cornucopia of emotion for Barrons. Whoever the thieves had been, whatever had transpired after V'lane had sifted me off to Faery, it had disturbed him profoundly. "Are you sure they aren't the ones who stole it?"

"If they'd been responsible for the killings, it wouldn't have been a massacre."

"What do you mean?"

"Although one of the men was versed in the black arts, both were Druid-trained. Unless blood is required for a specific purpose, a Druid kills cleanly. Whoever, whatever killed the guards and staff that night did it with either the detached sadism of a pure sociopath, or immense rage."

I stuck to the subject of the thieves to avoid the memory of those mutilated bodies. "There are Druids around today? I thought they died out a long time ago."

"That's what the world thinks about *sidhe*-seers, too," he said dryly. "You need to lose your preconceptions."

"How do you know one of them was into black magic?"

He shot me a sideways glance and I knew he was about to stop answering my questions. I was surprised he'd answered this many. "He was heavily tattooed. Black magic calls a price, Ms. Lane, that can be . . . diminished by working protection runes into the skin."

I thought about that a moment and followed it to its logical conclusion. "Don't you eventually run out of skin?"

"Precisely. Some payments can only be deferred, not denied. I warrant most tell themselves they'll only do 'one more small spell.' It's a drug, like any other."

I eyed him, wondering what his elegant Italian suit and crisp white shirt might conceal. He had all the tattooing implements. What did Barrons look like without his clothes on? "Well, if these thieves weren't at the auction," I hurriedly dispelled that image, "how did they learn about it?"

"You think we stood around and chatted, Ms. Lane? You'd just vanished and I had no idea where you'd gone. We made short work of each other and moved on."

Wondering what constituted "short work" in Barrons' book, I glanced out the window. We were passing through the Temple Bar District. The increase in crime had yet to impact the *craic*-filled party zone. It was bustling as usual.

And teeming with Unseelie.

There was at least one for every twenty or so people. I hoped that meant they favored the tourist zone, not that all of Dublin was infested to a similar ratio. This was significantly more Unseelie than I'd seen a few days, no — a *month* ago — when I'd last walked these boisterous cobbled streets. "Oh, God, the Lord Master brought more of them through while I was gone, didn't he? A lot more."

Barrons nodded. "Somehow. Not at LaRuhe. He must have constructed a new portal somewhere. I've been meaning to tell you the dolmen and the warehouse were destroyed. It looked as if someone dropped a bomb on them."

I narrowed my eyes. I'd just spotted the dainty, diaphanous Fae I'd seen sunning itself on the fountain the day I'd encountered Dani. It was standing outside a bar, in the middle of a group of young people. As I watched, it grew even more transparent and took a sort of flickering step toward a curvaceous, smiling brunette, turned — *and settled straight into her skin* — like slipping into a coat.

The brunette's eyes widened for a split second and she shook her head, as if trying to dislodge something from her ear. The Fae did not exit her body. I turned as we passed, watching through the rear window. Nothing came out. I flexed my *sidhe*-seer sense, tried to peer past the human shell and see the Fae within.

I couldn't. Couldn't see it and couldn't sense it. I might be able to penetrate their glamour, but I couldn't detect a Fae inside a human skin. Until this moment, I'd not known it was possible for a Fae to do such a thing.

I watched until the brunette disappeared from view. She was no longer smiling. I wondered what awful thing I'd just witnessed, wondered if I even wanted to know. I could hardly hop out of the car, race back down the blocks, and attempt to exorcise the girl. The whole street would think I was nuts and the Fae inside her would know I knew. "I know. V'lane did it for me," I told Barrons absently.

There was a moment of silence. I glanced over and I swear I saw steam coming out of his ears. "Too bad he wasn't there to save you the day you nearly died, Ms. Lane," he said coolly.

"He was there to get rid of the Shades. Where were you?"

"He demanded a price. I don't ask a price of you. Nor do I try to fuck you every time I see you."

"Yes, you do. Ask a price, I mean. You make me OOP detect. You both dress me in sleazy clothing, boss me around, and tell me as little as you have to in order to get what you want. You both tried to put a cuff on me. You succeeded. You're no different than he is. You're both using me. The way I see it, you've both saved my life once. That makes you even in my book."

He slammed on the brakes so abruptly that my seat belt cut into my breasts. If it had been a late-model car, I'd have been eating airbag. He reached across me and flung open my door. "If you really believe that, Ms. Lane, get out."

I glanced out at the night. We were well past Temple Bar now, and into a mixed neighborhood of commercial and residential that was tightly buttoned up for the night. Even armed with my spear and flashlights, I had no desire to be walking around those dark, deserted streets by myself.

"Oh, don't be so melodra — *AHHHH!*" I clutched my head with both hands as my skull was perforated by a thousand red hot ice picks.

The abbey was going to have to wait.

Bile exploded in the back of my throat. The alien part inside my head became a crematorium for my brain, the inferno spread to every cell in my body like someone was squirting me with gasoline, inside and out.

I could feel the skin on my body blistering, charring. I could *smell* myself burning.

Blessedly, blissfully, I passed out.

"It was the *Sinsar Dubh* again, wasn't it?" Barrons demanded, the moment I opened my eyes.

I would have nodded but my head ached too much to risk it. "Y-Yes," I whispered. Gingerly, I raised a hand to my face, felt my lips, my cheek, my hair. Contrary to what I'd expected, my skin was not covered with scabby blisters, and although my hair was short and the wrong color, at least it was still there. "Wh-Where are we?" It didn't feel like a car seat beneath me.

"Back in the store. You didn't regain consciousness this time, Ms. Lane. I assumed that meant the book was in our immediate vicinity, and unmoving, so I went hunting for it." He paused. "I had to stop. I wasn't sure it wasn't killing you."

"What do you mean?" Passing out was such a helpless thing. The world went on around you and you had no awareness of it.

"You were . . . twitching. Rather agitatedly."

I stared. "What did you do? Toss me over your shoulder and tote me around like a divining rod while I was unconscious?"

"What did you expect me to do? The last time you encountered the *Sinsar Dubh* it made you pass out, but as soon as it moved away from you, you regained consciousness. It was only logical to conclude that if you weren't coming around this time, it was because the book wasn't moving away, which meant we were probably on top of the damned thing. I thought your physical distress might visibly intensify as we got closer, even if you were unconscious. It did, and I was forced to retreat. What the bloody hell good are you if you can sense it, but can't stay conscious around it?"

"I've wondered the same thing myself. I

271

didn't choose this ability, any more than the stupid parameters accompanying it." I shivered. Now that the fire inside me was gone, I felt chilled to the bone and my teeth began to chatter. The last time I'd had a near miss with the book I'd felt the same thing, iced to the seat of my soul by the sheer evil of the thing.

He stepped to the fireplace, lit the gas flames, and returned with a blanket. I wrapped myself in it and gingerly sat up.

"Tell me what it feels like when it happens," he demanded.

I looked at him. For all his solicitude with the fire and the blanket, he was cold, remote, seeing professionally to my needs. I wondered to what extent he'd allowed my "distress" to intensify before retreating. What a quandary it must have been for him to be so close to the *Sinsar Dubh,* yet afraid that using me to locate it would kill me — before he'd located it — effectively putting his OOP detector permanently out of commission, and losing his advantage in the game.

If he'd had any kind of guarantee of keeping me alive till that last terrible moment, would he have sacrificed me for the book?

I had little doubt on that score. There was violence in him tonight. I could feel it. I had no idea why he wanted it, but I did know this: The Dark Book was the end-all, be-all to Barrons. He was obsessed, and obsessed men are dangerous men. "You've never been so close to it before, have you?" I guessed.

"Not that I was aware of," he said tightly. He whirled suddenly and punched the wall, a compact, careful blow — a controlled release of fury. Bits of plaster and lathing disintegrated around his fist, leaving it buried in the wall to the exterior brick. He leaned against it, breathing heavily. "You have no idea how long I've been hunting the cursed thing."

I went very still. "Why don't you tell me?" What might he say? Ten years?

Ten thousand?

His laughter was harsh, the brittle sound of chains being dragged across bones. "So, Ms. Lane?" he prompted. "What happens when you get close to it?"

I shook my head, and instantly regretted it. I was sick of Barrons' evasions, but my headache was a hostile squatter occupying every inch of my head, breaking ground behind my eyes with a pointy-bladed shovel. I closed them. The day was coming when I was going to get my answers, one way or another. For now I'd give him his, in hopes that he might be able to shed light on the glaring problem of my inability to approach the book my sister had demanded that I find in her dying message.

"It hits me so suddenly and with such force that I don't have time to think about it. All I know is one second I'm fine and the next I'm in such intense pain that I'd do anything to escape it. If it went on for very long and I didn't pass out, Barrons, I think I'd beg you to kill me." I opened my eyes. "But it's more complex than that. It's as if whatever I'm sensing is an utter anathema to everything I am. As if we're point and counterpoint, each other's antithesis. We can't occupy the same space. Like we're two magnets that repel, but it repels me with such force that it nearly crushes me."

"Polar opposites," he murmured. "I wonder . . ."

"Wonder what?"

"Dilute the opposite, would it still repel?"

"I don't see any way to dilute the power of the book, Barrons, and I just don't see myself getting that much stronger."

He waited for my brain to catch up.

I scowled. "You mean dilute *me?* Make me a little evil so maybe the book would let me near? What good would that do? Then I'd be evil and I'd get an evil book and I'd probably do evil things with it. We'd win the battle to lose the war."

"Perhaps, Ms. Lane, you and I are fighting different wars."

If he thought becoming evil was a solution, not a problem, he was right, we were.

THIRTEEN

"What the feck is going on in your back alley?"

I glanced up. Dani stood in the doorway of the bookstore with the early afternoon sunlight gilding her auburn curls, bathing her delicate features in light. A sprightly slip of a girl, she was wearing a uniform of light green trousers with a white and green pin-striped poplin shirt, emblazoned on the pocket with a shamrock and the letters PHI. She looked cute and sweet and innocent, and I knew better. I didn't know which startled me more: her presence, or the sunshine. Both had crept up on me while I'd been reading, absorbed in the day's news.

I returned my attention to the gruesome story. A man had killed his entire family — wife, kids, stepkids, even their dog — then driven his car halfway across town, straight into a concrete bridge abutment at eighty miles an hour, not far from where Barrons and I had been last night. According to friends, neighbors, and coworkers, no one could explain it. He'd been a loving husband, an excellent employee at the local credit union, and a model father who'd regularly made time for his children's sporting and academic events. "You want to cuss, Dani," I told her, "do it around someone else."

"Feck you," she retorted.

"Real mature there," I said, without looking up. "Trying on adulthood by cussing. You and a gazillion other teens. Do something original." Back home, I'd rarely read anything other than the Sunday paper, specifically the lifestyle and fashion sections. Had crimes like these always been going on, and I'd just never noticed? Had I been so criminally oblivious?

Dani wheeled her bike in the door. "I don't have to do something original, I *am* original." She hesitated. "So, what's going on out back?"

I shrugged. "You mean the cars? No clue." I wasn't about to admit to someone who was plugged into the *sidhe*-seer community that I'd stolen a Fae Hallow and in the process gotten sixteen humans killed. I'd been reading up on the paranormal and it

277

appeared there was a golden rule: Harm no innocents, and humans somehow seemed to unilaterally get accorded that status, an irony heavily underscored by the newspaper I was reading.

"No. I meant the half-wiped Grug."

"Grug?"

She described it, what was left of it. "I call them Rhino-boys." I dropped the paper. "There's one out back, half eaten?"

She nodded and her lips quirked. "Rhino-boys, I get that. They're gray and lumpy and make that funny noise in the back of their throats."

"Is Grug their Unseelie caste name?" Was this true *sidhe*-seer lore? I was starving for it. I wanted explanations, rules. I wanted someone to take my life and make sense out of it. I wanted a *Sidhe*-Seer Compendium.

She shrugged. "We don't know squat about the Unseelie. It's just what we call them. I like your name better. So, you gonna finish it off, or do you get off on torturing 'em? What do you do with the other parts? Keep 'em in a jar or something?" She glanced around, looking for those jars with an expression that said simultaneously "I'm so bored" and "Hey, way cool."

"Oh, God, you think I — *No*, Dani, I don't get off on torturing them! I didn't know it was out there." It bothered me immensely that something big and bad enough to eat Unseelie had been nearby, and I'd not even known it. It bothered me more that Dani thought I was so twisted. Who was this kid's role model? Where did she get her ideas? TV? Video games? Kids these days seem both dangerously impressionable and dangerously desensitized, as if their lives have somehow assumed comic book proportions, ergo, comic book relevance — or a complete lack thereof. If I had to read about one more group of teenage boys killing a homeless person and saying, "I don't know why we did it, it was like . . . hey, you know . . . that Internet game we play," I was going to start stabbing humans with my spear, golden rule be damned. "Did you kill it?" I asked.

"With what?" She poked out a slim hip. "You see a sword tucked into this uniform? Strapped on my bike somewhere?"

"A sword?" I blinked. Surely she didn't mean *the* sword. "You mean the Seelie Hallow, the sword of light?" I'd read about it in my research; it was the only other weapon capable of killing Fae. "That's what you've been getting your forty-seven kills with? You *have* it?"

She gave me a smug look.

"How on earth did you get it?" According

to the last book I'd read, it had been in the custody of the Seelie Queen herself!

The smug look faded a little.

I narrowed my eyes. "Rowena gave it to you." From her crestfallen expression, I continued guessing, "And she keeps it, and doesn't let you carry it much, does she?"

Dani scowled and propped her bike against the wall. "She thinks I'm too fecking young. I've killed more Fae than all her other little kiss-ass acolytes she sends out combined, and still she treats me like a child!" She stomped over to the counter, and looked me up and down. "I bet you can't kill the Grug. I bet Rowena's wrong about you. What kind of special powers do you have? I don't see anything special about you."

Without another word I skirted the cashier counter, pushed through the connecting doors, and headed for the rear of the store.

What was eating Unseelie outside my bedroom window? I didn't like it one bit. It was bad enough that I had to worry about Shades and whatever was beneath the garage but now I had to worry about a monster-muncher, too. Nor did I like that such a thing had happened twice now, with me in the immediate vicinity. Were such macabre feasts taking place across the city and I just didn't know it because I wasn't getting out much? Or was it happening specifically around me? Was it coincidence, or something more?

I pushed open the back door and scanned the alley, left and right.

It took me a few moments to spot it. Nearly two-thirds of it was gone and what remained — the head, shoulders, and stump of a torso — had been tossed into an overflowing Dumpster. Like the mangled Fae in the graveyard, it was in obvious agony.

I hurried down the stairs, scrambled up the small mountain of trash, and crouched over it. "What did this to you?" I demanded. No mercy killing this time. I wanted information in exchange.

It opened its mouth, made a wordless, whimpering sound, and I turned away. In addition to having no hands or arms left, it had no tongue. Whatever had stopped short of devouring it meant for it to suffer, and had left it unable to speak or communicate in any way.

I removed the spear from the holster I'd rigged beneath my jacket this morning, and stabbed it. It died with a rank gust of icy breath.

When I clambered back down the pile of

refuse, Dani was waiting for me, wide-eyed. "You have the spear," she said reverently. "And what an awesome holster! It's so compact I could carry it around all the time, everywhere. I could kill them twenty-four/seven! Are you superfast?" she demanded. "If not, I should probably have that spear." She reached for it.

I put it behind my back. "Kid, you try to touch my spear, I'll do worse things to you than you've ever seen done." I had no idea what I was talking about, but I suspected if anyone tried to take the spear from me, that savage Mac inside, the one that hated pink and hadn't particularly minded watching the Rhino-boy flail in eternal pain, might do something we'd both regret. Well, at least one of us would regret. I was becoming too complicated for my own peace of mind. Would Dani try to take it with her super-speed? Would I find something in that hot, alien place in my skull to fight her with?

"I'm not a kid. When are you fecking grown-ups going to see that?" Dani snapped, turning away.

"When you stop acting like one. Why did you come here?"

"You're in trouble," she tossed over her shoulder. "Rowena wants to see you."

■ ■ ■ ■

Turned out PHI was not the twenty-third letter in the Greek alphabet but Post Haste, Inc. Courier Services, and Dani a delivery girl, explaining the uniform and bike.

It was two in the afternoon on Thursday, when I hung my CLOSED EARLY placard on the bookstore door and locked up. "Shouldn't you be in school, Dani?"

"I'm home-schooled. Most of us are."

"What does your mom think about you running around killing Fae?" I couldn't imagine the mother of any young child being okay with it. But I guess when there's a war on and you're born a soldier, there's not much choice.

"She's dead," she said nonchalantly. "Died six years ago."

I didn't say I was sorry. I didn't mouth any of the platitudes people resort to in times of grief. They don't help. In fact, they chafe. I commiserated on her level. "It fecking sucks, doesn't it?" I said vehemently.

She flashed me a look of surprise and the nonchalance melted. "Yeah, it does. I hate it."

"What happened?"

Her rosebud mouth twisted. "One of them

283

got her. One day I'll find out which one, and kill the fecker."

Sisters in vengeance. I touched her shoulder and smiled. She looked startled, unaccustomed to sympathy. Six years ago, Dani would have been seven or eight. "I didn't know they'd been around that long," I said, meaning the Unseelie. "I thought they'd only recently been freed."

She shook her head. "It wasn't an Un that got her."

"But I thought the . . . other ones" — I spoke vaguely, mindful of the wind — "didn't kill us because of the . . . you know."

"Compact? That's a bloody crock. They never stopped killing us. Well, maybe some of them did, but most of them didn't."

We walked the rest of the way in silence, with Dani pushing her bike. She wasn't comfortable talking on the streets. We skirted Temple Bar and crossed the River Liffey.

PHI Courier Services occupied a three-story building painted the same light green of Dani's pants, trimmed in cherry, adorned by tall, arched windows. The sign above the entry sported the same emblem emblazoned on her shirt, but the shamrock looked misshapen, out of proportion. Something about the sign perplexed me. If I'd happened down this street on my own and seen it, I'd have walked straight into the building without hesitation, gripped by an irresistible compulsion.

"It's spelled," Dani explained, watching me study it. "It draws people like us. So does the ad in the paper. She's been gathering us for a long time."

"You think maybe you're telling me things she doesn't want me to know?" Where did her loyalties lie? Wasn't she Rowena's creation?

Dani thought about that a minute and I had a sudden insight into her character. Like me, she didn't trust anyone. Not completely anyway. I wondered why.

"Go to the back." The gamine redhead hopped on her bike. "I'm late for deliveries. See ya around, Mac."

Around back were dozens of green and white bicycles, four motorbikes, and ten delivery vans, all emblazoned with the same misshapen shamrock. If PHI was a cover, it was nevertheless a thriving business.

I walked up the rear steps of the building and knocked. A woman in her forties, with rimless glasses and a shiny cap of brown hair opened the door, ushered me inside, led me up two flights of stairs, to a room at the end of a hall, and left me at the door without saying a word. My *sidhe*-seer senses were getting a tingle. There was either a Fae or Fae OOPs through that door — and I doubted it was an actual Fae. Rowena probably kept Dani's close sword at hand, perhaps other relics as well.

I pushed it open and stepped into a handsomely appointed study with hardwood floors, paneled walls, and a huge fireplace. Sunlight spilled through tall windows framed with velvet. Floor and table lamps lit every nook and cranny. I would find this was a common trait among *sidhe*-seers, turning on all the lights we can. We hate the dark.

The old woman was seated behind an antique desk, but she wasn't looking so old today. On the two prior occasions I'd seen her, she'd been drably dressed. Today she wore a turquoise suit with classic lines and a white blouse, and looked twenty years younger, closer to sixty-something than eighty-something. Her silvery hair was pulled back from her face in a single plait that circled her head like a crown. The creamy pearls that glowed at her ears, throat, and wrist were the same lustrous color as her hair. She looked elegant, in charge, and, although diminutive of build, full of piss and vinegar as my father would have said. I guessed the dreary, aged appearance she donned in public was deliberate and useful; people tend to grant unkempt seniors a special invisibility, as if by not noticing them they won't have to acknowledge the same creature in themselves clawing closer to the surface with each tick of the clock.

Glasses on a beaded chain rested on her chest. She raised them now, slipped them onto a finely pointed nose. They magnified the size, fierce color, and the fiercer intelligence of her sharp blue eyes. "MacKayla. Do come in. Have a seat," she said briskly.

I gave her a curt nod and stepped into the room. I glanced around, wondering where the sword was. Something Fae was in this room. "Rowena."

Her eyes flickered and I knew she didn't appreciate the familiarity. Good. I meant to establish us as equals, not mentor and student. She'd lost the chance to mentor me when she'd turned her back on me. We looked at each other in silence. It stretched. I wasn't about to speak. This was our first battle of the wills. It wouldn't be our last.

"Sit," she said again, gesturing to a chair in front of the desk.

I didn't.

"Och, for the love of Mary, get your spine down, lass," she barked. "We're family here."

"Really?" I leaned back against the door and folded my arms. "Because where I come from, family doesn't abandon their own in need, and you've done that to me twice. Why did you tell me to go die that night in the pub? You gather *sidhe*-seers. Why not me?"

She tilted her head back and peered down her nose, assessing, measuring. "It had been a difficult day. I'd lost three of my own. And there you were, about to betray yourself, and the saints only knew how many of us, if you weren't stopped."

"It had to be obvious I had no idea what I was."

"What was obvious was that you were fascinated by a Fae. I told you, I thought you were *Pri-ya,* one of their addicts. I had no way of knowing it was the first Fae you'd ever seen, or that you were unaware of what you were. Those who are *Pri-ya* are beyond our help. By the time that kind of damage has been done, the will is demolished and the mind virtually gone. I will never sacrifice ten to save one."

"Did I look like my mind was gone?" I demanded.

"Actually, yes," she said flatly. "You did."

I thought back to that night, my first in Dublin. I'd been heavily jet-lagged, overcome with grief, feeling bitterly alone, and I'd just seen something that couldn't possibly have been there. Perhaps the expression on my face had been a bit . . . stupefied, maybe even blank. Still . . . "What about the museum? You abandoned me there, too," I accused.

She folded her arms and leaned back in her chair. "You appeared to be in league with a Fae prince — and again, *Pri-ya*. You were stripping for it. What did you expect me to think? It wasn't until I saw you threaten him with the spear that I began to understand differently. Speaking of which, I need to see that spear." She rose, skirted the desk with the agility of a much younger woman, and extended her hand.

I laughed. She was crazy if she thought I was handing my weapon over. I'd sooner put it through her heart. "I don't think so."

"MacKayla," she said sternly, "let me see that spear. We are your people. We are sisters in this war."

"My sister is dead. Did you see her, too? Did you make the same snap judgment and turn her away? Tell her to go die by herself? Because she did," I said bitterly. "The Fae ripped her to shreds."

Rowena looked startled. "What is this of a sister?"

"Oh, please." Here it was, the real reason I hated her. Not just for turning me away and shattering my beliefs about my family, but why hadn't she found my sister? With her spelled signs, her advertisements, and her bicycling spies, why hadn't she drawn Alina in? Taught her? *Saved* her? "She was in Dublin for months. She hung out in the pubs all the time. How could you not have run into her?"

"Would you expect me to encounter every single person in Chicago on a visit?" she snapped. "Dublin is a big city, and we have only recently become organized. Until a short time ago, I was busy elsewhere. How long was your sister here? What did she look like?"

"She was here for eight months. She was blond like . . . like I was the first time you saw me. Same color eyes. More athletically built. A bit taller."

Rowena searched my face, as if absorbing and breaking down my individual features, trying to place them in random arrangements on another woman. Finally she shook her head. "I'm sorry, MacKayla, but no. I never met your sister. You must tell me what happened. You and I are sisters in more than vision and cause; we are sisters in loss. Tell me everything."

"We aren't sisters in anything, and I'm not giving you my spear, old woman." She wasn't going to suck me in with sympathy.

She gave me a hard stare. "I sent you away the first time. The second time I tried to get you to come back here with me, but you refused. We've both turned the other away once. I won't make that same mistake again. Will you?"

"You should have found my sister. You should have saved her."

"You have no idea how much I wish I could have. Let me save you instead."

"I don't need saving."

"If you're working with Jericho Barrons, you do."

"What do you know about Barrons?"

"That there are not, and never have been, any male *sidhe*-seers, MacKayla. It is a gift of matriarchy."

I scoffed. "A gift? It killed my sister and ruined my life. As for Barrons, what is he, then? Because he sure can see the Fae, and he helps me kill them, which is more than you've ever done."

"Is that all one must do to win your trust, MacKayla? Battle alongside you? Let us go kill a Fae together then, right now. Do you know what's in his heart? His mind? Why he does it? What he's after?"

I said nothing because there was nothing to say to that. Most of the time I wasn't sure he even had a heart, and whatever thoughts he entertained he kept intensely guarded.

"I didn't think so. He tells you nothing, does he?"

"He's told me more about what I am than you have."

"You haven't given me a chance."

"I gave you two."

"Try again, MacKayla. I'm ready to talk. Are you ready to listen?"

"Do *you* know what he is?" I pressed.

"I know what he isn't, and that's all I need to know. He's not one of us. We are pure of heart, pure of purpose. You see that shamrock?" Rowena pointed to a picture behind her desk of a large green clover on a background of embossed gold. "Look at it. Do you know why it's considered lucky, and has been for longer than anyone can recall?"

I shook my head.

"Before it was the clover of Saint Patrick's trinity, it was ours. It's the emblem of our Order. It's the symbol our ancient sisters used to carve on their doors and dye into banners millennia ago, when they moved to a new village. It was their way of letting the inhabitants know who they were and what they were there to do. When people saw our sign, they declared a time of great feasting and celebrated for a fortnight. They welcomed us with gifts of their finest food, wine, and men. They held tournaments to compete to bed us." She strode to the picture, snatching a pencil from the desk on the way to it. "It is not a clover at all, but a vow." She traced the lines of the two bottom leaves, left to right, with the eraser. "You see how these two leaves make a sideways figure eight, like a horizontal Möbius strip? They are two S's, one right side up, one upside down, ends meeting. The third leaf and stem is an upright P."

So that was why the shamrock looked misshapen! It was. The upright leaf was flatter on the left side, the stem stiff.

"Over thousands of years they've forgotten us, added a few flourishes, occasionally a fourth leaf, and now they think it's a lucky clover." She snorted. "But we haven't forgotten. We never forget. The first S is for See, the second for Serve, the P for Protect. The shamrock itself is the symbol of Eire, the great Ireland. The Möbius strip is our pledge of guardianship eternal. We are the *sidhe*-seers and we watch over Mankind. We protect them from the Old Ones. We stand between this world and all the others. We fight Death in its many guises and now, more than ever, we are the most important people on this earth."

I almost broke into a rousing, emotional "Danny Boy," and I didn't even know the words. She'd made me feel part of something huge; she'd given me chills and I resented it. I'd never been much of a joiner and it's hard to want to join a club that's dissed you twice. Yes, I have a long memory and hold grudges. I would do with her what I did with everyone else: Mac Lane, P.I.: I would pump her for all the information I could get. Later I would take my journal somewhere quiet, make notes, decide who to trust . . . sort of, or at least who to throw in with for a while.

"I suppose you have a collection of stories and records somewhere?" If so, I'd love to get my hands on it.

She nodded. "We do. We have more information on the Fae than one person could sort through in a dozen lifetimes. Some of our . . . less physically inclined members have been recruited to bring us into the twenty-first century. They've begun the laborious task of converting it all to electronic files. Our library, though vast, is coming apart at the spines."

"Where is this library?"

She measured me. "In an old abbey, a few hours from Dublin."

An old abbey. Right. I was going to kill Barrons the next time I saw him.

"Would you like to see it?"

With every ounce of my being. I wanted to say take me, show me, right now, walk me up and down those halls, teach me who I am. But I didn't. What if she got me out there among hills and sheep and ruins, overpowered me with a coven of her faithful, and stole my spear? I understood the value of my weapon. There were only two capable of killing Fae. She had one — and countless followers who were unarmed. I had the other. Hardly seemed fair, even to me. I wasn't interested in fair. I was interested in my own survival. "Maybe sometime," I said noncommittally.

"Let me give you a taste of what you're missing." She moved to the desk, opened a drawer, and removed a thick volume bound in leather, tied with a cord. "Come." She placed it on the desk, motioned me over, and opened it, handling the time-stained pages with care. "I think this entry might interest you." She traced her finger down the page. It was an alphabetical record of some kind, a *sidhe*-seer lexicon, and we were in the *V*'s.

I gasped.

V'lane: Prince of the Court of the Light, Seelie. Member of Queen Aoibheal's High Council and sometimes Consort. Founder of the Wild Hunt, highly elitist, highly sexed. Our first recorded encounter with this prince took place in —

She closed the book and returned it to the desk drawer.

"Hey!" I protested. "I wasn't done reading. When and what was the first encounter? How sure are you of those notes? Are you positive he's Seelie?"

"The Fae prince you kept at bay in the museum was born to the Court of the Light and has been with his queen since the dawn of time. Join us, MacKayla, and we will share with you all we have."

"And demand what in return?"

"Allegiance, obedience, commitment. For that we will give you a home, a family, a sanctuary, a noble cause, and put all the lore of the ages at your disposal."

"Who was Patrona?"

She smiled faintly, sadly. "A woman for

whom I once had tremendous hopes, killed by the Fae. You've the look of her."

"You said I looked like an O'Connor. Are there O'Connors in your organization? People I might be related to?"

She tilted her head and gave me that look down her nose, with a vaguely approving air. "You spoke to your mother. Very good, I wasn't certain you would. And?"

My jaw locked. I couldn't bring myself to tell her she'd been right. "I want to know who I am, where I came from. Can you give me that?"

"I can aid you in your search for truth."

"Are there or aren't there O'Connors in your organization?" Why didn't anyone ever give me a straight answer?

A shadow crossed her face. She shook her head. "The bloodline died out, MacKayla. If you are an O'Connor, or an offshoot of that branch, you are the last."

I turned away, deeply affected. I hadn't realized how strongly I'd been nurturing the hope of blood relatives until it was summarily executed with a few words.

Her hand was gentle on my shoulder, although I knew it was made of iron. "We are your kin, MacKayla."

"Were the O'Connors killed by Fae, too?"

"You're in a doorway, child, one foot in,

one foot out. Make up your mind. That door may close."

I turned and looked at her. "Where is the *Sinsar Dubh?*"

"Och, now isn't that the question."

"Do you have it?"

"You are asking questions only The Haven have the right to know. I will not answer them."

"Who are The Haven?"

"Our Council, over which Patrona once presided. Are you a Null?"

"Yes." She'd shifted gears so swiftly I'd answered without hesitation. I employed her tactic and fired right back at her, "What are the Fae that slip inside humans and don't come out again?"

She sucked in a breath. "You've seen such a creature?"

I nodded.

"What do they look like?" I told her and she said, "Sweet saints, the one Dani described to me, the day she met you! So *that's* what it does. I've heard rumors such Unseelie exist. We don't know what they are, and have no name for them."

"I couldn't see it once it was inside her."

"It went beyond your *sidhe*-seer vision? You mean it wore humanity as a glamour, and you were unable to penetrate it?" She looked as troubled as I felt. "Did you kill it?"

"How could I, without killing the girl?"

Rebuke blazed in her eyes. "So, you left it walking around out there, looking like a human? How many humans will die now because you were too good to take a single life? Will you carry those deaths on your conscience, *sidhe*-seer? Or will you pretend not to own them? She was no longer human the moment that Fae stepped inside her!"

I both understood her point, and found it abhorrent. "First of all, you don't know that. And second, I can't just walk up to a perfectly innocent girl and kill her."

"Then turn that weapon over to someone who can! When you let her walk away, you didn't reject the blood of a life on your hands, you accepted the blood of dozens. It *will* kill. That's what the Unseelie do."

"It's all black and white to you, isn't it?"

"Gray is but another word for light black. Gray is never white. Only white is white. There are no shades of it."

"You scare me, old woman."

"You scare me, child," she retorted. She closed her eyes and took a deep breath. When she opened them, the rebuke was gone. "Come to the abbey. You've already met Dani. Meet more of your sisters. Learn about us. See what we do and why. We are not monsters. The Fae are. This is a war that is only going to get worse. If we do not meet their ruthlessness with unwavering resolve and equal ruthlessness, we will lose. Those who do not act react. Those who react die sooner."

"Do you know about the Lord Master and his plans for freeing all the Unseelie?"

"I won't answer any more of your questions until you make a choice. We have no renegades among us. I permit none. You are with us, or against us."

"There *are* shades of gray, Rowena. I'm neither with nor against. I'm learning and deciding who to trust. Instead of bullying me, convince me."

"I'm trying. Come to the abbey."

I wanted to. But on my terms, when and how I felt safe, and currently I couldn't imagine that situation. "I'll be in touch."

"Every moment you waste is a moment you might die alone out there, instead of banded with your sisters where you would be safe, MacKayla."

"I'll take that chance."

As I walked out, she called, "Why couldn't Dani find you for a month?"

I thought about lying but decided to let

the chips fall where they may. "Because I was in Faery with V'lane," I said, as I stepped through the door.

She hissed, "If you are *Pri-ya* and he has put you up to infiltrating us . . ."

"I am no one's puppet, Rowena," I said without looking back. "Not his. Not Barrons. Not yours."

FOURTEEN

I settled into the tufted leather seat of the high-backed snug, or booth as we call them back home in the States, and ordered a beer and a shot.

For the first time since I'd come to Dublin, I felt curiously at peace, as if a critical game piece had been placed on the board today, and the match was finally, fully under way.

On one side of the board was the Lord Master. He was bad. He was bringing Unseelie through. He planned to destroy our world.

On the other side of the board was me — tiny little hand waving here, a dot the size of a pencil tip on an aerial shot of the planet. I wanted vengeance for my sister and I wanted the Fae to get the feck, as Dani would say, out of our world. I was good.

There were three other major players on the board: V'lane, Barrons, and Rowena.

They all had one thing in common: They wanted me.

One was a Fae. One was an unknown. One was — I was pretty sure, though she'd not said and I'd not asked — the Grand Mistress of *sidhe*-seers.

They all had their private agendas and secrets.

And I had no doubt all three of them would lie to me as smoothly and easily as they'd put a knife through each other's backs.

I pulled out my journal and began writing.

I started with V'lane. According to Rowena, he'd been telling me the truth. He *was* a Seelie prince, a member of the queen's High Council, and working on her behalf to stop the Unseelie from entering our world and taking it over. That seemed to place him on my side of the board, the good side, which was a little hard to swallow because I knew that he was ruthless and would manipulate me to the brink of death to achieve his ends, in addition to trying to have potentially lethal sex with me along the way.

He was at least one hundred and forty-two thousand years old, probably substantially older. I wasn't sure it was possible for him to understand how a human felt about anything, therefore the damage he might do to me, even if he was trying to abstain from damaging me, was immense.

Barrons was next. Indisputably self-serving, could he be the most treacherous of the three? When Rowena had mentioned the abbey, a few hours from town, then said that Dani had been looking for me at the bookstore for the past month, I'd known instantly that Barrons must have followed the young girl and tracked her, or Rowena herself, back to the abbey at some point.

My abbey.

Then he'd had the gall to try to make me do a drive-by, no doubt to see if the *Sinsar Dubh* was perhaps secreted away beneath the abbey grounds — after all, who better to stand guard over a book of dark Fae magic than a horde of *sidhe*-seers who could see any and all of the monsters that might try to come after it? — without ever saying, Oh, by the way, I found the headquarters of *sidhe*-seers while you were gone and I bet they might be able to tell you something about yourself. No, there would be no voluntary sharing of useful information with me.

Barrons walked among Shades and came to no harm. Barrons could see the Fae; he knew about Druids; he had abnormal strength and speed; and although it had taken me some time to admit it to myself, what stared out at me from behind those jet eyes didn't seem thirty years old. Was he a human who'd somehow learned to cheat time? Was he Fae and I couldn't sense it? If so, how powerful a Fae was he, that he could out-glamour a *sidhe*-seer? Was it possible one of those diaphanous Fae had slipped inside him and taken over what *used* to be Barrons? I discarded that thought the instant I had it. I didn't believe anything, not even a Fae, could take over Jericho Barrons.

Fiona had disappeared after attempting to harm his OOP detector. An inspector who'd been snooping into his business was killed. People that interfered with Jericho Barrons had a convenient way of vanishing or dying. Still . . . I had no proof he'd done anything nefarious in either of those cases.

He didn't seem to want more Unseelie in our world. Nor, however, did he seem to have any interest in trying to save our world. Was he really so mercenary and ambivalent? Did he genuinely want the book just to sell it to the highest bidder?

Then there was the question of how he planned to touch it, assuming we found it.

The *Sinsar Dubh* was so evil it corrupted anyone who came in contact with it. Did he believe he could tattoo protection spells into his skin that would permit him to touch it without it corrupting him? Could he?

I rubbed my forehead and tossed back my shot. It burned all the way down my throat. I thumped my chest with my fist and drew a scorched breath.

The only thing that was certain about Jericho Barrons was that nothing was certain. With far more questions than answers, I couldn't place him on either side of the board.

With V'lane tentatively on the good side, and Barrons on the sidelines, next was Rowena. What a piece of work. Rowena should have been someone I could position firmly on my side of the game, and in terms of single-mindedly opposing the Unseelie and the Fae in general, I could. The problem was I didn't feel I could in terms of *my* welfare.

I knew V'lane and Barrons both wanted me alive, and had the ability to keep me in that condition. However, I wasn't so sure about Rowena. If she believed there was someone more qualified — and more malleable than I — to honor her holy triumvirate of See, Serve, and Protect with my spear, to what lengths might she go to take it from me? If humans met Fae ruthlessness with equal ruthlessness, how were we different from them? Didn't there have to be some defining factor? Was I really supposed to walk up to a human woman and kill her because a Fae had stepped inside her, without first trying to see if there was some way to get it out? Tonight when I went to sleep would I dream about the deaths I'd caused by letting her walk away?

Thinking about Rowena sucked. I added a little note with an asterisk: *if she isn't the Grand Mistress, who is?*

I moved on to making notes about the minor players like Mallucé, who'd been working for, and two-timing, the Lord Master. According to Barrons he'd still not been seen or heard from during the month I'd been gone, which I decided meant the vampire's memorial service had been for real, and he really was dead. If he'd survived what Barrons and I had done to him, he would have been back among his worshippers long before now. I wondered if the Lord Master had someone new serving his purposes. I brushed Mallucé off the board. One down!

I decided the McCabes, O'Bannions, and sundry collectors of Fae artifacts weren't part of the game. Only those seeking the *Sinsar Dubh* or working for someone who was merited their own square.

I accorded all the Unseelie in our world pawn status. It seemed their primary purpose was to indulge their twisted appetites, spy on humans, and create general chaos. To keep things stirred up while the Lord Master pursued his private agenda, and when he'd ultimately achieved his ends, serve him. If there was any single Unseelie more significant than another, either I hadn't yet encountered it, or was too dense to see it.

I paused with my pen above the page, wondering about the players behind the scenes, as yet unseen.

The Seelie Queen, I wrote. According to V'lane she wanted the *Sinsar Dubh*, but why? Did she need it to recontain the Unseelie? Were there spells in there that governed their darker brethren? What was the *Sinsar Dubh*, really? I knew it was a book of black magic authored by the Unseelie King, but what did it *do?* What did everyone want it for? Did each player have a different desire/use for it? What spells and enchantments were scribed in its pages that were so heinous they could corrupt anyone who came in contact with it? Could words and symbols wield such power? Could mere scribblings on parchment unmake a person's moral fiber? Weren't we made of sterner stuff?

I was in no hurry to find out. My two brushes with the Dark Book had pushed me beyond pain into unconsciousness, left me weak as a baby and wishing desperately that I'd never found my way onto this game board.

Where was the Unseelie King in all this?

Did he signify or was he an absentee landlord?

If *my* book of dark magic had gone missing, you could bet your petunia I'd be out there looking for it. Was he? Why hadn't he tracked me down, too? Everyone else had. How had his book gotten away from him in the first place? For that matter, indulging myself in perfect paranoia — which, in the world I inhabited, seemed perfectly reasonable — *had* it gotten away from him? What if it was nothing more than bait at the end of a very long fishing line? If so, what was he fishing for? Was the Lord Master himself a pawn, being moved about by a much darker, unspeakably ancient hand? Was the playing board bigger than I could see? Were we all pawns of something much larger than we knew?

Somewhere out there on the game board, the *Sinsar Dubh* was moving around. Who was moving it? How was it being moved? And why?

And what kind of ~~prankster~~ benevolent being — this was the one I really wanted to know — would create something like me that could sense the most dangerous of all relics, then give me a fatal flaw that caused me to pass out every time I got near it?

I ordered another shot and tossed it back, indulging myself in a ritual I'd witnessed too many times across my bar: swallow, shudder, breathe.

"Mind if I join you?"

I glanced up. It was the guy with the Scottish accent from the Ancient Languages Department at Trinity; "Scotty," the one I'd gotten the envelope about the illegal auction from. Small world. And everyone keeps telling me how large a city Dublin is.

I shrugged. "Sure, why not."

"Gee, thanks," he said dryly.

I suspected he was unaccustomed to such a blasé response from women. He was about the same age as the dreamy-eyed guy he worked with, but the resemblance ended there. His coworker was velvety-skinned, a sexy boy-on-the-cusp-of-man, but Scotty was broader, his body more filled out, and there was maturity in the way he walked and moved, a quiet self-assurance, as if, even at his age, he'd already been tested.

Six foot two or three, his hair was long and dark and pulled back at his nape. Gold tiger eyes swept me appreciatively. Estrogen responded to testosterone — this boy was a man — and I sat up a little straighter.

"To fine Scotch and lovely lasses." He clinked a glass of whisky to my mug of beer and we drank. I chased it with a third shot: swallow, shudder, breathe. That cold place in my stomach, where I felt alone and lost, was finally starting to warm up.

He extended his hand. "I'm Christian."

I took it. His hand swallowed mine. "Mac."

He laughed. "You don't look like a Mac to me."

"Okay, I give up. Why does everyone keep saying that? What *do* I look like?"

"In most places Mac is a man's name and you, lass, look nothing like a man. Where I come from you just introduced yourself to me as 'from the clan of' and I'm still waiting for the rest of your name."

"You're from Scotland."

He nodded. "From the clan of the Keltar."

Christian MacKeltar. "Beautiful name."

"Thanks. I've been watching you since

you came in. You look . . . pensive. And if I'm not mistaken, that was your third shot. When a lovely lass drinks shots alone I worry. Is everything okay?"

"Just a rough day. Thanks for asking." How sweet he was. A much-needed reminder that there were nice people in the world; I just didn't get to hang out with them often.

"You write?" He gestured to my journal. I'd closed it the moment he'd sat down.

"I keep a diary."

"Really?" A brow rose, his golden gaze shone with interest.

I almost laughed. I had no doubt he thought I wrote about cute boys and pretty clothes and the latest reality TV show hunk I had a crush on; all those things that used to occupy my mind. I was tempted to shove it across the table at him, tell him to read a page or two, then see if he still wanted to sit with me, and after three shots, I was just buzzed enough to do it.

I was tired of lies and tired of being alone and tired of feeling disconnected. I was tired of being with people I couldn't trust and wanting to trust people I couldn't be with, like this guy for example, or his coworker, the dreamy-eyed guy. I was hungry for normalcy and angry enough to want to destroy any chance I had at getting it.

"Check it out." I shoved my notebook across the table.

He looked startled, conflicted. I could tell he wanted to know my innermost thoughts — what man would turn down a chance to read what a woman really thought, uncensored? — yet knew he should preserve my dignity if I was too drunk to do it myself, and shove it back at me. Which would win: man or gentleman?

The man opened my journal to the first page, a page of descriptions of the latest Unseelie I'd been seeing, followed by a page of speculation about how they killed and how I might best kill them.

I let him finish both pages before reclaiming my notebook.

"So," I said brightly, "now that you know I'm nuts —" I broke off and stared at him. "You *do* know I'm nuts, right?" There was something very wrong with the way he was looking at me.

"MacKayla," he said softly, "come somewhere with me, somewhere . . . safer than this. We need to talk."

I sucked in a breath. "I didn't tell you my name was MacKayla." I stared at him, a little too toasted to deal with the panic I was feeling over this unexpected paradigm shift. I'd been trying to destroy my chances at normalcy only to find out I'd never had any chance at normalcy in this situation because the normal boy wasn't normal.

"I know who you are. And what you are," he said quietly. "I've met your kind before."

"Where?" I was bewildered. "Here, in Dublin?"

He nodded. "And elsewhere."

Surely not. Was it possible? He'd known my name. What else did he know about me? "Did you know my sister?" I was suddenly breathless.

"Aye," he said heavily, "I knew Alina."

My mouth dropped. *"You knew my sister?"* I practically screeched. How did he know us? Who *was* this man?

"Aye. Will you come with me, somewhere private we can talk?"

When my cell phone rang, even buried as it was in my purse, it was so loud it nearly scared me out of my skin, and pub patrons three booths down turned to glare. I didn't blame them; it was an obnoxious ring, a blaring band of celestial trumpets, set on full volume. Obviously Barrons hadn't wanted me to miss a call.

I fumbled for it, flipped it open, and pressed send. Barrons sounded pissed. "Where the fuck are you?" he demanded.

314

"None of your business," I said coolly.

"I saw two Hunters in the city tonight, Ms. Lane. Word is more are on the way. A great deal more. Get your ass home."

I sat there frozen with a dead line. He'd said what he had to say and hung up.

I can't explain what the word "Hunters" does to me, but it gets me where I live. It gets me in my most sacred place, the one where I used to feel safe but never will again so long as there are Fae in my world. It's as if certain things are programmed into a *sidhe*-seer's DNA and we have gut reactions that can't be diminished, controlled, or overcome.

"You've gone white as a sheet, lass. What's wrong?"

I considered my options. There were none. The pub I was in closed early on weeknights. It was either make a run for the bookstore now, or wait a few hours, and if more Hunters were on the way, in a few hours it would only be more dangerous.

"Nothing." I slapped down a few bills and some change. Why hadn't Barrons come after me? My phone rang again. I dug it out.

"I would only make us a bigger target, and I've got my hands a bit full at the moment," he said. "Stay close to the buildings, under overhangs when possible. Lose yourself in throngs of other people when you can."

What was he — a mind reader? "I could catch a cab."

"Have you seen what's driving them lately?"

No, but I sure was going to be looking now that he'd said that.

"Where are you?"

I told him.

"You're not far. You'll be fine, Ms. Lane. Just get here fast, before more arrive." He hung up again.

I stuffed my journal and phone in my purse and stood up.

"Where are you going?" Christian said.

"I have to leave. Something's come up." Whatever crimes I might lay at Barrons' feet, I believed he could protect me. If there were Hunters in the city tonight, I wanted the most dangerous man I knew at my side, not a twenty-something Scottish guy who'd known my sister — who was, grim case in point, dead — so obviously he'd been of no help to her. "I want to know everything. Can I come see you at Trinity?"

He stood. "Whatever's going on, Mac, let me help you with it."

"You'll only slow me down."

"You don't know that. I might be useful."

"Don't push me," I said coldly. "I'm sick

of being pushed."

He assessed me a moment, then nodded. "Come see me at Trinity. We'll talk."

"Soon," I promised. As I left the pub, I marveled at my ignorance. I'd been sitting there, believing Rowena the final, critical piece. While I'd been busy analyzing my board, making judgments and decisions, feeling pretty smart about myself, a player I'd known nothing about had strolled up and sat down, and like everyone else, he knew a great deal more about me than I knew about him.

I was back to feeling dumb.

Just where on the game board was I supposed to place Christian MacKeltar?

I took a mental swipe at it, toppled all the pieces, and stepped into the night. The heck with it. Right now I needed to get back to the bookstore, undetected by my mortal enemy, monsters whose sole purpose was to hunt and destroy people like me.

My dad had this thing he used to say to me when I'd try to convince him that a *D* on my report card was really close to a *C*. He'd say, *Mac, baby, close only counts in hand-grenades and horseshoes.*

I was really close; in fact, I was almost home when the Hunter found me.

FIFTEEN

It was as if a new Dublin had been born while I was inside the pub, and I realized, with the exception of our brief drive through Temple Bar the other evening, I'd not walked through the district in over a month. It had been that long since I'd taken a good look at my world.

Night was *their* time and they came out in droves.

Rhino-boys were driving the cabs.

A caste of Unseelie new to me, ghastly white and painfully thin with enormous hungry, wet eyes and no mouths, was running the street vendor stands.

Where had the original owners gone? I was pretty sure I didn't want to know.

There was one Unseelie for every ten humans on the street. Many of them wore glamours of attractive people and were paired off with real people, and I knew they were going into bars wearing the guise of sexy tourists and picking up the real tourists.

And doing what with them?

I didn't want to know that, either. I couldn't kill them all. In these numbers, I was useless against them. I forced myself to look straight ahead. There were too many Unseelie around me and I'd had too much to drink. My stomach was a roiling, queasy mess. I had to get out of here. Somewhere I could breathe. Maybe throw up.

The *sidhe*-seer coalition was starting to look better to me. We would need hundreds of us to fight what was happening in this city. And we only had two weapons. It was crazy; we had to find more ways to kill them.

I kept my head down and hurried through the streets, mixing in with other tourists, keeping tight beneath the eaves whenever possible, wondering what Barrons had his hands full of tonight.

The night was buzzing with Fae and I felt like a tuning fork, vibrating from their sheer numbers and nearness. I had an overwhelming desire to start screaming at everyone to run, to leave, to do . . . something . . . I couldn't remember . . . something that lurked somewhere in my genetic memory . . . a thing we'd learned to do . . . long ago . . . a ritual, dark thing . . . we'd paid a terrible price . . . it had been our greatest shame . . . we'd made ourselves forget.

Footsteps sounded behind me in the darkness as I turned down Dreary Lane and onto Butterfield, solid, intentioned footsteps like rank and file soldiers. I didn't dare look back. If I did and whatever was back there startled me, I was just buzzed enough that my face would betray me, and whatever it was couldn't possibly know I was a *sidhe-seer*, unless I gave myself away, so all I had to do was keep walking, as if nothing was wrong.

Right?

"Human," growled something behind me, "run. Run like the mangy cur you are. Run now. We like to chase."

The voice was straight out of a nightmare. And surely it was not talking to me.

"You. *Sidhe*-seer. Run."

It had called me *sidhe*-seer.

It knew I was one by sight.

The only Unseelie who knew my face were the Lord Master's minions, which meant he was back from wherever he'd been — and looking for me.

I'd believed any Hunters in the city tonight were there by coincidence, not design. I'd been wrong. They were there to capture me. I could fight, I had the spear tucked securely in my holster, but with the numbers of dark Fae I'd been seeing and no backup, I needed no encouragement to be a coward. I glanced over my shoulder. The street was packed with Rhino-boys, two abreast, stretching back farther than I could see.

There are times when brave is just stupid: I ran.

Down one street. Up the next. Through an alley. Across a park. I vaulted benches and splashed through fountains. I ran until my lungs burned and my legs were weak. I got turned around by the old brewery and tacked on an extra six blocks to my journey.

I ran.

I ran as if my feet had Dani's wings, and finally, blessedly the footsteps behind me faded and there was silence but for the pounding of my shoes on cement.

I spared a glance over my shoulder.

I'd lost them. I'd really, truly done it. Rhino-boys might be strong, but with their stumpy arms and legs, they were neither swift nor lithe of limb.

I turned a corner and drew up just short of plowing into a brick wall. Dead-end alleys spring up as unexpectedly as one-way streets in this city. I had to get out, before the soldiers tracked me down again. There was no way I could scale the wall. It was twelve feet of sheer brick and there were no convenient Dumpsters piled in front of it.

I was three blocks from Barrons Books and Baubles. It was just over this wall and down two streets. Close, so close.

I turned.

And froze.

It was as if a giant freezer had opened in the sky above me. The temperature plunged bitterly. Tiny, glistening bits of ice began to pellet my skin.

It was there. I knew what it was. Every cell of my being knew what it was. And not because I'd read about them, or Barrons had told me about them, or I'd seen sketches of them.

The beast above me hovered darkly. I could feel the great *whuf-whuf* of giant wings beating air. The scent of brimstone and ancient dusty things filled my nostrils. If Hell had dragons and they smelled, this was their scent.

Sidhe-seer, it said, without speaking at all. The voice was inside my head, in that hot, alien place. *Slave. We own you.*

"Get out," I snarled, and lashed out at it with all the hot, alien fire in my head.

It was gone from my mind, but not from above me. I could feel the air moving. I could smell its acrid stench.

I gauged the distance to the end of the alley, mentally calculated my run from there. How fast was it? For that matter, how *big* was it? The descriptions I'd read had varied widely. Could it fit between buildings? Could it swoop down and pluck me from the sidewalk in its talons? Might it rip the bookstore apart, rafter from eave, looking for me? Summon all its dark brethren to demolish the building? Would anyone even notice, or did Hunters have the same "cloaking" effect as Shades and Dark Zones? Did I dare lead it to Barrons? Did I dare not? If I got inside somewhere, anywhere, would it leave me alone or assume an eternal dark perch on my eave like Poe's raven, only far more macabre and deadly? Could it shift? Simply materialize wherever I was?

"Fuck," I said emphatically. Sometimes there's just no other word for it.

I had to know what I was trying to outrun. Knowledge is power. That is one truth I've learned that has never failed me.

Brushing ice flakes from my face, I looked up.

Straight into eyes that glowed like twin furnaces from Hell, staring malevolently back at me from a swirling fall of black ice.

The books I'd read had compared the

Royal Hunters to the classic human depiction of the Devil.

The books had been right.

Somewhere in our ancient human past a *sidhe*-seer, or a few, must have had something to do with recording religious myths and the Bible. They'd seen the Hunters, and had used their memories to scare the hell — literally — out of humanity.

For a moment it was hard to separate the thing from the night; they were both forged of blackness. Then my vision cleared and something in my genes kicked in, and it was clearly visible. Great, dark, leathery wings flapped from a great dark leathery body, with a massive satyrlike head, cloven hooves, and a forked tail. Its tongue was long and bisected down the middle. It had long curved black horns with bloody tips. It was black, but it was more than black; it was the absolute, utter, and complete absence of light. It *absorbed* the light around it, swallowed it up, took it into its body, devoured it, and spit it back out again as a miasma of darkness and desolation. And it was cold. The air paddled by its slow-moving wings churned with glittering black ice flakes, swirling beneath the great, leathery sails. It was the only Fae — besides V'lane, that first time we'd met — whose presence in our world altered our world around it. V'lane, too, had iced the air, though not so overtly or dramatically. It was powerful. It was making me feel so sick to my stomach that I almost couldn't breathe.

It laughed inside my head. I closed my eyes and forced it out again; this time it wasn't easy. It knew where to find me inside myself. Was that why we feared them so deeply — because these Fae could get inside our heads?

Would a *sidhe*-seer that wasn't as strong as me be able to withstand it, or would it rip her mind to shreds, one memory or personality trait or dream at a time, sift its talons through the tatters, before destroying her body as almost an afterthought?

I opened my eyes.

My personal Grim Reaper stood in the alley, directly in front of me, a dozen feet away, dark robes rustling softly in the unnatural wind generated by the beast's wings.

It stood in silence, as always, regarding me from beneath its deep black cowl, though it had no face, no eyes, nothing beneath that hood I could discern, with which to regard me. It was shadows and night, like the Hunter above me, only *it* wasn't there, and the Hunter was. What an absurd time to torture myself for my failings.

Ignoring it, I pushed back my jacket, slipped my spear from its holster, and fisted my hand around the hilt. It wasn't my problem. Dragon-boy from hell was.

Black hail began to fall, tiny pellets stinging my skin. The Hunter was incensed; its displeasure iced the night.

How dare you touch our Hallows? roared in my head.

"Oh, screw you," I snapped. "You want me? Come and get me." I focused on that foreign place in my mind, stoked the strange fire, and boxed up my mind as securely as I could. The thing's roar had nearly split my head.

Could the Hunter cram itself into the tight alleyway? Could it sift or resize itself?

We would see, and if it did, the moment it got close I would freeze and stab it.

I waited.

It hovered.

I looked up . . . and smiled.

Fury blazed in its fiery eyes, yet it made no move toward me. It wasn't about to risk getting near my spear, and we both knew it. I could kill it. I could take forever from it, and the thing's arrogance was immense as its wingspan; it didn't consider any master it might choose to serve worth dying for.

I realized then, or had some surfacing of a shred of collective memory, that the Hunters were feared even among their own kind. They had something . . . I wasn't sure what . . . but something that even their royal brethren didn't mess with. They were of the Fae . . . but perhaps not completely. They served whomever they wished, only if there was something in it for them, and stopped serving whenever they felt like it. They were mercenaries in the purest sense of the word.

It feared the spear. It would not risk death. I had a chance.

I broke into a run.

So long as the soldiers didn't find me, so long as more Hunters didn't show up, I would survive tonight. I could make it to the bookstore and Barrons would have some plan — he always did. Perhaps we could get out of the city for a few days. Perhaps, loath though I was to consider it, we would hook up with other *sidhe*-seers. There was safety in numbers.

As I sped past my Phantom Reaper, it did something so utterly unexpected and incomprehensible that my mind failed to process it.

It swung out its scythe and the blunt of the wood caught me in my midsection.

In my mind I screamed — *but you're not real* — even as I doubled over and lost the breath in my lungs.

Real or not, its scythe was.

For the second time tonight, my paradigm was brutally shifted: My Grim Reaper was *corporeal.*

Impossible! I'd thrown a flashlight through it, had watched it tumble end over end before crashing into a wall. It had no substance!

Laughing, it moved toward me. Now that I knew it was real, I could feel its malevolence, a dark, pulsating hatred, barely contained beneath the voluminous black shroud. Directed at me, *all* for me.

I stared in disbelief, laboring to suck air into my lungs. I'd exhaled to a painful point. My chest was locked down tight, my lungs deflated.

I'd been played. Lulled into believing my enemy wasn't an enemy, until it had been ready to make its move. Had it been spying on me all those times? Watching and waiting for the right moment?

I'd talked to it. I'd confessed my sins to it! What *was* it?

I wheezed violently, sucking down air.

It approached, dark robes shifting as it glided forward.

I sensed Fae — I didn't sense Fae. Perhaps I could nullify it, perhaps I couldn't.

It swung its scythe. I leapt. It whirled and parried, I ducked and jumped. The wood staff zinged as it sliced through air, and I knew if even one of those blows landed on me it would turn bone to dust.

It wasn't trying to get me with the curved blade. It wanted to pulverize, to maim. Why? Did it have a special death planned for me?

As we danced our macabre waltz, suddenly the alley was flooded with Rhinoboys; the rank and file soldiers had found us.

I was moments away from being hemmed in by dozens of Unseelie. Once they did that, I was doomed. I could freeze them but there were too many. Eventually they would overwhelm me. I needed Dani, I needed Barrons. I'd be absorbed into a horde of soldiers, borne on the crest of their dark wave, delivered to their master.

I did the only thing I could think of: When all else fails, try to take out the top dog. At this point, I was pretty sure Mr. Grim — heretofore utterly underestimated by me — was top dog, remaining innocuously in the background until now.

I charged the specter.

It parried my spear arm with inhuman

speed, and the flat of its scythe caught me. I felt the bones in my wrist powder. As I crashed to my knees, in spite of blinding pain, I managed to slam the palm of my other hand into its dark robe.

It didn't freeze.

In fact, what my hand encountered wasn't . . . quite . . . solid.

When I was five, I found a dead rabbit that had somehow gotten itself trapped in our playhouse. I guess it starved to death. It was spring, not too hot yet, and the animal hadn't begun to smell or show visible signs of decay — at least not side-up. It had looked so pretty lying there on my blanket, with its silky bunny fur and cottony tail and pink nose. I'd thought it was sleeping. I'd tried to pick it up to take in the house and show Mom, ask if we could keep it. My tiny hands had slid deep into its body, into a warm yellowish stew of decomposing flesh.

I'd hoped never to feel or smell such a thing again.

I felt and smelled it now.

My left hand slid straight into its abdomen, buried in its flesh. But the thing wasn't *entirely* rotted. Its arm wasn't soft at all when it snaked around my throat, but hard and unyielding as a steel cord.

I kicked and screamed, I fought and bit,

but the thing's strength was unbelievable. What was it? What was I fighting? How easily I'd believed what it had wanted me to believe! How it must have been laughing when I'd tallied the sins of my guilty conscience for it. Where was my spear?

For the second time in as many minutes, I couldn't breathe. It was choking me.

I stared up at the leathery underbelly of a Hunter as I died.

SIXTEEN

As I'm sure you've figured out, I didn't really die, twin to my sister's fate, alone in an alley, run down by monsters, in the dark heart of Dublin.

My parents would not have to claim another body from airport officials. At least not yet.

I'd *thought* I was dying, though. When the blood is being cut off to your brain in a choke hold, you don't know if your assailant plans to keep the pressure on your carotids for ten seconds — long enough to knock you unconscious — or longer still, until your heart stops and your brain dies. I'd assumed the specter wanted me dead.

It wouldn't be long before I would wish it had.

I came to with a sour, chemical taste in my mouth that made me suspect I'd been drugged, a burning pain in my wrist accompanied by a peculiar immobility and heaviness, and the dank odor of wet, mossy stone in my nostrils. I kept my eyes closed and my breathing even, trying to assess as much of myself and my surroundings as possible before betraying to anyone who might be watching me that I was conscious.

I was barefoot and cold, dressed only in my jeans and T-shirt. My boots, sweater, and jacket were gone. I had a dim memory of losing my purse in the alley. So much for the cell phone Barrons had given me. Speaking of Barrons — he would find me! He would trace my cuff and —

My heart sank. I couldn't feel the cuff on my arm. In fact the only thing I felt was something stiff and heavy around my wrist. I wondered when and where my cuff had been removed, where I was now, and how much time had passed. I wondered who or what the specter was. Although the Lord Master had worn a similar hooded robe of crimson the one time I'd seen him, I didn't believe these villains were one and the same. They shared some aspect of their nature in common, but there was something very different about the specter.

I lay perfectly still and listened. If someone lurked nearby, they were taking pains not to betray their presence.

I opened my eyes and stared up at stone.

No one said anything ominous like *Aha, you're awake, let the torturing begin,* so I risked a glance at my wrist. I was wearing a cast.

"I almost ripped your hand off," a voice said conversationally, and I nearly jumped out of my skin. "You were bleeding to death. It made repairs necessary."

I sat up slowly, carefully. My head was muzzy, my tongue thick. My wrist was a mass of screaming nerves, burning all the way up to my shoulder.

I looked around. I was in a cell of stone — an ancient grotto — behind iron bars, on a thin pallet on the floor. Beyond those bars my specter stood.

"Where am I?"

Its hood rustled as it spoke. "The Burren. Beneath it, to be precise. Do you know what the Burren is?" Its voice held a smile. Where had I heard that voice before? Sibilant, silky, it was familiar . . . but different . . . tone fluid, words loosely formed.

Yes, I knew what the Burren was. I'd seen it on my maps and read about it during the recent learning binge I'd gone on in an attempt to dispel my provinciality. From the Irish *Boireann,* which meant great rock or rocky place, it was a *karst* landscape in County Clare, Ireland, a limestone area of

334

roughly three hundred square kilometers, with the famous Cliffs of Moher at the southwest edge. On cracked limestone pavements chiseled by grykes, or fissures in the stone, one could find Neolithic tombs, portal dolmens, high crosses, and as many as five hundred ring forts. Beneath the Burren were active stream caves and miles of labyrinthine passages and caverns, some open to tourists, the majority unexplored, undeveloped, and far too dangerous for the casual potholer.

I was *beneath* the Burren.

It was a hundred times worse than being in the bomb shelter. I might as well have been entombed alive. I hate confined places as much as I hate the dark. The knowledge that there were tons and tons of rock above my head, dense and impenetrable, separating me from the air, from wide-open spaces and the ability to move freely about made me feel wildly claustrophobic. My face must have betrayed my horror.

"I see you do."

"Where are my things?" I couldn't think about where I was or I'd have a meltdown. I had to focus on getting out. Specifically, where was my cuff? Had it been removed here? Or back in the alley? I could hardly ask. I desperately needed to know.

"Why?"

"I'm cold."

"Cold is the least of your problems."

Undoubtedly true. Even if I managed to get free, how would I find my way out of this place? Down dark tunnels, through flooded caverns, with no compass, no sense of direction. As desperately as I wanted more information about my clothes, cuff, and spear, I was afraid to press; afraid too much interest might make my captor suspicious, and the last thing I wanted to do was cause the specter to dispose of something it might otherwise have left lying around — a thing that could save my life. How did the cuff work? Would Barrons be able to track it beneath the ground? "Who are you? What do you want?" I demanded.

"My life back," it said. "In lieu of that, I'll take yours. The same way you've taken mine. One piece at a time."

"Who are you?" I repeated. What was this thing talking about?

It raised a hand and pushed back its cowl.

I flinched violently. For a moment I was too horrified to do anything but stare. I searched the face for something, anything that I recognized. It took me several long moments to find it in the eyes.

They were dead, citron, inhuman.

Mallucé!

I'd been grossly premature in swiping him off my playing board. I'd been wrong, so wrong! The vampire wasn't dead.

He was worse than dead.

All those times I'd glimpsed the specter, seen it out a window late at night, or in the alley, or in the graveyard with Barrons, it had been Mallucé, watching me. All those times I'd discounted my Grim Reaper as a figment of my imagination, the vampire had actually been there, somehow. I shuddered. I'd been so close to him so many times, with no awareness of the danger I was in. He'd been in my back alley the night the Shades had gotten in, the night I'd broken into Barrons' garage. He'd been watching me since shortly after I'd stabbed him. I wondered why he'd waited so long to take action.

I struggled to hold his gaze, if only to keep from absorbing how grotesque the rest of him had become. It was no wonder he kept his hood up. No wonder he hid his face. I looked away. I couldn't take it.

"Look at me, bitch. See your handiwork. *You* did this to me," he snarled.

"No, I didn't," I said instantly. I may not know much, but I did know that I'd *never* do anything like that to anyone, not even my worst enemy.

"Yes, you did. And I'm going to do worse to you before I'm done. You'll die when I die. It might be weeks, it might be months."

I looked back at him and tried to speak but couldn't. His face, once handsome in a pale, Goth Byronic way, was now monstrous. "I didn't do that," I insisted. "There's no way. All I did was stab you in your gut. I don't know how the rest of you got so . . . so . . ." I let the sentence end there, the kinder for both of us. "Are you sure Barrons didn't do it?" Not very big of me trying to blame Barrons, but at the moment, under the circumstances, I wasn't feeling big. I was feeling small and terrified. Mallucé was holding me responsible for what he'd become, and what he'd become was worse than anything I'd seen in any movie I'd watched, or any nightmare I'd ever had.

"You stabbed me with a Fae-killing spear, you bitch!"

"But you're not Fae," I protested. "You're a vampire."

"*Parts* of me were Fae!" he hissed.

His mouth didn't completely close, and flecks of spittle flew through the bars, landed on my skin. They burned like acid. I scrubbed my arms on my T-shirt.

"What?" How could *parts* of someone be Fae? Yet that was exactly what it looked like.

As if the spear had killed parts of him. Portions of Mallucé's face were still marble white and handsome in a vampiric way; other parts had been ravaged by a foul leprosy: A blackened vein ran down his right cheek, over his jaw, and halfway down his neck, like rotted marbling in beef; a chunk above his left eye was gray, moist; most of his chin and lower lip had collapsed into a wet, septic decay. It was horrific. I couldn't stop staring. His long blond hair had fallen out, baring a bloated skull traced by a skein of thin, black veins.

I realized that must be why my hand had sunk into his abdomen — portions of his body were decomposing as well, which explained his altered gait and the change in his voice, not to mention a mouth that wouldn't close, which had to make diction difficult. Was he rotting from the inside, too? Revolted, I wiped my hand on my jeans.

"Look at me," he said, his yellow eyes burning lanterns in a misshapen skull. "Study me. Soon you'll know this face as well as your own. We're going to be intimate, so very intimate. We're going to die together." His eyes narrowed to slits. "Do you know what the worst part is?" He didn't wait for an answer. "At first you think it's watching parts of yourself rot. Staring in the mirror, poking your finger into melting pockets of your own flesh. Wondering if you should scrape out the rot or leave it alone. Bandage it up. Realizing that your cheek or your ear or part of your stomach is beyond repair. You lose yourself in degrees. You think, I can live with this, but then the next part goes and the next, and you find the worst part isn't the mornings when you wake up to discover another part of you is no longer alive, but the nights when you lie awake in terror of what you'll discover at dawn. Will it be my hand next? An eye? Will I go blind before I die? Will it be my tongue? My dick? My balls? It's not the reality that undoes you; it's the possibilities. It's the waiting, the hours you lie awake wondering what will be next. It's not the pain of the moment, but the anticipation of the next pain. It's not the dying itself — that will be a relief — but the desperation to live, the stupid fucking need to go on long after you hate what you've become, long after you can even stand to look at yourself. You'll feel that before I'm through with you." His lips — one sculpted, pink, and firm, one rotted — peeled back from fangs. "Look at me. I lived as Death for years. I played it for them. I delivered Death to my followers, dressed in grand Goth seduction. I gave it to them in velvet and lace and smelling of sex. I took them higher than they'd ever been on any drug. I danced them into death. I ripped out their throats and drank their blood and they came beneath my body as they died. Will no one do the same for me? Will no one dance *me* into the darkness?"

I couldn't find any words.

His smile was terrible, his laughter even worse: moist-sounding, wrong. He held out his arms, as if to waltz. "Welcome, dance partner. Welcome to my ball here in Hell's grotto. Death is not seductive. It does not come silk-clad and sweet-smelling as I did for my chosen. It is lonely and cold and merciless. It takes everything from you, before it finally takes you." He dropped his arms. "I had it all. I had the world by the balls. I fucked anything I wanted, anytime I wanted. I was worshipped, I was rich, and I was going to be one of the world's great new powers. I was the Lord Master's right hand and now I am nothing. Because of you."

He pulled up his cowl, adjusted it, then turned and walked away. "So think, lovely bitch," he tossed over his shoulder, "about how lovely you *won't* be soon. Think about the morning and what horrors await you there. Try to sleep. Wonder what might wake you. Dream. For they are all you have left now. I own your reality. Welcome to mine."

I lay on my pallet staring up at the stone ceiling. I'd gone to that *sidhe*-seer place in my head and discovered something: I was capable of illusion. Not the Fae kind of illusion that affected others, but a kind only I could see. It was enough. With my mind, I'd painted clouds and a blue sky on the stone ceiling of my grotto, and I could breathe again.

Was it really only three months ago that I'd been lying by the pool at my parents' house, in my favorite pink polka-dotted bikini, sipping iced sweet tea and listening to Louis Armstrong croon about what a wonderful world it was?

The song currently playing on my mental iPod was "Highway to Hell." I'd been on it and not even known. It was a fast road; made the Autobahn look like snail's play — three months total from Stateside to Tomb-side, and a month of that had been squandered in a single afternoon, playing volleyball with a facsimile of my sister in Faery.

"V'lane?" I said with soft urgency. I conjured a light wind to buffet my fluffy clouds on the ceiling. "Are you there?

Anywhere? I could *really* use some help right about now." For the next little while — I had no concept of time down here — I invoked the death-by-sex Fae fervently. I promised him things I knew I'd regret. I'd regret dying more.

It was no use.

Wherever he was, he wasn't listening.

What in the world had happened to Mallucé? What had he meant when he'd said parts of him were Fae? How could parts of a person — or vampire in this case — be Fae? My understanding was either you were Fae or you weren't. Could Fae and human reproduce and would the resulting offspring be half-Fae?

But that wasn't the read I was getting off Mallucé. Each time I'd encountered him, I'd focused directly on him, trying to get a sense of what he was. It had always been confused, and now it was even more so. However he'd become part Fae, he'd not been born to it. It was something he'd *become*. But how? Was it like vampirism? Did they bite you? Have sex with you? What?

My clouds were gone. Maintaining illusion was hard work, and between the pain of my wrist and the aftereffects of whatever drugs he'd given me to keep me unconscious while transporting me from Dublin to the Burren, I had little energy left. I was starving. I was cold and I was terrified.

I rolled over on my side and stared out of my cell.

I was imprisoned at one end of a long oval stone cavern lit by torches on the walls. At the other end a single metal door was hinged into the wall.

In the center of the cavern was a low stone slab that resembled a sacrificial altar more than anything else. There were knives, bottles, and chains on it. Three opulent, brocaded, Victorian-style chairs were drawn up around it. Mallucé had brought the tatters of his Goth past with him into the earth.

The walls of the damp cavern were lined with other cells or grottos; some so narrow and small that they were barely more than barred boxes in stone that a person might be stuffed into, others large enough to hold a dozen men. My cell was sandwiched between cells on both sides, with bars separating us, but they were empty. In a few of the cells across the way, occasionally something moved. I called out to other occupants but nothing replied. Had Mallucé created this place, or was I in some ancient dungeon, remnant of a more barbaric time, buried so deep in the earth it had been forgotten?

Clouds. I rolled over and painted them on the ceiling again. I was shaking. Phrases like "deep in the earth" just weren't working for me. I had a few friends who were spelunkers. I'd always thought they were nuts. Why go to the ground any sooner than we have to?

I added a sun and a dazzlingly white seashore to my illusion, I dressed myself in pink. I painted my sister into the picture.

Eventually I slept.

I knew he was in the cavern with me the moment I awakened.

Fae but not Fae: I could feel him there: a dark cancer, a wrongness.

My head ached from sleeping on a pillow of stone. My wrist pain had eased from the torture of screaming nerves, to flesh and blood pain, which was more bearable. I was so hungry I was almost too weak to move. Did he plan to starve me? I'd heard it took something like three days to dehydrate. How long did I have to go? I had no sense of time in this place. Would hours feel like days? Would days feel like months? How long had I been unconscious? How long had I slept? From how hungry I was, I knew at least a day had passed, perhaps two. I have a high metabolism and need to eat frequently. Assuming he fed and watered me, what would I be like after a week down here? A month?

I rolled over gingerly. There was bread and a small pail of water inside my cell. I fell on them like an animal.

As I tore off chunks of dry, crusty bread and stuffed them in my mouth, I watched Mallucé through the bars. His back was to me. His hood was down. The back of his hairless, swollen head looked gangrenous. Froths of lace rimmed his neck and black-gloved wrists where his robe fell away. Even decaying, he was still dressing in the height of Goth. He was seated at the low stone slab and if I wasn't mistaken, he was eating something, too, making disgusting noises while he did it. I saw the flash of silver slicing, the sound of blade against stone, crunching sounds. I wondered what decaying vampires dined upon. According to the authors of *Vampires for Dummies,* they *didn't* eat. They drank blood. His body and the chairs blocked my view of the slab.

I finished the bread too quickly, resulting in a hard, sour lump of dough in my stomach. Despite raging thirst, I sipped the water carefully. There was no bathroom in my cell from Hell. Ironic, the humiliations that occur to us in the midst of significantly larger problems, as if being killed by one's enemy isn't quite as terrible as being forced to urinate in front of him.

Where was Barrons? What had he done when I'd not shown up at the bookstore that night? Gone hunting for me? Was he still out there looking? Had Malluce and the Hunters captured him, too? I refused to believe that. I needed hope. Surely if Malluce had gotten Barrons, he'd be bragging about it, would have imprisoned him somewhere I could see him. Was he back at the bookstore, furious with me, thinking I'd gone off with V'lane again and would turn up next month, bikini-clad and suntanned?

Where was the cuff?

Why, oh, *why* hadn't I let him tattoo me? What was my problem? He could have branded me between the cheeks of my petunia for all I cared, if it'd get me out of here! What had I been thinking? I was such an idiot!

A cuff can be removed, Ms. Lane; a tattoo can't.

I'd learned that lesson the hard way. Question was would I survive it?

"Where's my spear?" I asked Malluce. If it was here, perhaps the cuff was, too.

"Not your spear, bitch," the vampire said, raising an arm, bringing another bite to his

347

mouth. I caught a glimpse of his hand; he was wearing shiny, stiff black gloves. I wondered if his hands had begun to rot and he wore gloves to contain their shape. He chewed a moment. "You were never worthy of it. I've put word out that I have it. Whoever restores me gets it."

"Do you really think you *can* be restored?" He looked like something that had been resurrected from a grave. I couldn't see such damage being undone.

He didn't answer me, but I felt his anger; it chilled the room.

"If you were the Lord Master's right hand, why doesn't *he* heal you? He leads the Unseelie. He must be very powerful," I fished.

He spat something from his mouth. I caught a glimpse of a red gristly thing before it hit the floor beyond the slab. Was he eating raw meat?

"He is nothing compared to the Fae! It's a true Fae I need now, a full-blood. Perhaps the queen herself will come for the spear, and give me the elixir of life in exchange for it, make me truly immortal."

"Why would she do that when she could just kill you and take the spear?"

He whirled and glared at me, citron eyes maddened with fury. Clouds were my illusion. The queen granting him eternal life was his, and I'd just shattered it.

My body retched before my brain processed what I was seeing. Some things don't have to be filtered through the consciousness; they get you in the gut. A chunk of raw flesh dangled, half in, half out his rotting mouth, and he held another piece of it in his hand. The flesh was pinkish gray, seeping, and glistened with white pustules. I could see beyond his half-turned body to the slab. I knew now what he was eating.

A Rhino-boy was chained to the slab. Alive. What was left of it writhed in agony. Mallucé was eating Unseelie!

My bread metamorphosed instantly to a spoiled lump of yeast that expanded and threatened to disgorge. I refused to give it up. I needed my energy. I swallowed, hard. Who knew when he would bother to feed me again? *"You!* You're the one who's been eating them! But why?" Of course. It was no coincidence the half-eaten bodies had been found where my specter was seen. It had been Mallucé eating the Rhino-boy in the graveyard that night I'd searched it for Barrons. It had been him right outside my bookstore, who'd left the half-eaten nightmare in the Dumpster! So close and I'd never even known!

He shoved the bite into his mouth with

his fingers. It quivered, resisting the entire time. I could see his "food" moving behind his cheeks. The flesh he was eating wasn't just raw; like the Unseelie on the slab, it was still alive. "Do you wonder about me, bitch? I wondered about you. After you stabbed me, I sickened immediately. I didn't know what was wrong with me. I lay in my lair, poisoned, realizing in slow degrees what your spear had done to me. It was then that I projected myself to you, spied on you. I was too weak at first to do more than watch you and plan, but vengeance made me strong. That and eating most of my followers." He laughed. "While I lay in that room, stinking to high hell, watching myself rot, I had so many conversations, so many intimate little encounters with you while I waited for this moment. In all of them you worshipped me before you died. You want to know me? You'll know everything soon. You'll call *me* Lord Master." Around another mouthful, he said, "He's the one who taught me to eat them."

"Why? For what?" Here, at last, was some information about my enemy!

"So I could see them."

"Who them? Do you mean the Fae?" I said, incredulous.

He nodded.

"Are you saying that if person eats Unseelie they develop the ability to see the Fae? A perfectly normal person, or do you have to be a vampire?"

He shrugged. "I made two of my bodyguards eat it. It worked on them."

I wondered what he'd done to the bodyguards. I didn't ask. I couldn't see him letting competition in any form live to potentially challenge him. If Mallucé really was a vampire, I highly doubted he'd ever "sired" anyone. "Why did the Lord Master want you to see them?"

"To recruit me to his cause. He wanted my money, my connections. I wanted his power. And I was about to take it — all of it — until you came along. I'd won many of his minions to my side. They serve me still." He stuffed another bite in his mouth and closed his eyes. For a moment, there was an obscene expression of sensual pleasure on his ruined face. "You can't imagine what it feels like," he said, chewing slowly, half smiling. Then his eyes snapped open, febrile with loathing. "Or what it *used* to feel like, before you damaged me. It was the ultimate high. It gave me power in the black arts, the strength of ten men, heightened my senses, and healed mortal wounds as quickly as they were inflicted. It made me invincible.

351

Now none of the ecstasy is there. It makes me strong. It keeps me alive, if I eat it constantly, but nothing more. Because of you!"

One more reason to hate me: I'd taken away his drug of choice. On top of that, I'd inflicted an *im*mortal wound on him, one that eating Unseelie obviously couldn't heal. A wound that was killing him slowly, one Fae part at a time. I didn't quite understand that aspect of it.

"Does eating Unseelie turn you Fae eventually? Is that what you and the Lord Master were doing? Eating Fae to become Fae?"

"Fuck the Lord Master," he snarled. "*I'm* your world now!"

"He abandoned you, didn't he?" I guessed. "When he saw you like this, he sent you away to die. You didn't serve his purposes any more."

Fury hummed in the air. The vampire turned and carved off another slice of flesh. As he moved, his dark robes parted and I caught the flash of something gold and silver, encrusted with onyx and sapphires, hanging around his neck.

Mallucé had the amulet! *He* was the one who'd beaten us to the Welshman's estate that night!

But if he had the amulet, why hadn't he used it to heal himself? The answer came swiftly on the heels of the question: Barrons had told me the Unseelie King had fashioned it for his concubine, who wasn't Fae, and that humans had to be epic to invoke its power. Mallucé was part Fae now. Which meant either the Fae part of him prevented him from being able to access the power of the amulet, or, despite his machinations to elevate himself to such ranks, John Johnstone, Jr., just wasn't epic.

Perhaps *I* was.

I needed to get my hands on that amulet.

A much grimmer thought followed the first: it had been Mallucé who'd so brutally killed all those people. How had Barrons summed it up? *Whoever, whatever killed the guards and staff that night did it with either the detached sadism of a pure sociopath, or immense rage.*

So, what was I dealing with? Sociopath or hair trigger? Neither boded well for me. I might be able to manipulate a hair trigger. I wasn't sure anyone could survive a sociopath.

Mallucé stood, turned, withdrew a delicately embroidered handkerchief from the voluminous folds of his robe, and dabbed at his chin. Then he smiled, baring his fangs.

"How does your wrist feel, bitch?"

It had been feeling better actually, until he broke it again.

I'm going to leave a little to your imagination now.

Although it may not seem like it, this isn't a story about darkness. It's about light. Kahlil Gibran says *Your joy can fill you only as deeply your sorrow has carved you.* If you've never tasted bitterness, sweet is just another pleasant flavor on your tongue. One day I'm going to hold a lot of joy.

Bottom line is Malluce didn't want me dead. Not yet. He knew many inventive ways to cause pain without doing permanent, debilitating injury. He wanted me to anticipate the horrors he had planned for me, more than he wanted to begin those horrors, so I would feel the same helpless terror he'd endured. All those weeks he'd lain in his lair, fighting the poison in his body, he'd planned my death in exacting detail, and now he meant to take a long time enacting it. Only after he'd hurt me as much as he could without disfiguring me would the maiming begin. For every piece he'd lost, he told me, I would lose a piece. He had a doctor on hand to tidy up after his barbaric surgeries, to keep me alive.

I was going to be as insane as him by the time we died.

He had two Unseelie restraining me at first. Eventually he sent them away, entered my cell, and began a more personal assault. He seemed to feel we had a special, intimate bond. He talked incessantly while he hurt me, told me things that didn't penetrate my pain-muddied mind, but might later, in clearer waters, resurface, and I realized he really *had* passed a great deal of time having conversations with me in his head. His words had been rehearsed, and were delivered with impeccable timing for maximum horrific impact. The vampire Mallucé, with his Addams Family Goth mansion, his steampunk clothes, and his seductive, fanged portrayal of Death, had always been a showman and I was his final, captive audience. He was determined that his last show would be his greatest. Before he was done with me, he told me, I would cling to him, seek succor from him, beg him for comfort, even as he destroyed me.

There is torture and there is psychological torture. Mallucé was a master of both.

I was holding up. I wasn't screaming too much. Yet. I was clinging tenaciously to the side of a tiny lifeboat of optimism in my sea of pain. I was telling myself that everything would be all right, that Malluce might have taken my cuff, but he would never discard a relic that might prove useful to him somehow, especially not an ancient one, worth money. I assured myself that he'd tossed it in a cave nearby and that Barrons would track it, and find me. The pain would stop. I wouldn't die here. My life wasn't over.

Then he dropped the bomb on me.

With a leprous smile, his face so close to mine that the putrid odor of rotting flesh nearly choked me, he sank my lifeboat, drove it straight to the bottom of the sea. He told me to forget about Barrons, if that was my hope, if that was what was keeping me from succumbing to mindless panic, because Barrons was *never* coming for me. Malluce had seen to it himself when he'd stripped off my "clever little locator cuff" back in the alley where he'd run me to ground, along with my purse and clothing. He'd left it lying there, amid broken bottles and debris.

Hunters had flown us here; we'd left no trail on the ground to follow. Pure mercenaries that they were, Malluce had outbid the Lord Master for their temporary services. There was no chance that Jericho Barrons or anyone else would ever find or rescue me. I was forgotten, lost to the world.

It was him and me, alone, in the belly of the earth, until the bitter end.

Phrases like "belly of the earth" really get to me. The thought of my cuff lying back there in that alley, useless, got to me even worse. I was hours from Dublin, beneath tons of stone.

Mallucé was right; without the cuff, I would never be found, alive or dead. At least Mom and Dad had gotten a body back with Alina. Mine would never show up. What would it do to them, to lose their second daughter without a trace? I couldn't bear to think about it.

Barrons was out. I couldn't count on V'lane. If he was hovering in whatever manner he hovered, he would have stopped this by now. He wouldn't have let Mallucé do these things to me, which meant he was off somewhere, probably on some errand for his queen, and it could be months in human time before he came around again. That left Rowena and her group of tightly controlled *sidhe*-seers, and she'd made her sentiments plain: *I will never risk ten to save one.*

Mallucé was right. No one was coming for me.

I was going to die down here, in this miserable, dark hellhole with a rotting monster. I would never see the sun again. Never feel grass or sand beneath my feet. Never listen to another song, never draw another breath of sweet Georgia blossom-drenched air, never taste my mother's pecan chicken and peach pie again.

He was going to turn me into a quadriplegic, he told me, by slow, infinitesimal degrees. The suffering he planned to inflict on the remnant of my body was too horrific for my brain to allow my ears to hear. I turned them off. I heard no more.

Hope is a critical thing. Without it, we are nothing. Hope shapes the will. The will shapes the world. I might have been suffering a dearth of hope but I had a few things left: will, desperation in spades, and a chance.

A glittering, gold and silver, encrusted with sapphires and onyx chance.

I'd eaten today, I wasn't too badly beaten yet, and one of my arms still worked. Who knew what shape I'd be in tomorrow? Or the next day? I couldn't think about a future in this place. I might never be as strong again as I was right now. Would he really begin torturing me with psychotropic drugs, as he'd said? The thought of having control of my mind stripped from me was worse than the thought of more pain. I wouldn't even possess the wits to *try* to fight. I couldn't let that happen.

It was now or never. I needed to know: Was I epic? I might never have another opportunity to find out. He might chain me up the next time. Or worse.

He was still talking, didn't seem to care that I'd willed myself deaf and was no longer even responding with flinches to what he was saying. This was the performance he'd been living for. His sickly yellow eyes burned with psychotic zeal.

When he reached for me again, I threw myself forward, as if seeking his embrace. It startled him. I plunged my good hand beneath his robes, groped for the amulet, and locked down tight on it when I found it. It was like closing my hand around dry ice. The metal was so cold it burned, felt like it was eating straight through my flesh to the bone. I pushed through the pain. For a moment nothing happened. Then a dark fire, a blue-black light began to pulse from the folds of his robe, from between my fingers.

I had my answer: MacKayla Lane had potential for greatness!

I'd settle for a little superstrength and a map to get me out of here. I yanked, but the chain was forged of thick links. I couldn't snap it. I remembered how the old man's head had been nearly ripped off. Were the links reinforced by magic? I focused my will, tried to jerk it through his rotting neck. The translucent stone inside the amulet blazed, bathing the grotto with dark radiance.

"You bitch!" The vampire looked incredulous.

I'd been right. He hadn't been able to make it work. I smirked. "Guess you just don't have the right stuff."

"Impossible! You are no one, *nothing!*"

"This nothing is going to kick your ass, vamp." Bluff, bluff, bluff. And pray there was some truth in it. When the chain snapped abruptly, I stumbled backward into the wall, clutching the amulet.

For a moment, he stared blankly; his gloved hand went to his neck, and I knew he was wondering how I'd gotten it off him when he'd had to nearly behead the last owner to tear it free, then his face contorted with rage. He fell on me, fangs tearing, fists flying, trying to take the amulet back before I was able to use it.

I curled in on myself, clutching it, protecting it, focusing on it fiercely.

Nothing happened.

I flexed that hot place in my brain and

tried to impose my will on it. *Destroy him,* I commanded it. *Rip him apart. Kill him. Save me. Make him die. Let me live. Make him stop hitting me make him stop make him stop make him stop!*

Still the blows rained down. I wasn't impacting reality one bit.

The amulet was colder than death in my hand, seeping up my arm. It radiated dark light, offering me its chilling, immense power. It had some kind of shadowy life, this arctic thing in my hand. I could feel it pulsating, the thud of an impatient dark heartbeat. I could feel that it *wanted* to be used by me. It was hungry for purpose, but there was something I didn't understand about it, something I had to do to make it mine. I realized then that I'd not broken the chain; it had snapped of its own dark accord, *chosen* to come to me because it had sensed I could use it.

But that was where it stopped. *I* had to figure out how to make it work.

What did I need to do?

Mallucé's teeth were in my neck, tearing. His stiffly gloved fists were eighty-mile-an-hour hardballs in my sides, trying to force me to uncurl so he could take the amulet back. The pain was rapidly becoming more than I could think past.

The Dark Hallow was useless.

If I'd had time to learn how to make it work for me, I'd have had a chance.

As it was, I'd managed to do just enough to really piss Mallucé off: I'd proven myself epic when he wasn't.

As he continued to pound me, I had a sudden insight into his character: At the core of it, beneath the monstrous villainy, the vampire was a self-indulgent, spoiled bully. Not a sociopath at all, but an out-of-control, petulant child that couldn't stand anyone else having better toys, more wealth, or greater power or, in my case, being more epic than him. If he couldn't own it, do it, or be it, he would destroy it.

My mind revisited the bodies he'd left at the Welshman's estate. The terrible ways they'd been killed.

No one was coming for me. I couldn't make the amulet work. Rotted though he may be, I was not and would never be a physical match for Mallucé. There was no way out for me. That was just the truth of it.

When all the control you have over your world gets stripped away, leaving you no choice but to die — the only difference how you do it: quickly or slowly — life distills to a bitter pill. The pain I was in made it easier to swallow.

I would not let him make me a quadriplegic.

I would not let him take my mind away from me. Some things are worse than death.

He was in a blind rage, more intense than I'd felt coming off him yet. He was on the brink of total loss of control. I braced myself to fuel it, to push him over the edge.

I remembered what Barrons had told me about John Johnstone, Jr.'s past. The mysterious "accidental" death of his parents, how rapidly he'd disassociated himself with everything they'd stood for and been. I remembered how Barrons had provoked Mallucé with references to his roots, and the vampire's instant, livid fury, his irrational hatred of his own name. "How long have you been insane, J.J.?" I gasped out, between blows. "Since before you killed your parents?"

"It's Mallucé, bitch! Lord Master, to you. And my father deserved to die. He called himself a humanitarian. He was squandering my inheritance. I told him to stop. He didn't."

Barrons had provoked Mallucé by calling him Junior. That was my name, bestowed upon me by Alina. I wouldn't pervert it by using it on him. "You're the one that deserves to die. Some people are just born wrong, *Johnny.*"

"Never call me that! You will NEVER call me that!" he screamed.

I'd nailed it, a name the vampire hated even worse than Junior. Was it his mother's special name for him? Had it been his father's belittlement? "*I'm* not the one that made you a monster. You came that way, Johnny." I was nearly out of my mind with pain. I couldn't feel one of my arms. My face and neck were dripping blood. "Johnny, Johnny, Johnny," I chanted. "Johnny, little Johnny. You'll never be anything but a —"

The next blow turned my cheekbone into a blossom of fire. I dropped to my knees. The amulet slipped from my hand.

"Johnny, Johnny," I said, at least I think I did. Kill me, I prayed. Kill me now.

His next blow smashed me into the rear wall of the grotto. Bones snapped in my legs. I sank mercifully into oblivion.

Seventeen

I don't know where dreams come from. Sometimes I wonder if they're genetic memories, or messages from something divine. Warnings perhaps. Maybe we *do* come with an instruction booklet but we're too dense to read it, because we've dismissed it as the irrational waste product of the "rational" mind. Sometimes I think all the answers we need are buried in our slumbering subconscious, in the dreaming. The booklet's right there, and every night when we lay our heads down on the pillow it flips open. The wise read it, heed it. The rest of us try as hard as we can upon awakening to forget any disturbing revelations we might have found there.

I used to have a recurring nightmare when I was a child. A dream of four distinct, subtly varied tastes. Two of them weren't entirely unpalatable. Two of them were so vile I would wake up choking on my own tongue.

I tasted one of the vile ones now.

It saturated my cheeks and tongue, made my lips draw back from my teeth, and I finally understood why I'd never been able to put a name to it. It wasn't the taste of a food or drink. It was the taste of an emotion: regret. Profound, exquisite sorrow that bubbles from the wellspring of the soul over the mistakes we've made, over the actions we should or shouldn't have taken, long after it's too late and nothing can be done or undone.

I was alive.

But that wasn't my regret.

Barrons was bending over me.

That wasn't my regret, either.

It was the look on his face that told me more frankly than a doctor's prognosis that I wasn't going to make it. I was alive, but not for long. My rescuer was here, my knight-errant had arrived to save the day, but I'd blown it.

It was too late for me.

I could have survived — if only I'd not given up hope.

I wept. I think. I couldn't feel my face much.

What was it he'd said to me, that night

we'd robbed Rocky O'Bannion? I'd listened. I'd even thought it had sounded terribly wise. I just hadn't understood it. *A sidhe-seer without hope, without an unshakable determination to survive, is a dead* sidhe-*seer. A* sidhe-*seer who believes herself outgunned, outmanned, may as well point that doubt straight at her temple, pull the trigger, and blow her own brains out with it. There are really only two positions one can take toward anything in life: hope or fear. Hope strengthens, fear kills.*

I got it now.

"Are you . . . r-real?" My mouth had been badly lacerated by my teeth. My tongue was thick with blood and regret. I knew what I was trying to say. I wasn't sure it was intelligible.

He nodded grimly.

"It was . . . Mallucé . . . not dead," I told him.

Nostrils flared, eyes narrowed, he hissed, "I know, I smell him in here, everywhere. This place reeks of him. Don't talk. Bloody hell, what did he do to you? What did you do? Did you piss him off on purpose?"

Barrons knew me too well. "He t-told me you . . . weren't . . . coming." I was cold, so cold. Other than that, there was oddly little pain. I wondered if that meant my spinal cord was damaged.

He glanced wildly about as if looking for something, and if he'd been any other man, I would have called his emotional state frantic. "And you *believed* him? No, don't answer that. I said don't talk. Just be still. Fuck. Mac. *Fuck.*"

He'd called me Mac. My face hurt too bad to smile, but I did inside. "B-Barrons?"

"I said don't talk," he snarled.

I put all my energy into getting this out. "D-Don't let me . . . die . . . down here." *Die . . . down here,* echoed weakly back at me. "Please. Take me . . . to the . . . sunshine." Bury me in a bikini, I thought. Lay me next to my sister.

"Fuck," he exploded again. "I need things!" He was standing, looking around the cavern again, with that frantic air. I wondered what things he thought he might find here. Splints wouldn't help this time. I tried to tell him that but nothing came out. I also tried to tell him I was sorry. That didn't come out either.

I must have blinked. His face was close to mine. His hand was in my hair. His breath was warm on my cheek. "There's nothing here that I can use, Mac," he said hollowly. "If we were somewhere else, if I had certain things, there are . . . spells I could do. But

368

you won't live long enough for me to get you there."

A long silence ensued, or he was speaking and I just wasn't hearing him. Time had no relevance. I was floating.

His face was over me again, a dark angel. Basque and Pict, he'd told me. Criminals and barbarians, I'd mocked. A beautiful face, for all that savagery. "You can't die, Mac." His voice was flat, implacable. "I won't let you."

"So . . . stop . . . me," I managed, although I wasn't sure the irony I meant carried through in my tone. My voice was weak, reedy. At least my sense of humor wasn't gone. And at least Mallucé hadn't gotten to turn me into a monster before I died. That was a silver lining. I hoped my dad would take good care of my mom. I hoped someone would take care of Dani. I'd wanted to get to know her better. Beneath all that bristle I'd sensed a kindred soul.

I hadn't avenged Alina. Now who would?

"This isn't what I wanted," Barrons was saying. "This isn't what I would have chosen. You must know that. It's important you know that."

I had no idea what he was talking about. There was a kernel of something gnawing at the back of my mind. Something I needed to think about. A choice to be made.

I felt his fingers on my eyelids. He eased them closed.

But I'm not dead yet, I wanted to tell him.

His hand was a warm pressure on my neck. My head lolled to the side.

D-Don't let me . . . die . . . down here, was echoing back at me again in my head. I was astonished by how weak and stupid I sounded. How helpless. All fluff and no steel. I was pathetic with a capital *P.*

I tasted the second vile taste in my mouth. It drew tight the insides of my cheeks, and saliva pooled in my mouth. I examined the taste, rolling it on my tongue like spoiled wine. This time I recognized the poison before I drank it: cowardice.

I was still making the same mistake. Giving up hope before the fight was over.

My fight wasn't over. I might not like my choices — in fact, I might despise my choices — but my fight wasn't over.

It gave me power in the black arts, Mallucé had said of eating Unseelie, *the strength of ten men, heightened my senses, healed mortal wounds as quickly as they were inflicted.*

I could pass on the black arts. I'd take the strength and heightened senses. I was especially interested in the healing mortal wounds part. I may have blown one chance to live tonight. I would not blow another. Barrons was here now. The cell was open. He could get to the Fae on the slab, feed it to me.

"Barrons." I forced my eyes open. They felt heavy, weighted by coins.

His face was in my neck and he was breathing hard. Was he grieving me? Already? Would he miss me? Had I, in some tiny way, come to matter to this enigmatic, hard, brilliant, obsessed man? I realized he'd come to matter to me. Good or evil, right or wrong, he mattered to me.

"Barrons," I said again, this time more strongly, infusing it with everything I had left which wasn't much, but enough to get his attention.

He raised his head. His face was all harsh planes and angles in the torchlight, his expression bleak. His dark eyes were windows on a bottomless abyss. "I'm sorry, Mac."

"Not your . . . fault," I managed to get out.

"My fault in more ways than you could possibly know, woman."

Woman, he'd called me. I'd grown up in his eyes. I wondered what he'd think of me soon.

"I'm sorry I didn't come for you. I shouldn't have let you walk home alone."

"L-Listen," I said. I would have clutched urgently at his sleeve, but I couldn't move either arm.

He bent nearer.

"Unseelie . . . slab?" I asked.

His brows drew together. He glanced over his shoulder, looked back at me. "It's there, if that's what you mean."

My voice was terrible when I said, "Bring . . . it . . . me."

He raised a brow and blinked. He glanced at the twitching Unseelie and I could see his mind working. "You — what — was Mallucé —" He broke off. "Exactly what are you saying, Mac? Are you telling me you want to *eat* that?"

I was beyond speaking. I parted my lips.

"Bloody hell, have you thought this through? Do you have any idea what it might do to you?"

I strove for one of our wordless conversations. I said, *Pretty good one. Like make me live.*

"I meant the downside. There's always a downside."

I told him a bigger one would be being dead.

"There are worse things than death."

This isn't one. I know what I'm doing.

"Even *I* don't know what you're doing, and I know everything," he snapped.

I would have laughed if I'd been capable of it. His arrogance knew no bounds.

"It's dark Fae, Mac. You're planning to eat Unseelie. Do you get that?"

I'm dying, Barrons.

"I don't like this idea."

Got a better one?

He inhaled sharply. I didn't understand the things that flashed across his face then — thoughts too complex, beyond my grasp — thoughts he discarded. But he hesitated a few seconds too long, before jerking his head in a single, violent negation, and I knew that he'd had some other idea, and had deemed it worse than this one. "No better ideas."

There was a knife in his hand. He gave me a tight, mocking smile as he moved to the slab. "Wing or a thigh? Ah, I'm afraid we don't have any thighs left." He sliced into the Fae.

They didn't have wings either, but I appreciated the humor, black as it was. He was trying to lessen the terrible reality of my impending meal.

I didn't want to know what parts of it I was eating so I closed my eyes when he raised the first slice of Unseelie flesh to my lips. I couldn't look at it. It was bad enough that it crunched in places and continued to move the entire time I chewed it. And the entire time I swallowed it. The tiny pieces fluttered in my stomach.

Unseelie flesh tasted worse than all four of my nightmare tastes combined. I guess our instruction booklets only cover this world, not Faery, which is fine with me. I'd hate to have to dream all the bad tastes of their world, too.

I chewed and gagged, gagged and swallowed.

MacKayla Lane, bartender and glam-girl, was screaming at me to stop, before it was too late. Before we could never again go back to being the uncomplicated, happy young southern girl we'd been. She didn't get that it was already way too late for that.

Savage Mac was squatting in the dirt, stabbing her spear into the ground, nodding and saying, *Yesss, finally, some real power! Bring it on!*

Me — the one who tries to mediate between the two — wondered what price I was going to pay for this. Were Barrons' concerns founded? Would eating dark Fae do something terrible to me, make me dark, too? Or do you only turn dark if you have the seeds of darkness in you to begin with? Perhaps eating it a single time wouldn't change me at all. Mallucé had eaten it constantly. Perhaps frequency was the killer. There were many drugs a person could do a few times without paying too high a price. Perhaps the living flesh of a dark Fae would heal me, make me strong, and do little else of consequence.

Perhaps it didn't matter, because the bottom line was that I'd made the mistake today — or tonight, or whatever it was — of giving up hope too soon, and I wasn't about to make it again. I would fight to live with whatever means I had at my disposal, and pay whatever price I had to pay without complaining. I would never again accept death. I would battle it until the last second, no matter the horrors confronting me. I was ashamed of myself for giving up hope.

You can't go forward if you're looking backward, Mac, Daddy always said. *You run into walls that way.*

I dropped my regrets, a burdensome piece of baggage. Looking forward, I opened my mouth.

He sliced off another piece of flesh and fed it to me, and another. I chewed more strongly, swallowed more vigorously. A chilling heat suffused me and I trembled, as if in the grip of a brutal fever. After several more pieces, I felt my body begin the painful process of knitting itself back together. It was not pleasant. I cried out. Barrons covered my mouth with his hand, wrapped his arms around me, and crushed me against him while I thrashed and moaned. I guessed his efforts to keep me quiet meant Mallucé was somewhere nearby, or some of his minions were.

When the worst of it had passed, I ate more, and endured the brutal cycle again and again. Against his hot skin, I healed. Bracketed by his arms, I shuddered and writhed, and grew back together. The lacerations on the inside of my mouth faded into smooth, unbroken skin. Bones straightened and fused, tendons and torn flesh knitted itself, contusions melted. It was an agony. It was a miracle. I could feel the living Unseelie flesh doing things to me. I could feel it changing my innate structure, affecting it on a cellular level, infusing me with something ancient and powerful. Healing every ill, taking it farther, past perfect mortal health, into the realm of the extraordinary.

A slow, sweet rush of euphoria began to build inside me. My body was young, stronger than it had ever been, stronger than anything could be!

I stretched, gingerly at first, then with growing elation. There was no pain left in my body. As I moved, my muscles bunched with coiled power. My heart thundered, flooding my brain with potent, Fae-spiked blood.

I sat up. *I sat up!* I'd been on the brink of death and now I was whole again! Better than whole. Wonderingly, I ran my hands over my face and body.

Barrons sat up with me. He was staring at me as if waiting for me to suddenly sprout a second, monstrous head. His nostrils flared; he ducked his face to my skin and inhaled. "You smell different," he said roughly.

"I *feel* different. But I'm fine," I assured him. "In fact, I feel amazing!" I laughed. "I feel fantastic. I feel better than I've ever felt in my life. This is *incredible!*"

I stood, stretched out my arm, and flexed my hand. I fisted it and punched the stone wall. I hardly even felt it. I punched it again, hard. The skin on my knuckles tore — and healed instantly. Blood scarcely had the time to well before it was gone. "Did you see that?" I exclaimed. "I'm strong. I'm like you and Mallucé, I can kick ass now!"

His expression was grim as he rose and moved away. He worried too much. I told him so.

"You don't worry enough," he retorted.

It was hard to worry when I'd just been knocking on Death's door and now felt like I was going to live forever. I'd been jerked between the two, a badly weighted pendulum, jarringly fast. I'd ricocheted from the depths of despair to euphoria, from pulverized to stronger than ever before, from terrorized to the one capable of terrorizing. Who could hurt me now? No one!

I finally felt like being a *sidhe*-seer had some perks. Better than Dani's astounding speed, I had superhuman strength. I couldn't wait to test myself, discover what I could do. I was giddy with fearlessness. I was drunk on power, on how good it was to be me!

I danced on light boxer's feet over to Barrons. "Punch me."

"Don't be absurd."

"Come on, punch me, Barrons."

"I'm not punching you."

"I said, punch — *Ow!*" He'd decked me. Bones vibrating, my head snapped back. And forward again. I shook it. No pain. I laughed. "I'm amazing! Look at me! I hardly even felt it." I danced from foot to foot, feinting punches at him. "Come on. Punch me again." My blood felt electrified, my body impervious to all injury.

Barrons was shaking his head.

I punched him in the jaw and his head snapped back.

When it came back down his expression said *I suffer you to live.* "Happy now?"

"Did it hurt?"

"No."

"Can I try again?"

"Buy yourself a punching bag."

"Fight me, Barrons. I need to know how strong I am."

He rubbed his jaw. "You're strong," he said dryly.

I laughed, delighted. This southern belle was a force to be reckoned with! It was amazing. I had power. I was a player. Once I had my spear again, I'd be even better. The playing field against evil had just been leveled.

Speaking of leveling, I wanted Mallucé. Dead. Now. The bastard had shattered my will to live. He was a living, breathing reminder of my shame.

"Did you happen to see Mallucé on the way in? Speaking of the way in, how did you find me? He lied about the cuff, didn't he?"

"I didn't see him, but I was more concerned with finding you. The cave system beneath the Burren is vast. I'll lead you out." He glanced at his watch. "With luck, we'll be out of here in an hour."

"After we kill Mallucé."

"I'll come back and take care of Mallucé."

"I don't think so," I said icily. I shot him a look that dared him to argue. I was pumped up, flying on adrenaline. There was no way I was letting someone else fight this battle for me. It was mine. I'd paid for it in blood.

"Give a woman a little power," he said dryly.

"He broke me, Barrons." My voice shook.

"Anyone worth knowing breaks once. Once. No shame, no foul, if you survive it. You did."

"Did you break once?" Who, what could have broken Jericho Barrons?

He stared at me through the dimly lit cavern. The torchlight flickered across his dark face, hollowing out his cheeks, making flame-filled coals of his eyes. "Yes," he said finally.

Later I would ask how, who. Now all I wanted to know was "Did you kill the bastard?"

I wasn't sure that twist of his mouth was a smile, but I didn't know what else to call it. "With my bare hands. After I killed his wife." He waved his hand at the door of the cell. "You lead, Ms. Lane. I've got your back."

I was "Ms. Lane" again. Apparently I was only Mac when gravely injured or dying. We'd talk about that later, too.

"He's mine, Barrons. Don't interfere."

"Unless you can't handle him."

"I'll handle him," I vowed.

The cave system *was* vast. I wondered how Barrons had ever found me. Carrying torches we'd lifted from the wall, we ascended and descended through tunnels and caverns without apparent rhyme or reason. I'd seen pictures of the tourist parts of the Burren. They were nothing like these parts. We were much deeper beneath the ground and way off the beaten path, in the unexplored parts of the labyrinthine cave system. I imagined that if any foolhardy potholers ever found their way here, Mallucé simply removed the problem by eating them.

I never would have found my way out.

Although I was barefoot, either the rocks weren't cutting my feet, or they were healing as quickly as they were being damaged. Under normal circumstances I found both darkness and confined spaces highly disturbing, but the Unseelie I'd eaten had done something to me. I felt no fear. It was exhilarating. My senses were extraordinary. I could see in the dim, flickering torchlight as well as daylight. I could hear creatures burrowing in the earth. I smelled more scents than I could identify.

Mallucé had moved in. He'd brought many of the Victorian furnishings I'd seen at his house into the caves. In a chamber he'd converted into a sumptuous Goth boudoir, I found my brush on a table, near a bed covered by a stained satin spread. Next to the brush was a black candle, a few of my hairs, and three small vials.

Barrons opened a vial, sniffed. "He was spying on you, projecting himself. Did you ever feel you were being watched?"

I told him about the specter. I shoved the brush in my back pocket. I hated touching what he'd touched but I was leaving no part of me here, beneath the earth, in his hellish domain.

"And you never told me this?" he exploded. "How many times did you see it?"

"I threw a flashlight through it. I thought it wasn't real."

"How can I keep you alive if you don't tell me everything?" he snapped.

"How can you expect me to tell you everything when you never tell me anything? I don't know the first thing about you!"

"I'm the one that keeps saving your life. Doesn't that tell you something?"

"Yes, but why? Because you need me. Because you want to *use* me."

"For what other reason would you have me save you? Because I *like* you? Better to be useful than liked. Like is an emotion. Emotions" — he raised a hand, made a fist, clenched it tightly — "are like holding water. You open your hand, there's nothing there. Better to be a weapon than a woman."

Right now I was both. And I wanted Mallucé. "You can chew my petunia later. I've got an earful for you, too."

We found the spear in a velvet-lined box, near his laptop. I wondered how a laptop could possibly be working down here, until I realized all the lights on it were that strange blue-black shade of cold light the amulet had given off. Mallucé was powering it with black magic.

"Wait." Barrons punched in a few commands, brought up the screen. A page of text was visible for a split second before icy sparks erupted from the computer and it went dead.

"Did you catch any of that?"

"He had multiple bidders on the spear. I saw two of the names." He glanced at his watch again. "Get the spear and let's move."

I reached for the spear, nestled in velvet, and was just about to remove it from the box when I drew up short, struck by a sudden terrible thought.

I snapped the lid shut. When I picked up the box and tucked it beneath my arm, Barrons gave me a strange look. I shrugged and we moved on.

We left the boudoir, and entered another cavern, crammed with books and boxes and jars with contents that defied description. From the look of things, Mallucé had been dabbling in black magic since long before he'd met the Lord Master. There were boyhood treasures scattered among the vampire's collection of potions, powders, and brews. I could almost see the young British child, invisible in the shadow of his prominent, powerful father, hating it. Rebelling. Becoming fascinated with the Goth world, so different from his. Studying black magic. Planning his parents' murder at twenty-four. Mallucé had been a monster long before he'd rechristened himself.

The storage cavern opened into a long, wide tunnel lit by torches. There was a steel door in the wall. It was locked. Neither Barrons nor I could kick it in. He placed both palms against it. After a long moment, he said, "Ah," and muttered a swift string of unintelligible words. The door swung open, revealing a long, narrow cave that looked to be a quarter of a mile long. It contained cell after cell of Unseelie. Here was Mallucé's personal larder. I wondered how he'd trapped them all.

Suddenly I sensed him, a maelstrom of decay and fury, gusting down the tunnels toward us.

"He's coming this way," I told Barrons. "I think he needs food. He said he has to eat constantly."

Barrons gave me a sharp look.

I knew exactly what he was thinking. "Not because it's addictive," I defended, "but because parts of him had turned Fae from eating Unseelie and the spear poisoned those parts."

Barrons stared at me. "Parts of him had turned Fae? And the spear poisoned him? And you knew this before you ate Unseelie?"

"Bear in mind the alternative, Barrons."

"*That's* why you left the spear in the box and tucked it beneath your arm. You're afraid to carry it now, aren't you?"

"Before, I had a weapon. Now I *am* a weapon." I turned and stalked from the cavern, not about to reveal how deeply it disturbed me that I might have gained the power of a Fae — and the weakness of one. I never wanted to touch the spear again. If I accidentally pricked myself, would I, too, begin to rot? What had I become? Kin to my enemy in how many ways? "He's on the way," I tossed over my shoulder. "I'd rather he didn't eat again."

Barrons stepped through behind me and closed the door. He slipped a vial from his pocket and I realized he'd been pilfering some of the vampire's things. He splashed a few drops on the door and spoke again in that language I didn't understand. He glanced around, and I could tell he didn't like what he saw. "A good soldier chooses the terrain of his battle. You've shared the same flesh with him. If you can sense him, I'll bet he can sense you. He'll follow."

"What are we looking for?"

"A place with no way out. I want this over with fast."

The cavern we chose was small, narrow, and spiked with stalactites and stalagmites. There was a single entrance that Barrons planned to bar once Mallucé had entered. I handed him the box with the spear. He gestured for me to conceal it behind a fall of rubble. There was no way I was giving Mallucé the opportunity to use the weapon against me. Besides, I'd already established that it only killed parts of him, and parts weren't enough. I wanted *all* of him dead.

"How do I kill a vampire?" I asked Barrons.

"Hope he's not."

"I really don't like that answer."

He shrugged. "It's the only one I have to offer, Ms. Lane."

I could feel Mallucé approaching. Barrons was right, somehow the meal we'd shared had linked us. I had no doubt he could sense me as clearly as I could him.

The vampire was incensed . . . and hungry. He'd been unable to enter his larder. Whatever Barrons had done had successfully sealed the entrance. I told you my inscrutable host has a bottomless bag of tricks. I'm really beginning to wonder where he gets them.

He was near. My body hummed with anticipation.

Mallucé stepped into the opening. His hood was down and his smile was beyond gruesome. "You're still no match for me, bitch."

He was framed in the doorway, backlit by torchlight, his dark robes rustling, and I could smell the emotions wafting from his rotted flesh. He smelled as fearless as I felt.

He believed what he'd just said. I would prove him wrong. I narrowed my eyes, assessing him. He might think himself my superior, but my escape bothered him and he wasn't going to step into the cavern until he knew how I'd managed it.

I taunted, "Come and get me then."

"How did you get out of your cell?"

"You left it unlocked," I lied.

He considered that a moment. "There's no way you could have moved. I broke both your legs. And your arms. How did you get the Unseelie?"

"The same way I spelled your little 'refrigerator' down there. I did a good job, didn't I? You couldn't get in. I know a little black magic of my own. You underestimated me."

He studied me. He knew how powerful the spell on his larder was, and if I was capable of performing black magic to that degree, I was capable of a great deal. I felt him relax infinitesimally. "This makes things much more interesting. You know, I toyed with this idea. Now we'll rot together. I'll feed you more and stab you with your own fucking spear."

Obviously he didn't know it was missing yet. "Bring it on," I purred.

He unfastened his robe and let it drop to

the floor. His frothy lace shirt was badly stained. He was wearing stiff, tight leather pants, I suspected for the same reason he wore the stiff gloves. I needed him inside the cavern. Then Barrons would spell the exit and there would be no way out.

I did my boxer dance. "Come on, Johnny, let's play."

He lunged through the entrance with inhuman speed, and closed one of his stiff-gloved hands around my throat. I saw Barrons loom up behind him and shot him a wordless command: *Don't interfere.*

I grabbed Mallucé's wrist and kneed him in the groin with the strength of ten men. The flesh between his legs was too soft. My knee slid a few inches into his body.

"No feeling there, bitch," he spat.

"What about here?" I punched him in the ear with all my strength. Blood spurted from his skull, and he reeled sideways and staggered. I watched the wound heal as quickly as it had opened. Would I do that?

I found out soon enough. He broke my nose. It reassembled itself. I nearly tore his arm from his shoulder. It dangled uselessly for a few moments then he punched me with it again, strong as ever.

"When I finish with you, bitch, I'm going to Ashford. Remember your little confession?" he taunted. "Telling me you had a mother there? Maybe I'll keep you alive long enough to see what I do to her."

I pummeled his hated face into a mass of bloody flesh. It would end here, now. Mallucé was never walking out of these caves again if I had to stay down here for all eternity killing him. He tried to rip my ear off. I almost bit him but thought twice, not exactly clear on vampire rules. I didn't want his blood anywhere near my mouth. I kicked him in the knee. When it shattered and he went down I fell on him, kicking, punching, snarling.

I felt something inside me de-evolving, and I liked it.

Time lost all meaning to me. We were virtually indestructible machines. We beat each other senseless, long past the point of reason. I existed for one thing: to make him go down, stay down, and never move again. I no longer knew who he was. I no longer cared who I was. Things had deconstructed to the basest terms. Mallucé no longer even had a name or a face. He was Enemy. I was Destroyer. I understood only the imperative of battle, the appetite to kill.

I slammed him into the cavern wall. He smashed me into a man-sized stalagmite. It crumbled from the impact. I picked myself up and we crashed together again, punching, kicking, grunting.

Suddenly Barrons was between us, forcing us apart.

I turned on him, snarling, "What the hell are you doing?"

"You!" Mallucé looked stunned. "How did *you* get here? I left the cuff in the alley! There's no way you tracked me!"

I stared at Barrons. How *had* he found me? "Stay out of this, Barrons! It's my fight."

Barrons caught me completely off guard with half a dozen rapid-fire punishing blows to my head and stomach.

I doubled over, dazed.

Mallucé laughed.

I was bent low, ribs cracking and rehealing for several seconds. My chest burned like a lung had been pierced.

Mallucé stopped laughing, with a strangled sound.

When I shot up, Barrons had Mallucé by an arm around his neck. He hit me again and I went right back down. Barrons had held back when he'd punched me before. Given me a love tap compared to what he was dishing out now.

The bastard did it to me three more times; each time I straightened, his fist pistoned into my face before I could even get all the way up. It felt like my brain was rattling in my skull.

The fifth time I rose, Mallucé was on the ground, unmoving. I could see why. His head was no longer attached to his shoulders. He'd killed him! Barrons had stolen my revenge, cheated me of the pleasure of destroying the one who'd nearly destroyed me!

I whirled on him. He was spattered with blood, breathing hard, head down, eyes narrowed, and fury was rolling off him in thick, dangerous waves. How dare he be furious with me? I was the wronged party! My battle was interrupted, bloodlust was bottled up inside me, a turbo engine revved to redline.

"The vamp was *mine*, Barrons!"

"Inspect his teeth, Ms. Lane," he said tightly. "They were cosmetic enhancements. He was no vampire."

I punched him lightly in the shoulder. "I don't care what he was! It was my fight, you bastard!"

He punched me back with the same light, warning force. "You were taking too long to finish it up."

"Who are *you* to decide how long is too

long?" I gave him another tap in the shoulder.

He returned the blow with equal force. "You were enjoying it!"

"I was not!"

"You were smiling, bouncing on the balls of your feet, egging him on."

"I was trying to end the fight!" I punched his shoulder, hard this time.

"You were way past trying to end it," he snapped, punching me back. I nearly fell over. "You were prolonging it. You were glorying in it."

"You don't know what the feck you're talking about!" I shouted.

"I couldn't tell the difference between the two of you anymore!" he roared.

I smashed my fist into his face. Lies roll off us. It's the truths we work hardest to silence. "Then you weren't looking hard enough! I'm the one with boobs!"

"I know you're the one with boobs! They're in my fucking face every fucking time I turn around!"

"Maybe you need to get a grip on your libido, Barrons!"

"Fuck you, Ms. Lane!"

"You just try. I'll kick the shit out of you!"

"You think you could?"

"Bring it on."

He grabbed a fistful of my T-shirt, and dragged me up against him until our noses touched. "I'll bring it on, Ms. Lane. But remember you asked for it. So don't even think about trying to tap out on the mat and quit the fight."

"You hear anybody crying 'Uncle' here, Barrons? I don't."

"Fine."

"Fine."

He swapped the fistful of my shirt for one in my hair, and ground his mouth against mine.

I exploded.

I shoved at him, and clawed him closer. He shoved me back, and yanked me tighter to his body. I pulled his hair. He pulled mine. He didn't fight fair. Actually, he fought exactly fair. He didn't extend courtesies, not a single one.

I bit his lip. He tripped me and pushed me down to the stone floor of the cavern. I punched him. He straddled me.

I ripped his shirt down the front, left it hanging in tatters from his shoulders.

"I liked that shirt," he snarled. He rose over me, a dark demon, glistening in the torchlight, dripping sweat and blood, his torso covered with tattoos that disappeared beneath his waistband.

He grabbed the hem of my shirt, tore it straight up to my neck, and inhaled sharply.

I punched him. If he punched me back, I was past feeling it. His mouth was on mine again, the hot silk of his tongue, the sharp, deliberate abrasion of his teeth, the exchange of breath and the small, desperate sounds of need. A tsunami of lust — no doubt amplified by the Fae in my blood — crashed into me, knocking me from my feet, and dragging me out to a dangerous sea. There was no lifeboat here in these deep, killing waters, not even a lighthouse, marking the way back to shore with its soft amber promise. There was only the storm of Barrons and the one I seemed to be, and if there were dark shapes moving in the waters beneath my feet that I should probably take a good hard look at and possibly reconsider trying to swim here, I didn't care.

He fitted himself to me and began a driving, erotic, rhythmic bump and grind. *A lonely boy. A lone man. Alone in a desert beneath a blood-red moon. War everywhere. Always war. A breath-stealing sirocco sweeping down over treacherously sifting sands. A cave in a cliff wall. Sanctuary? No sanctuary left anywhere.* Barrons' tongue was inside my mouth, and somehow I was inside Jericho Barrons. The images were his.

We both heard the noise at the same time and exploded away from each other as quickly as we'd come together, scrambling to opposite sides of the small cavern.

Panting, I stared at him. He was breathing hard, his dark eyes narrowed to slits.

Is it still spelled? I mouthed, meaning the entrance to the cave.

To contain only. Not to expel.

Well, spell it again!

Isn't that easy.

He melted into the shadows behind a stalagmite.

I focused my attention on the door, tried to sense what was coming, and stiffened.

Fae . . . but not Fae. Followed by at least ten Unseelie.

I stared past Mallucé's body at the entrance, tensed to spring. A glint of gold and silver caught my eye in the flickering torchlight.

The amulet! How could I have forgotten? It was pooled in a pile of chain, between his body and the door. It must have fallen off when Barrons had beheaded him.

The footsteps drew nearer.

I sprang for the Hallow.

A booted foot came down on it just as I reached it.

I stared up the leg and looked straight into the eyes of my sister's murderer.

EIGHTEEN

The Lord Master's gaze flicked away from me, passed with cursory interest over Mallucé. "I'd come to finish him myself," he said. "He'd become a liability. You saved me the trouble. How did you do it?" He studied me, the blood splattered on my face, clothing, and hands, the glaring lack of injuries. A slow smile spread over his exotic, beautiful face. "You ate Unseelie, didn't you?"

I said nothing. I guess something in my eyes did, though. Framed behind him in the doorway were a dozen or so Unseelie of a caste I'd not seen before, wearing black uniforms with red insignia, clearly his personal guard.

He laughed. "What a surprise you are. Lovely like your sister, but Alina would never have done it."

My sister's name on her murderer's lips incensed me. "Don't even say her name. Nothing about her is yours. Nothing about her ever was." If Barrons took this fight from me, I'd kill him.

But I wasn't going to get this fight. Not here. Not tonight.

The Lord Master's voice deepened, hardened, rolled with the thunder of a legion of voices. It did something inside my head; echoed, whispered, rearranged things. "Hand me the amulet. Now."

I picked it up and handed it to him, wondering even as I did it what I was doing, why I was obeying. It glowed a faint blue-black invitation the moment I touched it. His eyes widened fractionally. He took it from me swiftly.

"Another surprise," he murmured.

That's right, you bastard, I *am* epic, so watch out, I wanted to say, but my vocal cords weren't under my control any more than anything else was at the moment.

"Stand," he commanded. The amulet blazed in his hand, eclipsing the feeble light I'd managed to make and been so proud of.

I stood as jerkily as a puppet on strings, mind resisting, flesh obeying. I swayed before the red-robed Lord Master, stared into his too-beautiful-to-be-human face, and waited for him to rule me. Had he done this to my sister? Had she been not duped by him, but stripped of choice like I was now?

"Come." He turned and, automaton-like, I began to follow.

Barrons exploded from the shadows and hit me like a missile, taking me to the ground beneath him.

The Lord Master turned in a whirl of robes.

"She stays with me," said Barrons. His voice, too, rolled with the thunder of a multitude, reverberating inside my skull. Of course I was staying with him. What had I been thinking?

What the Lord Master did next was so incomprehensible to me that I was still blinking blankly at the opening, several minutes after he was gone.

He took a long look at my enigmatic mentor, jerked his head at his guard — and left.

NINETEEN

We raced back to Dublin in the sleek, stolen stealth of Rocky O'Bannion's black Maybach.

I made no attempt at conversation, nor did Barrons.

I'd been through too much in the past, however many hours it had been. Twenty-seven, I would learn later. I'd faced a Hunter, discovered my specter was not only real but a greater threat than the Unseelie chasing me; been locked in a cave, tortured, beaten to the brink of death, rescued; eaten the living flesh of an Unseelie, gained superhuman strength and power and lost God only knew what, battled a vampire, gotten into a fight with Barrons that had skewed dangerously toward the end, lost a powerful Dark Hallow to my sister's murderer, and worse, been unable to function with any will at all in his presence, and if Barrons hadn't been there to save me yet again, I would have trundled off behind my archenemy, ensorcelled by the crimson-cowled Pied Piper.

Then when I'd thought nothing else could possibly startle or surprise me, the Lord Master had taken one look at Barrons — and walked away.

That worried me. A lot. If the Lord Master walked away from Barrons, how much danger was I in on a daily basis? I'd been feeling invincible up until those last few moments in the cave. Until one man in the room with me had stripped away my will with mere words, and the other man in the room with me had apparently intimidated that one into leaving. Bad and badder.

I glanced across the front seat at Badder. I opened my mouth. He looked at me. I closed it.

I don't know how he continued driving, because we stared at each other for a long time. The night whizzed by, the air inside the speeding car pregnant with all the things we weren't saying. We didn't even have one of our wordless conversations this time; neither of us was willing to betray a single thought or feeling.

We looked at each other like two too-intimate strangers who've woken after the lovemaking and don't know quite what to say to each other, so they say nothing at all and go their separate ways, promising, of course, that they'll call, but each time they look at the phone over the next few days, the discomfort and mild embarrassment of having taken off their clothing in front of someone they didn't really even know rises up, and the phone call never gets made.

Barrons and I had taken our *skins* off around each other tonight. Shared too many secrets, and none of them the important ones.

I was about to look away when he reached across the seat, touched my jaw with his long, strong, beautiful fingers, and caressed my face.

Being touched by Jericho Barrons with kindness makes you feel like you must be the most special person in the world. It's like walking up to the biggest, most savage lion in the jungle, lying down, placing your head it its mouth and, rather than taking your life, it licks you and purrs.

I turned away.

He returned his attention to the road.

We completed the drive in the same strained silence it had begun.

"Hold this," said Barrons, as he turned to lock the door on the garage. He had an alarm system on it now, and punched some numbers in on the keypad.

It was nearly dawn. I could see the Shades out of the corner of my eye, down at the edge of the Dark Zone, moving as restlessly and desperately as flies stuck on flypaper.

I accepted the delicate glass ball. Eggshell thin and fragile, it was an impossible color, the ever-changing hues of V'lane's robes on the beach that day in Faery. I handled it carefully, aware of my heightened strength. I'd bent the door of the Maybach when I'd shut it too hard. Barrons was still pissed about it. Nobody likes a door-slammer, he'd growled.

"What is it?" I asked.

"The D'Jai Orb. A relic from one of the Seelie Royal Houses."

"Can't be. It's not an OOP," I told him.

He looked at me. "Yes, it is."

"No, it's not," I said. "I know these things, remember?"

"Yes," he repeated carefully, "it is."

"No, it's not."

For a moment I thought we were going to get into a "is to/is not" squabble. We glared at each other, resolute in our opinions.

Then his eyes widened as if with a startling thought. "Remove the spear from the box, Ms. Lane," he snapped.

"I hardly see the point, and I'd really rather not." I never wanted to touch it again. I was excruciatingly aware of the Unseelie flesh inside me, and that I had no idea how profoundly eating it had changed me, and until I understood what my new limits were, I meant to studiously avoid anything capable of damaging a Fae.

"Then just open it," he gritted.

I could do that, although I still didn't see the point. I slipped it from beneath my arm and lifted the lid. I looked at the spear. It took a moment to sink in.

I couldn't sense it.

At all.

In fact, I realized, I hadn't sensed it back in Mallucé's boudoir. I'd merely *seen* it, lying there in the box.

I focused on it, hard. I wasn't getting the faintest tingle. My *sidhe*-seer sense was dead. Not numb. Not tired. Gone. Stricken, I cried, "What's wrong with me?"

"You ate Fae. Do the math."

I closed my eyes. "A Fae can't sense Fae OOPs."

"Precisely. And do you know what that means? That means, Ms. Lane, that you can no longer find the *Sinsar Dubh*. Bloody hell." He turned sharply on his heel and stalked into the bookstore.

"Bloody hell," I echoed. It also meant that Barrons no longer had any use for me. Nor did V'lane. For all my superhuman abilities, I suddenly wasn't so special at all.

There's always a downside, he'd warned.

This was one hell of a downside.

I'd lost everything I was to become part Fae with a fatal weakness.

I stayed in bed all day Sunday, slept for most of it. The horrors I'd endured had drained me. It seemed my rapid, preternatural healing had taken a toll as well. The human body wasn't meant to nearly die and regenerate. I couldn't begin to comprehend what had happened to me on a cellular level. Despite my exhaustion, the Fae inside me kept me feeling on edge, aggressive, like I was bristling with tiny soldiers inside my skin.

Fitfully, I dozed, I dreamed. They were nightmares. I was in a cold place from which there was no escape. Towering walls of ice surrounded me, hemmed me in. Creatures had carved out caverns in the stark, sheer cliffs above me, and were watching me. Somewhere there was a castle, a monstrous fortress of black ice. I could feel it drawing me, knew if I found it and entered those forbidding doors I would never be the same again.

I woke up shivering, stood under a scalding shower until the hot water ran out. Bundled in blankets, I set up my laptop and tried to answer e-mails from my friends, but I couldn't relate to anything they'd written about. Parties and Jell-O shots, and who was sleeping with who, and he-said/she-said just didn't compute in my brain right now.

I slept. I dreamed again of the cold place. I repeated the scalding shower to thaw myself. I glanced at the clock. It was Monday, nine a.m. I could stay in bed all day and hide or I could lose myself in the solace of routine.

I opted for routine. Sometimes it's dangerous to stop and think. Sometimes you just have to keep going.

I forced myself to groom. Exfoliated, masked, and shaved. I nicked my knee in the shower and smeared it with toothpaste when I got out, a trick Alina had taught me when I'd first begun shaving and butchered my ankles more than a few times. As the blood welled in the pale blue gel, tears threatened. At that moment, if I'd had the ability to slip into Faery and spend time with her again, I might have been too weak.

Blood welled in the pale blue gel.

I stared at it.

I was bleeding. I wasn't healing. Why? I scraped the toothpaste off my wound. It bled freely, pooling in the trickles of water on my still-wet leg.

Frowning, I made a fist and punched the doorjamb. "Ow!"

Stunned, disbelieving, I punched it again. It hurt again, and my abraded knuckles began to bleed, too.

My superhuman strength was gone! And I was not regenerating!

My thoughts whirled. Mallucé had talked as if he'd eaten Unseelie constantly, even before I'd stabbed him. I'd assumed it was because it was somehow addictive.

Now I knew how: If you didn't keep eating it, you reverted to your natural human state. Of course, Mallucé hadn't been willing to let that happen.

I stared in the mirror, watching myself bleed. It made me think of another time I'd stood in front of this mirror, examining myself. Of crimson I'd glimpsed on myself once before.

It's hard to say what causes things to come together in a startling flash of clarity but images suddenly bombarded me —

Splint dropping from my arm, smudges of crimson and black ink on my skin; tattoos on Barrons' torso, Mallucé screaming that he'd left the cuff in the alley, demanding to know how Barrons had tracked us; me chained to a beam in the garage, tattooing implements nearby —

— and I had a small epiphany.

"You bastard," I breathed. "It was all a ruse, wasn't it? Because you were afraid I'd find out that you'd *already done it*." Games within games, true Barrons form.

I began examining every inch of my skin in the mirror. *I'd planned to hide it,* he'd said.

I poked, I prodded. I looked beneath my breasts. I checked between the cheeks of my behind with a hand mirror and heaved a huge sigh of relief. I looked in my ears. I checked behind my ears.

I found it on the nape of my neck, high up in the slight indentation of my skull, nearly invisible beneath my hair.

It was an intricate pattern of black and red ink with a faintly luminescent *Z* in the middle, a mystical bar code, a sorcerous brand.

He must have done it the night he brought me out of the Dark Zone, the night he'd splinted and healed me. The night he'd told me to sleep and kissed me. I'd been unconscious for a long time.

Then something must have made him begin to worry that I'd find it. Worry that if

I did, it might push me too far. He was right, it would have. So when I'd returned from Faery, he'd seized the perfect opportunity to insist on tattooing me *for my own good.* No doubt he would have just touched up the old one, perhaps added something nefarious to it.

When I'd made it plain that if he trespassed against my boundaries so egregiously I'd leave, he must have been in a double bind. Unwilling to push, because I'd leave — knowing if I found out what he'd already done, I'd leave.

He'd branded me without my knowledge and consent, like a piece of property. *His* property. There was a fecking *Z* on the back of my skull.

I traced the pads of my fingers over the tattoo. It was warmer than the skin around it. I remembered lying in the hellish grotto, regretting with every ounce of my being that I hadn't let him tattoo me.

If he hadn't tattooed me, I'd be dead now.

Ironically, the very thing I'd been determined to leave him over if he'd done it to me was the only thing that had kept me alive.

I stared at myself in the mirror, wishing that anything in my life were one-tenth as clear as my reflection.

Rowena was wrong. She was so wrong. There are only shades of gray. Black and white are nothing more than lofty ideals in our minds, the standards by which we try to judge things, and map out our place in the world in relevance to them. Good and evil, in their purest form, are as intangible and forever beyond our ability to hold in our hand as any Fae illusion. We can only aim at them, aspire to them, and hope not to get so lost in the shadows that we can no longer aim for the light.

Power is. If you don't use it, someone else will. You can either create with it or destroy. Creation is good. Destruction is evil. That's my bottom line.

I could sense the spear behind me, quietly chafing my *sidhe*-seer senses.

I could sense OOPs again. I had only normal human strength and healing abilities again. I was me. One hundred percent MacKayla Lane, for better or for worse.

I was back — and I was *glad.* I hoped the dark flesh had passed through me and left no mark.

Life is not black and white. The closest we ever get to either of those colors is wearing them.

I got dressed, went downstairs, and opened my store for business.

■ ■ ■ ■

It was a busy day. A little rainy but not too bad.

I found the cell phone Mallucé had dumped in the alley when he'd abducted me lying on the counter next to the cash register, beside my boots, jacket, and purse; Barrons must have gone searching for me and found them. It had two bars so I plugged it in to recharge it; I don't take my cell phone responsibilities lightly anymore. I will forever be haunted by the reminder of one floating in a sky blue swimming pool, and the spoiled young woman I used to be.

I threw the boots and jacket in the Dumpster out back, along with everything else I'd been wearing during my interment beneath the Burren. Mallucé had touched them; they stank of him and I would never wear them again.

The cuff was not on the counter.

I smiled faintly. Barrons knew I'd figured out from Mallucé's little slip that he'd had some other way to find me. Good. He didn't underestimate me. He shouldn't.

I'd had nearly sixty customers by four o'clock.

I was about to flip the sign for a bathroom

break when I sensed someone, or something, outside my front door.

Fae — but not Fae!

I stiffened.

The cherry-framed, diamond-paned door moved, the bell above it tinkled.

Derek O'Bannion stepped in, dripping aggression and arrogance. I wondered how I'd ever found him attractive. He wasn't darkly handsome; he was swarthy. His movements weren't macho; they were saurian. He gave me that sharp-bladed smile and I saw my death waiting on those ivory knives.

I knew what he was feeling. I'd been there recently myself. He was pumped up on Unseelie.

I was getting better at putting things together; my deductive reasoning skills had improved a hundredfold since I'd stepped off that plane from the States.

Facts: Derek O'Bannion is not a *sidhe*-seer. He can't see the Unseelie. If you can't see the Unseelie, you can't eat the Unseelie. Which means that if a human who is not a *sidhe*-seer shows up, pumped up on Unseelie, someone who *can* see the Unseelie must have fed it to that person, deliberately opening their eyes to a whole new dark realm, like the Lord Master did with Mallucé. A normal human can't choose to be turned into a hybrid; he or she must be *made* into it, initiated into the dark rite by someone in the see and know.

"Get out of my store," I said coldly.

"Got a lot o' balls for a walking dead woman."

"Who fed it to you? Red robe? Pretty boy? Did he tell you about Mallucé?"

"Mallucé was a fool. I'm not."

"Did he tell you Mallucé rotted from the inside out?"

"He told me you killed my brother and that you have something that belongs to me. He sent me for it."

"He sent you to die, then. The thing he sent you for is the one thing capable of killing Unseelie — which parts of you are now — which is how and why Mallucé rotted from the inside out. I stabbed him with it." I smiled. "Did your new friend tell you that? You have no idea what you've gotten yourself into." Had I just sounded exactly like Barrons? Had I just said something to the mobster's brother Barrons had said to me when I'd first begun pushing my way into the realm of the Fae? Please tell me my mentor wasn't rubbing off on me. Please tell me we don't grow up and turn into the adults that drive us crazy.

I slipped the spear from my shoulder

holster and slammed it, point first, into the counter. It quivered in the wood, shimmering with alabaster light, nearly white. "Go ahead, O'Bannion, come and get it. I'm fed up with jack-petunias like you and would like nothing more than to watch you rot, slowly and painfully. I know you're all juiced up on your new powers right now, but you should know that I'm way more than just a pretty face. I'm a *sidhe*-seer and I have a few kick-ass powers of my own. There's no way you can stop me from stabbing you with this if you get within a dozen feet of me. So, if you don't mind rotting from the inside out — did I mention that his dick went before his mind did? — step one inch further inside my store."

Indecision flickered in those cold reptilian eyes.

"Your brother didn't see me as a threat. Your brother's dead. So are fifteen of his henchmen. Think about that. Think hard."

He stared at the spear, glowing with its soft, unnatural luminescence. Rocky hadn't known anything about the dark forces around him. Derek had been recently awakened to it, and wouldn't make the same mistakes. I could see it in his face. This O'Bannion wouldn't rush blindly to his death. He would retreat now. His withdrawal would only be temporary. He would regroup and return, even more dangerous than before.

"This isn't over," he said. "It won't be over until you're dead."

"Until one of us is," I agreed. "Get out." I pulled the spear from the counter, fisted my hand around the hilt.

I should have let him walk into the Dark Zone that day. Instead, out of guilt for past sins, I'd saved his life. What an idiot I'd been.

I stared at the door after he was gone. My heart rate hadn't even accelerated. I flipped the sign, went to the bathroom, then reopened for business.

Barrons didn't show up Monday night or Tuesday. Wednesday came and went with no sign of him. By Thursday evening it had been five days since I'd seen him, longer than he'd ever stayed away before.

I was growing impatient. I had questions. I had accusations. I had memories of a fight that had ended in disturbing lust. I'd been sitting in the rear conversation area of the bookstore, every evening for hours, before a softly hissing gas fire, pretending to read, waiting for him.

The bookstore was huge and silent and I

felt alone and a million miles from home.

After five days, I broke down and dialed JB on the cell phone he'd given me. There was no answer.

I stared at the display, thumbed through my short contact list: JB; IYCGM; IYD.

I didn't quite have the balls to try the last one.

I punched up IYCGM instead.

"Ryodan," a voice barked.

I hung up instantly, feeling embarrassed and guilty.

The phone blared with the thunder of a hundred celestial trumpets in my hands, and although part of me had fully expected it, it still scared me out of my skin.

The display blinked: IYCGM.

I sighed and pressed send.

"Mac? Are you all right? Talk to me," a deep voice growled.

Ryodan: the mysterious man who talked about Barrons to people he shouldn't talk to, the man Barrons had been fighting the day I'd gone to Alina's apartment.

I hesitated.

"Mac!" the voice roared.

"I'm here. I'm fine. I'm sorry," I said.

"Why did you call?"

"I wondered where Barrons was."

There was a soft laugh, a deep, rumbling

purr. "Is that what he's calling himself these days? Barrons?"

"Isn't that his name? Jericho Barrons?"

More laughter. "Is he using a middle name?"

"The initial *Z*." I'd seen it on his license.

"Ah, the Omega. Ever the melodramatic one."

"And the Alpha?" I said drolly.

"He'd probably try to make a great case for it."

"What's his real name?"

"Ask him yourself."

"He wouldn't answer me. He never does. Who are you?"

"I'm the one you call when you can't get Barrons."

"Duh. Thanks. Who's Barrons?"

"The one who keeps saving your life."

I wouldn't have believed two men could sound so much alike, both masters of circuitous answers that went nowhere. "Are you brothers?"

"In a manner of speaking."

I didn't have to press further to understand that, like Barrons, Ryodan would only tell me what he intended to tell me and all the questions in the world would fall on deaf ears unless he wanted me to know something. "I'm leaving, Ryodan. He lies to me, he bullies me. He never tells me anything. He betrayed me."

"I don't believe that."

"What? The lying, bullying, or betraying?"

"Betraying. The rest of it is classic . . . what did you call him? Barrons. But he doesn't betray."

"You don't know him as well as you think you do."

"Open your eyes, Mac."

"What do you mean?"

"Words can be twisted into any shape. Promises can be made to lull the heart and seduce the soul. In the final analysis words mean nothing. They are labels we give things in an effort to wrap our puny little brains around their underlying natures, when ninety-nine percent of the time the totality of the reality is an entirely different beast. The wisest man is the silent one. Examine his actions. Judge him by *them*. He thinks you have the heart of a warrior. He believes in you. Believe in him."

"In what? A mercenary? He wants the book to sell it to the highest bidder! The Hunters are mercenaries, too!"

"If I were in your shoes, I'd never call him that. Who are you to talk? You think your motives are so pure? You have such a noble calling? Bullshit. What's good about you?

You want blood. You want revenge. You don't care about the fate of the world. You just want your happy little place in it back. People who live in glass houses . . ." He trailed off as if I should know what came next. I didn't.

"What? People who live in glass houses what?"

"Fuck, you *are* young, aren't you?" He laughed. "Shouldn't throw rocks, Mac. People who live in glass houses shouldn't throw rocks."

The line went dead.

The bell jingled. Barrons walked in.

"Barrons." I hastily shoved the phone between the cushions.

"Ms. Lane." He inclined his dark head.

"You tattooed me, you bastard." I got right to the point.

"So?"

"You had no right!"

"Would you rather I hadn't?"

"That doesn't make it okay!"

"But it does, doesn't it? And that's what rankles you. I overruled your wishes. I took care of you in the way a man used to take care of a woman before the world was a place where children could sue to divorce their parents, and if I hadn't, you'd be dead. Are you going to pretend to wish you were dead? I know you. You're crammed full of life and selfishly glad you're alive, and you always will be. If you need a stage and an audience to play the maiden nun who would sacrifice her life to preserve her virginity to appease your conscience, find it somewhere else, I'm not going to applaud. Will you hang your life on values that have none in the final analysis? When you were too young and naïve to see the risks, I incurred your wrath to protect you. Scream at me for it if you must. Thank me for it when you finally grow up."

I changed the subject. He hits me with so much sometimes that it's easier to veer on to some other topic, one that would put me on the offensive, and him on the defensive instead of vice versa. "Why did the Lord Master take one look at you and leave? What are you, Barrons?"

"The one who will never let you die, and that's more, Ms. Lane, than anyone in your life has ever been able to say to you. More than anyone else can do."

"V'lane —"

"V'lane sure as fuck didn't come get you in the grotto, did he? Where was your golden prince then?"

"I'm sick of your evasions! What *are* you?" I stalked over to him, punched him in the shoulder. "Answer me!"

He knocked my hand away. "I just did. That's all you're getting. Take me or leave me. Stay or go."

We glared at each other. It seemed like all we did anymore. But there was no real fight in me, and he sensed it.

When I went to the sofa and sat down, he turned away.

"I assume you are yourself again," he said, staring into the fire.

"How did you know that?"

"I spent the past few days researching the ramifications of what you'd done, to find out if it was reversible. I learned the effects of eating Unseelie are temporary."

"If you'd bothered showing up on Monday, I could have told you that myself."

He turned. "It wore off that quickly?"

I nodded.

"Are you entirely restored? Can you sense the spear again?"

"Never fear, your OOP detector is back," I said bitterly. "Oh, and it looks like O'Bannion replaced Mallucé for the Lord Master." I filled him in on the younger brother's visit, that he'd eaten Unseelie.

Barrons took a seat on the opposite end of the sofa. Even with all that space between us, we were too close. I remembered the feel of his wild, electric body on top of mine. I remembered lying beneath him with my shirt ripped to my neck, the look on his face. I looked away.

"I'll ward the store against him. You'll be safe so long as you're inside."

"If I was already tattooed, why couldn't you find me when V'lane had me in Faery?" This was a bit of illogic that had been nagging at me.

"I knew you were in Faery but I couldn't track you there. The realms shift constantly, making it impossible to follow the . . . beacon."

"Why did you make me wear the cuff if I was already tattooed?"

"So I could explain being able to find you if I had to."

I snorted. "What a tangled web we weave, huh? Does it really work as a locator cuff?"

He shook his head.

"Does it do anything?"

"Not that concerns you."

"What did the Lord Master do to me that made me obey him?"

"Parlor tricks. It's called Voice. A Druid skill."

"You knew that parlor trick yourself. Is it something someone else can learn to do? Me, for example?"

"I doubt you'll live long enough to learn it."

"You did."

"You have no training."

"Try me."

"I'll think about it."

"Did you use it on my father? Is that what made him leave the next morning, after he and I had argued all night and I couldn't get him to go?"

"Would you have had him stay?"

"Did you use it again when he called here, when I was in Faery for a month?" I was beginning to understand his methods.

"Should I have let him fly over and get himself killed?"

"Why didn't you tell me about the abbey, Barrons?"

"They are witches and liars. They would tell you anything to woo you to their side."

"Sounds like somebody else I know." Actually it sounded like *everybody* else I knew.

"I make you no promises I won't keep, and I gave you the spear. They would take it from you. Give them half a chance and see what they do. Don't come whining to me when they screw you."

"I'm going to the abbey in a few days, Barrons," I told him, and it was a challenge. It was a "You'd better give me whatever freedom I want." After everything I'd been through, my feelings about things had changed. He and I were partners, not OOP detector and director, and partners had rights. "I'm going to spend some time there and see what they can teach me."

"I'll be here when you get back. And should the old woman try to harm you, I'll kill her."

I almost muttered a "thanks" but caught myself. "I know there are no male *sidhe-seers.*" When he opened his mouth I said, "Spare me," before he could toss a pithy comment my way. "I know you're male and I know you see them. We don't need to revisit that. I also know you're superstrong and that you rarely touch the spear. So how long have you been eating Unseelie, Barrons?"

He gaped a moment, then his shoulders began to shake, his chest rumbled, his dark eyes glittered with amusement, and he laughed.

"It is a perfectly logical assumption," I bristled.

"Yes," he said finally, "it is. It startled me with its logic. But it's not true."

I studied him through narrowed eyes. "Maybe that's why the Shades don't eat you. They're not cannibals and you're full of their brethren. Maybe they don't like dark meat."

"So, stab me," he said softly.

I slipped my hand beneath my jacket, fisted my hand around the hilt of the spear. It was pure bluff. We both knew I wouldn't.

Behind the counter the phone rang. I stared into Barrons' dark eyes while the phone rang and rang. I remembered kissing him, remembered the images: the desert; the hot, killing sirocco; the lonely boy; the endless wars. I wondered whether if I kissed him again, I'd get inside him again. The phone rang. It occurred to me that it could be my dad. Jerking my gaze away with an effort, I pushed off the sofa and grabbed the phone.

"Hello?" It wasn't my dad. "Christian! Hi, yes, actually I'd love to. No, no, I didn't forget! I got tied up."

I'd had other things on my mind, been wound tight as a knot.

But I was okay now. Things were back to normal. I was Mac Lane, *sidhe*-seer, armed to the teeth with spear, knives, and flashlights. Barrons was . . . well, Barrons, and the hunt for the *Sinsar Dubh* was back on.

And tonight would be a fine night to spend with a good-looking young Scotsman who'd known my sister, and learn what he knew.

"I'll be there in forty minutes." I wanted to change and freshen up. "No, no need to come get me. I'll walk. Don't worry, I'll be fine."

"A date, Ms. Lane?" Barrons said, when I hung up. He was motionless. In fact, for a moment I wasn't certain he was breathing. "You really think that's appropriate in the midst of our current circumstances? There are Hunters out there."

I shrugged. "They fear my spear."

"The Lord Master's out there."

I gave him a dry smile. "Then I guess it's a good thing you won't let me die."

He returned my smile with the ghost of one, even dryer. "He must be something, if he's worth walking Dublin's night."

"He is." I didn't tell him he'd been my sister's friend. Volunteering information isn't something Barrons and I do with each other. We let each other stew in whatever messes we've created for ourselves. The day he stops, I'll stop.

"Shouldn't I be giving you a curfew?" he mocked.

"Try." I turned for the connecting doors. I would wash my face, brush on blush, mascara, and lip gloss, and put on something pretty and pink. Not because I thought of this as a date. I didn't. Scotty might have known my sister and he might know a little about what we were, but he couldn't live in my world. It was too dangerous for the average man, even one armed with a bit of knowledge.

I would wear pink because I knew my future was anything but rosy. I would accessorize myself to the hilt, and I would wear flirty shoes because my world needed more beauty to counter all the ugliness in it. I would wear pink because I hated gray, I didn't deserve white, and I was sick of black.

As I reached the connecting door, I stopped. "Jericho."

"Mac."

I hesitated. "Thank you for saving my life." I slipped through the door. Before I pulled it closed, I added softly, "Again."

TWENTY

I had to walk through Temple Bar to get to Trinity where I was meeting Christian.

I passed Inspector Jayne on the way. He and two other Garda were attempting to subdue a group of combative drunks. He gave me a sharp, furious look as I passed, making it clear he'd not forgotten about me, or his brother-in-law's murder. I had no doubt I would be seeing him again soon. I didn't blame him. I was hunting a murderer, too, and I knew how he felt. Problem was, he was targeting the wrong person. I wasn't.

Although you might think after everything I'd been through I would fear the night, I didn't. Night's just Day's other cheek. It's not the darkness that frightens me; it's the things that come out in it, and I was ready for them.

I had a spear the Hunters didn't want to get too close to. I had a tattoo at the nape of my neck that Barrons could use to find me anytime he wanted to, anywhere. And if I were in Faery, I suspected news would travel swiftly to V'lane on a Fae wind and I knew he wanted me alive, too. I might have powerful enemies but I had powerful protectors. Then there was Ryodan — a man capable of surviving a fight with Barrons — who was a mere phone call away in case Barrons wasn't around, and I had IYD, in case things got really bad. After what I've seen from Barrons, I was confident that IYD would be a real petunia-kicker.

If things got stupendously bad, I'd bite the nearest Unseelie instead of stabbing it, and start chewing.

Speaking of Unseelie, they were everywhere in the busy party zone tonight, but I didn't focus on them. I focused on the humans instead.

They were my people.

I had a job, a purpose, more so than the task of finding the *Sinsar Dubh* with which my sister had charged me. I knew now that she'd never meant it to end there, anyway. I'd just been interpreting her message from my selfish viewpoint.

Everything depends on it, she'd said. *We can't let them have it! We've got to get to it first!*

I knew her message by heart. I'd listened

to it over and over in my head. We had to get to it first so that we could *do* something with it. Exactly what, I had no idea, but I had no doubt my job would be far from over when it was finally found.

Question: When you're one of the few people who can do something to fix a problem, just how responsible does that make you for it?

Answer: It's how you choose to answer that question that defines you.

I walked through the bustling crowds dressed in pink and gold, my dark curls fluffed, my eyes sparkling, looking everywhere, inhaling the scents, enjoying the sounds. The spring was back in my step. I'd never felt more alive, more charged, more part of the world. I decided I would stop at an all-night Internet café on the way home, soak up the late-night Irish *craic,* and download some new tunes for my iPod. I was making a salary now. I was entitled to spend a little of it.

I'd been knocking on Death's door recently and I was exhilarated to be alive, no matter how bad the current state of my world, no matter how fecked-up my life.

I stared curiously, interestedly into the faces as they passed by. I offered smiles, collected many in return. I got a few whistles, too. Sometimes the small pleasures in life are the sweetest.

I mentally assessed the current state of my game board as I walked. Mallucé was now off it for real, a dark, headless rook, slain on the sidelines. Derek O'Bannion had risen up in his place on the shadowy side of the board ruled by the Lord Master.

I was still willing to keep Rowena mostly on my side — the light side — and I hoped Christian MacKeltar might fit there somehow, too. It would be nice to have a little company. I was certain Dani was a light warrior.

Barrons?

Sometimes I wondered if he'd built the darned board, set the game in motion.

I was three blocks from Trinity, down a side street shortcut I'd decided to take, when it happened.

I clutched my head and moaned. "No. Not now. No!" I tried to step backward, to retreat from it, but it wouldn't let me. My feet locked down right where they were.

The pain in my head swelled to a vicious crescendo. I wrapped both arms around my face and cradled my aching skull.

Nothing compares to the agony the *Sinsar Dubh* causes me. I ducked my chin to my chest, knowing in moments I would be on the sidewalk, curled up in a gibbering ball, then unconscious, vulnerable to anyone and anything in the night.

The pressure ratcheted up violently, and just when I was certain the top of my skull was going to blow off and rain bone shrapnel across the street, a thousand red hot ice picks perforated my head, releasing the pressure, creating a new hell of its own, an internal inferno.

"No," I whimpered, staggering. "Please . . . no."

The ice picks had jagged edges and rotated like roasting skewers. My lips moved soundlessly and I collapsed to my knees, toppled into the gutter, and fell facedown into a sour-smelling puddle; so much for pretty in pink and gold. A wintry wind howled down between the buildings, chilling me to the bone. Old newspapers cartwheeled like dirty, sodden tumbleweeds over broken bottles and discarded wrappers and glasses.

I clawed at the pavement with my fingernails, left the tips of them broken in gaps between the cobbled stones.

With immense effort, I raised my head and looked down the street. It was nearly deserted, scourged clean of tourists by the dark, arctic wind, leaving only me . . . and them.

I watched in speechless horror at the tableau that played out before my eyes.

After a few interminable minutes, the pain began to ebb and I dropped my chin in the sour dark puddle, panting from the aftermath of agony.

After a few more minutes, I managed to crawl from the puddle and drag myself back up onto the sidewalk, where I threw up until nothing was left.

I knew now where the *Sinsar Dubh* was.

And I knew who was moving it around.

As momentous and mind-boggling as that information was, it wasn't my primary concern at the moment.

I'd been within fifty yards of the Dark Book, closer to it than I'd ever been before, I'd seen it with my own eyes — and I *hadn't passed out.*

I wonder, Barrons had said, *dilute the opposite, would it still repel?*

The *Sinsar Dubh* had existed for a million years and although, according to Barrons, Fae things change in subtle ways over time, I was quite certain it was never going to get any nicer. In fact, I had no doubt it would only continue to grow consistently more evil.

Previously it had repelled me so violently that it had knocked me out within seconds.

Tonight I had remained conscious the entire time, closer to it than ever before, and that could mean only one thing.

What had changed was *me.*

GLOSSARY FROM MAC'S JOURNAL

*Amulet, The: Unseelie or Dark Hallow created by the Unseelie King for his concubine. Fashioned of gold, silver, sapphires, and onyx, the gilt "cage" of the amulet houses an enormous clear stone of unknown composition. A person of epic will can use it to impact and reshape reality. The list of past owners is legendary, including Merlin, Boudica, Joan of Arc, Charlemagne, and Napoleon. Last purchased by a Welshman for eight figures at an illegal auction, it was all too briefly in my hands and is currently in the possession of the Lord Master. It requires some kind of tithe or binding to use it. I had the will; I couldn't figure out the way.

Barrons, Jericho: I haven't the faintest fecking clue. He keeps saving my life. I suppose that's something.

*Cauldron, The: Seelie or Light Hallow from which all Seelie eventually drink to divest memory that has become burdensome. According to Barrons immortality has a price: eventual madness. When the Fae feel it approaching, they drink from The Cauldron and are "reborn" with no memory of a prior existence. The Fae have a record-keeper that documents each Fae's many incarnations, but the exact location of this scribe is known to a select few and the whereabouts of the records to none but him. Is that what's wrong with the Unseelie — they don't have a cauldron to drink from?

Cruce: A Fae; unknown if Seelie or Unseelie. Many of his relics are floating around out there. He cursed the Sifting Silvers. Unknown what the curse was.

Cuff of Cruce: A gold and silver arm cuff set with blood-red stones; an ancient Fae relic that supposedly permits the human wearing it "a shield of sorts against many Unseelie and other . . . unsavory things" (this according to a death-by-sex Fae — like you can actually trust one).

Dani: A young *sidhe*-seer in her early teens whose talent is superhuman speed. She has to her credit — as she will proudly crow from the rooftops given the slightest opportunity — forty-seven Fae kills at the time of this writing. I'm sure she'll have more by tomorrow. Her mother was killed by a Fae. We are sisters in vengeance. She works for Rowena and is employed at Post Haste, Inc.

Dark Zone: An area that has been taken over by the Shades. During the day it looks like your everyday abandoned, run-down neighborhood. Once night falls, it's a death trap. (Definition Mac)

Death-by-Sex-Fae: (e.g., V'lane) A Fae that is so sexually "potent" a human dies from intercourse with it unless the Fae protects the human from the full impact of its deadly eroticism. (Definition ongoing)
Addendum to original entry: V'lane made himself feel like nothing more than an incredibly sexy man when he touched me. They *can* mute their lethality if they so choose.

Dolmen: A single-chamber megalithic tomb constructed of two or more upright stones supporting a large, flat, horizontal capstone. Dolmens are common in Ireland, especially around the Burren and Connemara. The Lord Master used a dolmen in a ritual of dark magic to open a doorway between realms and bring Unseelie through.

Druid: In pre-Christian Celtic society, a Druid presided over divine worship, legislative and judicial matters, philosophy, and education of elite youth to their order. Druids were believed to be privy to the secrets of the gods, including issues pertaining to the manipulation of physical matter, space, and even time. The old Irish "Drui" means magician, wizard, diviner. (*Irish Myths and Legends*)

Addendum to original entry: I saw both Jericho Barrons and the Lord Master use the Druid power of Voice, a way of speaking with many voices that cannot be disobeyed. Significance?

Fae: (fay) See also Tuatha Dé Danaan. Divided into two courts, the Seelie or Light Court, and the Unseelie or Dark Court. Both courts have different castes of Fae, with the four Royal Houses occupying the highest caste of each. The Seelie Queen and her chosen consort rule the Light Court. The Unseelie King and his current concubine govern the Dark. (Definition J.B.)

Four Stones, The: Translucent blue-black stones covered with raised runelike lettering. The key to deciphering the ancient language and breaking the code of the *Sinsar Dubh* is hidden in these four mystical stones. An individual stone can be used to shed light on a small portion of the text, but only if the four are reassembled into one will the true text in its entirety be revealed. (*Irish Myths and Legends*)

Glamour: Illusion cast by the Fae to camouflage their true appearance. The more powerful the Fae, the more difficult it is to penetrate its disguise. The average human sees only what the Fae wants them to see, and is subtly repelled from bumping into or brushing against it by a small perimeter of spatial distortion that is part of the Fae glamour. (Definition J.B.)

Gray Man, The: Monstrously ugly, leprous Unseelie that feeds by stealing beauty from human women. Threat assessment: can kill, but prefers to leave its victim hideously disfigured, and alive to suffer. (Personal experience)

Addendum to original entry: Allegedly the only one of its kind, Barrons and I killed it.

Hallows, The: Eight ancient relics of immense power fashioned by the Fae: four light and four dark. The Light or Seelie Hallows are the stone, the spear, the sword, and the cauldron. The Dark or Unseelie Hallows are the amulet, the box, the mirror, and the book (*Sinsar Dubh* or Dark

Book). (*A Definitive Guide to Artifacts, Authentic and Legendary*)

Addendum to original entry: I still don't know anything about the stone or the box. Do they confer powers that could help me? Where are they? Correction to above definition — the mirror is actually the Silvers. *See* Sifting Silvers or Silvers. The Unseelie King made all the Dark Hallows. Who made the Light ones?

Haven, The: High council of *sidhe*-seers.

Lord Master: My sister's betrayer and murderer! Fae but not Fae, leader of the Unseelie army, after the *Sinsar Dubh.* He was using Alina to hunt it like Barrons is using me to hunt OOPs.

MacKeltar, Christian: Employed in the Ancient Languages Department of Trinity. He knows what I am and knew my sister! Have no idea what his place in all this is, nor do I know his motives. Will find out more soon.

Malluce: born John Johnstone, Jr. On the heels of his parents' mysterious death, he inherited hundreds of millions of dollars, disappeared for a time, and resurfaced as the newly undead vampire Malluce. Over the next decade, he amassed a worldwide cult following, and was recruited by the

Lord Master for his money and connections. Pale, blond, citron-eyed, the vampire favors steampunk and Victorian Goth.

Many-Mouthed Thing, The: Repulsive Unseelie with myriad leechlike mouths, dozens of eyes, and overdeveloped sex organs. Caste of Unseelie: unknown at this time. Threat assessment: unknown at this time but suspect kills in a manner I'd rather not think about. (Personal experience)

Addendum to original entry: Is still out there. I want this one dead.

Null: A *sidhe*-seer with the power to freeze a Fae with the touch of his or her hands (e.g., me). While frozen, it is completely powerless. The higher and more powerful the caste of Fae, the shorter the length of time it stays frozen. (Definition J.B.)

O'Bannion, Derek: Rocky's brother and the Lord Master's new recruit. Should have let him walk into the Dark Zone that day.

OOP: Acronym for Object of Power, a Fae relic imbued with mystical properties. (Definition Mac)

OOP Detector: Me. A *sidhe*-seer with the special ability to sense OOPs. Alina was one, too, which is why the Lord Master used her.

Orb of D'Jai: No clue, but Barrons has it. He says it's an OOP. I couldn't sense it when I held it, but I couldn't sense anything at that particular moment. Where did he get it and where did he put it? Is it in his mysterious vault? What does it do? How does he get into his vault, anyway? Where is the access to the three floors beneath his garage? Is there a tunnel that connects buildings? Must search.

Patrona: Mentioned by Rowena, I supposedly have "the look" of her. Was she an O'Connor? She was at one time the leader of the *sidhe*-seer Haven.

PHI: *Post Haste, Inc.,* a Dublin courier service that serves as a cover for the *sidhe*-seer coalition. It appears Rowena is in charge.

Pri-ya: A human addicted to Fae sex. (I think. Definition ongoing)

Rhino-boys: Ugly, gray-skinned Fae who resemble rhinoceroses with bumpy, protruding foreheads, barrel-like bodies, stumpy arms and legs, lipless gashes of mouths, and jutting underbites. They are lower mid-level caste Unseelie thugs dispatched primarily as watchdogs for high-ranking Fae. (Personal experience)

Addendum to original entry: They taste horrible.

Rowena: In charge to some degree of a coalition of *sidhe*-seers organized as couriers at Post Haste, Inc. Is she the Grand Mistress? They have a chapter house or retreat in an old abbey, a few hours from Dublin, with a library I *must* get into.

Royal Hunters: A mid-level caste of Unseelie. Militantly sentient, they resemble the classic depiction of the devil, with cloven hooves, horns, long satyrlike faces, leathery wings, fiery orange eyes, and tails. Seven to ten feet tall, they are capable of extraordinary speed on both hoof and wing. Primary function: *sidhe*-seer exterminators. Threat assessment: kills. (Definition J.B.)

Addendum to original entry: Encountered one. Barrons doesn't know everything. It was considerably larger than he'd led me to expect, with a thirty- to forty-foot wingspan and a degree of telepathic abilities. They are mercenary to the core and serve a master only so long as it benefits them. I'm not sure I believe they're mid-level, and in fact, I'm not sure they're entirely Fae. They fear my spear and I suspect are unwilling to die for any cause, which gives me a tactical edge.

Ryodan: Associate of Barrons and IYCGM on my cell.

Seelie: The "light" or "fairer" court of the Tuatha Dé Danaan governed by the Seelie Queen, Aoibheal. (Definition J.B.)

Shades: One of the lowest castes of Unseelie. Sentient, but barely. They hunger — they feed. They cannot bear direct light and hunt only at night. They steal life in the manner the Gray Man steals beauty, draining their victims with vampiric swiftness, leaving behind a pile of clothing and a husk of dehydrated human matter. Threat assessment: kills. (Personal experience)

Addendum to original entry: I think they're changing, evolving, learning.

Shamrock: This slightly misshapen three-leaf clover is the ancient symbol of the *sidhe*-seers, who are charged with the mission to See, Serve, and Protect mankind from the Fae.

Sidhe-seer (SHE-seer): A person Fae magic doesn't work on, capable of seeing past the illusions or "glamour" cast by the Fae to the true nature that lies beneath. Some can also see *Tabh'rs,* hidden portals between realms. Others can sense Seelie and Unseelie objects of power. Each *sidhe*-seer is different, with varying degrees of resis-

446

tance to the Fae. Some are limited, some are advanced with multiple "special powers." (Definition J.B.)

Addendum to original entry: Some, like Dani, are superfast. There's a place inside my head that isn't . . . like the rest of me. Do we all have it? What is it? How did we get this way? Where do the bits of inexplicable knowledge that feel like memories come from? Is there such a thing as a genetic collective unconsciousness?

Sifting: Fae method of locomotion, occurs at speed of thought. (Seen this!)

Addendum to original entry: Somehow V'lane sifted me without my awareness that he was even there. I don't know if he was able to approach me "cloaked" somehow, then touched me at the last minute and I just didn't realize it because it happened so fast, or if perhaps instead of moving me, he moved the realms around me. Can he do that? How powerful is V'lane? Could another Fae sift me without my having any advance warning? Unacceptably dangerous! Require more information.

*Sifting Silvers or Silvers, The: Unseelie or Dark Hallow, an elaborate maze of mirrors created by the Unseelie King once used as the primary method of Fae travel between realms, until Cruce cast the forbidden curse into the silvered corridors. Now no Fae dares enter the Silvers. (Definition J.B.)

Addendum to original entry: The Lord Master had many of these in his house in the Dark Zone and was using them to move in and out of Faery. If you destroy a Silver does it destroy what was in it? Does it leave an open entry/exit into a Fae realm like a wound in the fabric of our world? What exactly was the curse and who was Cruce?

***Sinsar Dubh**, **The (She-suh-DOO):** Unseelie or Dark Hallow belonging to the Tuatha Dé Danaan. Written in a language known only to the most ancient of their kind, it is said to hold the deadliest of all magic within its encrypted pages. Brought to Ireland by the Tuatha Dé during the invasions written of in the pseudohistory *Leabhar Gabhåla,* it was stolen along with the other Dark Hallows, and rumored to have found its way into the world of Man. Allegedly authored over a million years ago by the Dark King of the Unseelie. (*A Definitive Guide to Artifacts, Authentic and Legendary*)

Addendum to original note: I've seen it now. Words cannot contain a description of it.

It is a book but it lives. It is aware.

*Spear of Luisne, The: Seelie or Light Hallow (a.k.a. Spear of Luin, Spear of Longinus, Spear of Destiny, Flaming Spear): The spear used to pierce Jesus Christ's side at his crucifixion. Not of human origin; it is a Tuatha Dé Danaan Light Hallow, and one of few items capable of killing a Fae — regardless of rank or power. (Definition J.B.)
Addendum to original note: It kills *anything* Fae and if something is only part Fae, it kills part of it, horribly.

*Sword of Lugh, The: Seelie or Light Hallow, also known as the Sword of Light, a Seelie Hallow capable of killing Fae, both Seelie and Unseelie. Currently, Rowena has it, and dispatches it to her *sidhe*-seers at PHI as she deems fit. Dani usually gets it.

Tabh'rs (TAH-vr): Fae doorways or portals between realms, often hidden in everyday human objects. (Definition J.B.)

Tuatha Dé Danaan or Tuatha Dé (TUA day dhanna or Tua DAY) (*See* Fae): A highly advanced race that came to Earth from another world. (Definition ongoing)

Unseelie: the "dark" or "fouler" court of the Tuatha Dé Danaan. According to Tuatha Dé Danaan legend, the Unseelie have been confined for hundreds of thousands of years in an inescapable prison. Inescapable, my ass.

V'lane: According to Rowena's books, V'lane is a Seelie Prince, Court of the Light, member of the Queen's High Council and sometimes Consort. He is a death-by-sex Fae and has been trying to get me to work for him on behalf of Queen Aoibheal to locate the *Sinsar Dubh.**

* Denotes a Light or Dark Hallow.

PRONUNCIATION GUIDE

An Garda Sioch'na: In Dublin, garda, or on garda shee-a-conna. Outside Dublin, gardee.

Aoibheal: Ah-*veel* (not Irish Gaelic but an older language unique to the Fae)

Craic: crack

Cuff of Cruce: like the cruc in crucify

Drui: Dree

Firbolg: Fair *bol* ugh

Leabhar Gabhala: Lour *Gow* ola (lour-like flower, Gow-like cow)

Mallucé: Mal-*loosh**

* Irish pronunciations obtained from sources in Dublin at the Garda and Trinity. Any errors in pronunciation are mine.

ABOUT THE AUTHOR

Karen Marie Moning is the internationally bestselling author of the Highlander and Fever novels. Her books have appeared on the *New York Times, USA Today,* and *Publishers Weekly* bestseller lists, and have won numerous awards, including the prestigious RITA. She lives in Georgia and Florida with her husband Neil and the world-traveling cat, Moonshadow.

SIDHE-SEERS, INC.™

SEE, SERVE, & PROTECT

Be the first to get the inside scoop on Seelie and Unseelie sightings around the world, the inner workings of PHI, and the occasional tidbit from Mac about what's going on in Dublin and where she is now.

Visit www.sidhe-seersinc.com and sign up to become an official member of *Sidhe-Seers, Inc.*™